i

other books by this author

The Great Wall of New York
O'Rourke: another slopsink chronicle

THE
GREAT
REDSTONE

THE
GREAT
REDSTONE

KEVIN BARTELME

coolgrovepress

All rights reserved under the International and
Pan-American copyright conventions. Published in the United States by
Cool Grove Press, an imprint of Cool Grove Publishing, inc., New York.
512 Argyle Road, Brooklyn, NY 11218
http://www.coolgrove.com
All inquiries to info@coolgrove.com

ISBN 10: 1-887276-59-9

ISBN 13: 978-1-887276-59-7

Printed in the USA

For Mayumi

FOR SHELLYP

2011

It is—or seems to be—a wise sort of thing, to realise that all that happens to a man in this life is only by way of joke, especially his misfortunes, if he have them. And it is also worth bearing in mind, that the joke is passed round pretty liberally & impartially, so that not very many are entitled to fancy that they in particular are getting the worst of it.

- Herman Melville

CHAPTER ONE

As I sat on the veranda of the old house overlooking the bay, watching the yachts and motor launches return from the sound as twilight settled, I saw a glittering candy apple red speedboat racing towards a marina across the way. The driver did not slow down as required by the rules of the harbor and other boaters caught in his jarring wake as he roared by shook their fists and made obscene gestures. The speedboat disappeared from view and I thought no more of it. I went into the large house, which was not mine, and made myself a drink. I was staying in a converted outbuilding down the driveway that had once served as a carriage house. My landlord rarely showed up at his place and was outspokenly disdainful of "these new people" who had invaded the neighborhood so I pretty much had the run of the property. Down the coast, one of these new people had constructed a fantastically vulgar mansion and on weekends the street was lined with the cars of revelers attending the loud and lengthy parties held on the grounds. I learned in town that the house was owned by the financier, Dacron Redstone, already legendary at the age of thirty-five for his daring investment strategies that always seemed to pay off. But more about Redstone later.

I had come to the island to ghostwrite for a hysterical woman whom you may have heard of, Sheridan March, the noted author of several best sellers who'd made her fortune and reputation penning "inspirational" books. She was now so rich she didn't write anything but the occasional check and I was the lucky recipient of her largesse. Frankly I needed the job but the very thought of sitting down and writing *Buddha; The First Entrepreneur* had left me in a funk of procrastination. My cousin Alicia was staying at an artists' retreat run by the famous conceptualist, Fuzzwick Offenfusser, and I decided to take a spin around the bay and pay her a visit. I had never been there before but she gave me precise instructions and I soon arrived at the gates of the Illuminatus estate, former convent, but now home to the Offenfusser Foundation. I drove in and came upon a work in progress, a wildly bent and twisted radio tower that had a crew of hardhats busy booming up giant red klieg light to the top with a crane. I drove on further and arrived at the old convent, a sprawling stucco building that now served to house the visiting artists. I parked the car — a loan from my landlord — and entered into the cool precincts of this mission style dormitory. In the expansive living room, my cousin was arguing with a wild haired, middle-aged man.

"You can't just treat people like that," she scolded.

But I had caught the wild-haired man's attention.

"Can I help you?"

Alicia turned around. "Oh, it's you, Martin. Wick, this is my cousin."

"I'm glad to meet you," said Offenfusser, standing up and affably offering his hand. "Now, if you'll excuse me, I've got some things to do." The man was not being brusque. He seemed relieved that I had interrupted them and let him off the hook.

"It's so good to see you, Martin." She took my arm. "Let me show you around."

Alicia is the daughter of my mother's sister who married a rich man. She grew up in great privilege and seemed to be headed directly for the Junior League and all the rest but something happened along the way. She disappeared into an entirely different world of art and drugs and excess. Her mother tried to put her in rehab but Alicia was too clever for that. She hired a psychiatrist, had the old bag committed to a deluxe rest home for the feeble-minded, and ran back off to *la vie bohème*. Now here she was ensconced in this peculiarly lavish estate directly across the harbor from my own humble abode. We chit-chatted our way around the grounds to the water where there was a small dock with a boathouse. At the time I didn't know it housed a candy apple red speedboat. Alicia asked me what I was doing and I told her. She was appalled.

"But you're far too talented for that, Martin!"

"I agree, but my stuff doesn't sell and I have to pay the bills."

"I think you should apply for a grant from the Offenfusser Foundation and write the great American novel. Believe me, I'll make sure you get it."

"That's very kind of you, Alicia."

"Don't patronize me, Martin. I'm not kidding."

"If I've said anything to offend you..." I teased.

"Stop that. How's your mother?"

"She's fine. Yours?"

"She's crazy as a loon. A few seconds before my father died, he whispered, 'Don't panic.' She thinks he was talking to her."

"Wasn't he? What do you mean?"

"He was talking to himself, of course. But enough about the relatives."

There was something perversely charming about Alicia's callous disregard of what I believe they refer to these days as "family values."

"I haven't told anyone yet but I'm getting married," she said offhandedly.

"Really? Who's the lucky guy?"

"What makes you think it's a guy?"

"Oh, well..." I phumphed.

She laughed. "I'm marrying Fuzzwick."

My cousin is pretty in a certain way but rather plain in another, not fat but not as thin as most young women would like to be. Her expression is perky and vivacious but her face can also appear as haggard as an old crone. It was easy yet not so easy to see what Offenfusser saw in her. He seemed to have his own money.

"Congratulations," I said. "When's the wedding?"

"Later this week. I'd invite you but we're just going to city hall. You must come to the reception though."

"Of course. I wouldn't miss it for the world."

We continued on our tour of the estate and came upon a large, square hole in the middle of a rolling lawn. The hole was about four feet deep and a single granite boulder sat within on a bed of gravel. The walls of the hole were lined with concrete. A short distance from this earthwork, a massive steel plate leaned at an angle that seemed to defy the law of gravity. Painted on the plate were the words: "COMMON SENSE."

"These are site specific pieces," Alicia explained. "They can't be moved anywhere else."

"Yes, it would be difficult to move a hole in the ground," I agreed, "but you could always dig another."

Alicia looked at me in mock horror. "Good God, Martin.

That's like saying a cheap print of the Mona Lisa is the same as the original."

"I hadn't thought of it that way."

"Such a philistine," she huffed, then broke into laughter. "Come back up to the house and we'll have lunch with Wick."

When we arrived, Offenfusser was conferring with his attorney at the far end of the cavernous living room. "Just ironing out the details of the pre-nup with Arlington," he called out to Alicia. "I'll meet you on the patio."

Alicia and I adjourned to an outdoor stone terrace overlooking the harbor where a man with tousled, spiky hair, dressed all in black, was sitting with his feet up on the railing. He didn't turn until Alicia hailed him.

"Harry!"

He shook his head and looked up at her with bleary eyes. Apparently he'd been asleep.

Alicia took my arm and introduced me. "Martin, this is Harry Poon. He just did Ahmed Jifhraz's yacht."

I had no idea what she was talking about. What did she mean by "did"? "Pleased to meet you," I said.

"Yeah, right," was his peculiar response. "Where's Fuzzwick?" There was something very slightly British about his accent.

As if conjured, Offenfusser appeared on the terrace. He did not seem happy to see Poon. "What are you doing here, Harry?"

"Just in the neighborhood. I came out with A.J. He's visiting some guy across the bay."

"You call him A.J.?"

"Hey, I did all the sculpture on the boat. We're pals."

"Well, you know, Harry, we're all hungry and since you're such a great pal of A.J. why don't you have us all over to the yacht for lunch?"

Poon smirked and called Offenfusser's bluff. "Sure, why not?"

"How did you get here anyway?" Offenfusser wanted to know.

"Helicopter, Wick."

It turned out that Poon had taken a cab, so we all piled into Offenfusser's mint condition 1956 Chevy Nomad and drove over to the marina where the giant power yacht Sulema was berthed. It dwarfed anything else in the harbor. Poon led the way up the gangplank to the enclosed main deck, which featured a stone fireplace, a mottled pink and black marble floor, and lots of garish, aggressively gold fixtures. The perimeter of the room was decorated with small, frankly pornographic sculptures on blue granite pedestals.

"So, what do you think?" said slightly leering Poon, placing his hand on an onyx statue of a goat having its way with a buxom woman from the rear.

Offenfusser stroked his chin. "You've done it again, Harry. You've definitely done it again."

Poon fairly beamed at this backhanded assessment of his work. "Not your cup of tea, Wick, but A.J. knows what he likes. Come on, I'll show you the rest of the place."

I had never heard a boat referred to as a "place" before, but the word somehow fit this floating palace. Poon led us into a room where swarthy young men in white shirts and ties were seated before computer consoles yelling frantically into telephone headsets.

"This is A.J.'s trading floor!" Poon shouted over the din. "Let's get out of here and let these guys make some money!"

We proceeded down a corridor lined with staterooms to a circular staircase that led to a glass-enclosed dome with a very nice view of the bay. I imagined it might look something like a planetarium at night if you could see the stars through the haze. There was a low table in the center nestled in a pile of overstuffed cushions.

"This is where A.J. gets down with his harem."

"Harem? You're kidding," said Alicia.

"Just a figure of speech," Poon tut-tutted. "A.J. thinks it's rude to call them whores."

"I should think."

We went back downstairs to a spacious dining room attended by Filipino servants in full waiter mufti and sat down at one end of the long table.

"You've really come up in the world, Harry," said Offenfusser with unconcealed irony. "Don't let it go to your head."

"I won't," Poon agreed. "I've seen too many guys go down the tubes to forget my natural humility."

This jibe didn't sit well with Offenfusser. He'd enjoyed his day in the sun some time ago and now rested uneasily on his shaky laurels, tossed and turned by the fickle whims of critics, curators, and, above all, collectors. He didn't take Poon's bitch slap lying down. "Humility becomes you, Harry. It suits a man of your talent."

Poon let it go. "Foie gras anyone?"

When I drove back to my little house across the bay, I was surprised by the unexpected appearance of my landlord, Mr. Wilberforce, with a real estate agent in tow, who, as I learned, had been engaged to sell the property.

"This is Mr. Paine. You don't mind if he brings people traipsing around to look at the place, do you?" Wilberforce asked me.

"No, of course not," I replied. I didn't see that I was in position to complain.

He leaned toward me confidentially. "I don't mean to inconvenience you, Martin, but there's no point in having a house where you can't stand your neighbors. Too many of the chosen people, if you know what I mean."

Yes, I knew what he meant and wondered if he'd sell the property to a Jew for the right price. Of course he would.

After they'd left, I made a futile attempt to put some thoughts in order for the Buddha book but was defeated at every turn by sheer ennui. My mind wandered across the bay to the ostentatious display of wealth that everyone out here took for granted. I have no mercantile sense and could never possibly engage in the sort of pursuits that made these movers and shakers rich, but I nevertheless felt envious about the degree of freedom their mysterious activities afforded. If I had that kind of money I probably wouldn't do anything at all. I lack both the appetite and the stamina required to play the adolescent games that most so-called successful people do and I suffer moral qualms inappropriate to untrammeled greed and worldly desire. That's what I'd like to think anyway. Actually, I'm just lazy.

This reverie on my own shortcomings was interrupted by the ringing telephone. It was Alicia. "Martin, there's someone I want you to meet. She's a dancer. I don't like the idea of you being all alone over there."

"Alicia, really," I protested.

"Don't argue. She's going to like you and you're really going to like her. She's Croatian."

I was now thoroughly befuddled. "You know, Alicia, there's this woman I see back in the city - "

"Forget about her. Danica's going to knock your socks off. She should be there any minute."

"What?!"

"I've got to go." No sooner had she hung up than a car turned into the driveway and pulled to a stop in front of the house. Danica, which I later learned means morning star or, more accurately, Venus, since Venus is not actually a star at all and, as you can see, even writing about her makes me nervous, knocked on the door and I opened it.

"Martin?"

"Yes."

"My name's Danica. I'm a friend of Alicia's. May I come in?"

Now, I've got to tell you this was one of the sexiest women I'd ever seen in my life. Blond, leggy, not so tall, as if a busty fashion model had been shrunk to five foot three with no changes in the dimensions.

"Yes, of course," I managed.

"Such a nice house," she said.

"Well, it's not mine. I just live in the cottage down there." I couldn't believe I was saying the word "cottage."

"May I sit down?"

"Oh, yes, of course. Would you like something to drink?"

"A raspberry cosmopolitan?" she said playfully.

"I'm sorry. I really don't know what that is."

"Neither do I. Do you have any white wine?"

And so we sat there for the next few hours in which time I learned a thing or two. Danica was a former girl friend of Fuzzwick Offenfusser and she highly disapproved of the impending wedding.

"I don't want to say anything against your cousin, but she's making a big mistake if she marries Fuzzwick."

My cynicism got the better of me. "All marriages are a big mistake."

"So we agree. Where do I sleep?"

"I thought you were staying with Alicia."

"Are you kidding? She doesn't want me anywhere near Fuzzwick."

"Yes, I see, but as I told you, this isn't my house. I'm staying at that little place down the road."

She paused before she responded. "Now I understand why

Alicia sent me here. But I don't mind. I'll sleep with you."

Without going into the details of that voluptuary evening with this little minx, suffice to say no orifice went unpenetrated and no spermatozoa were left behind. The next morning she brewed a pot of green tea and roused me to sit with her at the sheet of plywood on sawhorses that served as my desk and dining table. She pointed at my laptop. "Alicia told me you're a writer. You write other people's stuff for money."

"When I have to," I allowed.

"You don't like to do it."

"No."

"I have an idea for a book," she said.

I smirked. "Don't tell me. Your autobiography."

She smiled kittenishly. "Please, it's not pornography."

"Okay, shoot," I humored her.

"It's about this mysterious rich guy, no one knows where he got his money, but when he was poor he fell in love with a rich girl who wouldn't marry him because rich girls don't do that sort of thing. Actually, she wouldn't marry him because he was complete bore. It all ends quite tragically. At least for him. What do you think?"

I wondered if she was the rich girl in the story. In my limited experience I've found that rich girls are far more likely to jump in bed with you right away than women of more modest means who are angling for some-thing more than a quick roll in the hay. "Quite original, but what's the market?" I asked.

"You never know until you put it out there. So, what if you write my book?"

"I don't know if you can afford me."

She laughed. "Well, I guess we'll just have to lie down and negotiate."

Now, I am not some sort of Lothario. Actually, I'm rather shy and awkward around women, especially good looking ones, but Danica made me feel at ease precisely because she was obviously so promiscuous there was no point in even contemplating a so-called "serious" relationship and that made everything very serious indeed. Does that make any sense?

When she left, she asked me if I minded if she came back in the next few days. "I don't want to impose," she said.

"No imposition at all," I stammered.

"I like you, Martin," she said. "You're so easy to manipulate. What would you write if you didn't have to be a hack?"

I wasn't going to take that lying down. "Well, I've been working on this book set in the future called Babyland where everybody's been reduced to the level of infants who can only whine and make demands."

"Ummm, sounds delicious," she purred.

With that and a peck on the cheek she was gone. After her departure I drove into the village to buy a newspaper and there was my neighbor Redstone on the front page escorting a young woman to a premiere at the local film festival. Actually, I'd never seen a picture of him before. It was hard to tell whether he was waving to or warding off the photographer. The smile on his ruggedly chiseled face seemed tight and uncomfortable as if he weren't accustomed to this sort of public exposure. I bought a six-pack and drove back to the house to confront my responsibilities as a hack.

My employer had written down a few pages of notes, which were a combination outline and pep talk. The book's premise, if you could call it that, was that the Buddha had first lived in profligate luxury and then became a complete ascetic until he was enlightened and found the middle way, the foundation for commerce as we now know it. The enlightened businessman must follow the Buddha's teachings and not live it up like certain recently indicted corporate executives nor become such a frugal bean counter that life is no fun at all. The middle way was the ticket to success, happiness, and a hot sex life. The notes also included suggestions for chapter headings such as, "If Buddha Could Do It, Why Not You?!" or, "From The Mud Grows The Lotus" or, "The Dharma: Your Road To Wealth And Power." All this food for thought rendered me unable to continue and I immediately headed down the middle way to the veranda overlooking the bay and plopped myself down in a deck chair to conduct surveillance.

Across the way, I spotted the bright red speedboat erratically bobbing and weaving through the harbor out to sea. Shortly after it cleared the breakwater and took off with a startling burst of acceleration, the giant Sulema appeared headed in the same direction. I wished I could be out on the water instead of confined to my distasteful labors. The phone rang inside the house and I answered. It was Mr. Paine who wanted to drop by with a potential buyer if it wasn't an intrusion.

"No, no," I assured him. "No problem." Actually, I didn't like the idea at all but what could I do?

He soon arrived with a couple who were dressed identically in white, vinyl jumpsuits which they must have thought were very chic but didn't work at all. In fact, they looked ridiculous. Paine apologized for bothering me and introduced the Zelenskys who oohed and aahed at the view of the bay, admired the kitchen, inspected the bedrooms, and hemmed and hawed about the asking price. Paine assured them it was very reasonable considering the desirability of the neighborhood. Then they departed leaving me to wonder how many people would be invading the property in the days to come. But I had other things to worry about, namely my stubborn resistance to sitting down and cranking out the silly book that was paying my rent.

I returned to my lodgings and sat down at the laptop, made a few tentative stabs at the introduction, and gave up in despair. I simply could not get in the proper groove to blatantly patronize the poor saps who would be poring over the thing in some vain attempt to escape from the confines of their painfully vacuous lives. That was my excuse, anyway, to leave off typing and call Alicia.

"Martin, how are you? How was Danica?"

"Everything worked out fine but please don't do that to me again."

"Do what? You just said everything worked out fine."

"You know, send strangers over here."

Alicia laughed. "I guess you're not strangers any-more. Did you get laid? Danica will fuck just about anyone."

"Just how am I supposed to take that?"

She laughed again. "Let me take you to town for lunch. You can tell me all about it."

So she picked me up in the Chevy Nomad and we drove to a little restaurant on a hill overlooking the sound. Let it be said that the restaurants in the area are not very good but they are at least twice as expensive as their counterparts in the city and Alicia must have seen me wince when I looked at the menu.

"God, Martin, don't worry. I'm paying."

I still ordered the least expensive offering, a simple hamburger with fries. Alicia was in no mood to be frugal. She ordered lobster and an expensive bottle of wine. "You're such a dud," she mock scolded me. "I can't imagine what Danica saw in you. Was she good in bed?"

"You ought to know that gentleman don't talk, Alicia."

She snorted. "Where on earth did you get the idea you're a gentleman? Come on. You don't have to get clinical."

She wasn't going to get anything out of me. "Why is it that women are so curious about other peoples' sex lives?"

"Don't answer a question with a question. I'm not paying for lunch to have you clam up on me. Was she good in bed?"

"Maybe you should ask Fuzzwick."

"He's just like you. He won't talk about it."

"So let's change the subject. When are you getting married?"

She rubbed her chin. "I'm not sure. Wednesday, I think."

"You're not sure? What about the reception?"

"We're not having it the same day, maybe in a week or two. What's the matter? You need a party to go to?"

"Well, no, not really."

"Don't worry. You'll be the first to know."

The waitress returned with the bottle of wine and poured it for us.

"Cheers," Alicia said holding up her glass. "Don't you want to know why I'm marrying Fuzzwick? I'm not in love with him, you know."

"No?" Actually, I was wondering why he wanted to marry her.

"It's purely a career move. Wick is famous and I'm not. His publicist will get both of us in all the papers and before you know it my name will be a household word. My work will sell for astronomical prices and I'll get richer than I already am. You understand, don't you?"

"I understand that you're putting me on."

"You're so clever, Martin," she chuckled. "If that's all I wanted, I'd go after Harry Poon. Or even Ahmed Jifhraz."

"Why are you doing it then?"

"I want to get control of the foundation. Fuzzwick is so hopeless when it comes to business. He could be one of the most important people in the whole art world but he just fritters away his time and money on toys and women. I've got different plans. As soon as I take over, I'm going to remake the foundation into one of the biggest cultural institutions in the world. What do you think of that?"

Now I wasn't sure if she was putting me on or not. "That sounds pretty ambitious."

"But of course, Martin. I am ambitious. Just think if I controlled the foundation's endowment. I wasn't kidding when I said I'd get you a grant so you could stop writing that silly stuff you're working on now."

I wish I could start writing that silly stuff I was not working on now, I thought ruefully.

"Right now you're just treading water, Martin. You need to focus, set a goal for yourself."

This motivational lecture reminded me of the book I wasn't writing and I complained. "Stop sounding like some television self-improvement guru."

"Stop hiding behind ironic detachment," she ad-monished. "You've got to engage the world to get what you want."

There was no use in arguing so I quietly acceded. "Yeah, right."

"Don't be sarcastic."

Later, after she'd dropped me off at the big house, the only thing I could do was turn on the television and watch the Hitler Channel where tanks never ceased rumbling through Poland as waves of Stukas roared overhead. I dozed off and didn't wake until the early evening. What roused me was a knock on the door. I thought it was another prospective second home buyer but it turned out to be someone else entirely.

"Hey there, sport, I'm your neighbor. Just down the road there," he said with nervous affability. It was none other than Dacron Redstone. "I just thought we should get acquainted. Being neighbors and all, I mean."

I didn't know what to say. Strictly speaking, we were neighbors but it wasn't my house we were standing in. "Oh yes, come in."

"Dacron Redstone," he said, extending his hand, "but just call me Dack. You're..?"

"Martin, Martin Seward."

"Oh, yes, the Chowderhead Bay Sewards, right?"

I chuckled at what I thought was a joke but he didn't seem aware he'd said something funny and he wanted to know what I found so amusing about his inquiry into my genealogy.

"Have I said something to offend you? I was only curious."

"I'm sorry," I said. "It's just that so few people guess my lineage straight off."

My response seemed to please him. "I'm good at that sort of thing," he said. "Excellent family you've got."

I couldn't tell if he had no sense of humor or he was putting me on. "Would you like something to drink?"

"Whatever you're having, sport."

Behind this oddly gregarious façade I sensed a sort of inattentive obsession with appearances that had nothing to do with what was really going on in his mind. In fact, it was unclear if anything was going on in his mind, as if he were a basso profundo automaton programmed to play the part of a country club swell. He looked just like his picture in the newspaper, caught somewhere between a good fellow well met and terrible discomfort. I fetched a couple of beers and bade him sit down.

"Thanks so much. This is a very nice place you've got."

"Well, it's not mine really. I'm just a summer guest."

"Lucky you. I can feel the history in this house. Mine's all brand new. No history at all. So, what's your game, Martin?"

"Excuse me?"

"What business are you in?"

"Well, I don't know if you can call it a business. I'm a writer."

His hearty laugh was slightly unnerving. "I knew it," he said. "It's written all over you." He laughed again at his own lame joke. "Seriously though, sport, I need someone to write something for me. Have you ever played football?"

"Not since I was a child."

"Well, I did. Defensive back, Notre Dame. In the big game against USC we were ahead by one point but the Trojans had driven to our ten yard line. With seconds left in the game, their quarterback fell back for a pass to the end zone and I sensed exactly where he was going to throw it. I leaped high for the interception and was carried off the field in triumph on the shoulders of my teammates. When I got to the sidelines, my coach gave me a bear hug and said, 'That's you all the way, Dack! My golden retriever!' It was a truly great moment."

"I can imagine," I agreed. I only found out later that Redstone had never attended Notre Dame. "Is that what you want me to write about?"

"No, no, this is a financial thing. What I need is a short piece, just a few pages, on why I should be appointed to the board of Moloch and Feeney."

Moloch and Feeney was and, even after a series of scandals, still is a major player in the bond market. "I'm sorry, Mr. Redstone…"

"Dack. Call me Dack, sport."

"All right, Dack, I don't know anything about the financial world."

"Who cares? I'll tell you what to write. You just pretty it up a little bit. What do you say?"

"Well…"

"I know what you're thinking, sport. You're saying to yourself, 'What's in it for me?' Am I right? You're saying, 'This guy's going to offer me some kind of chump change to help him get into a position where he'll make millions.' That's what you're thinking, right? Well, let me tell you, I'm prepared to make you a very substantial offer to help me out. Let's say ten thousand dollars."

I must say I was flabbergasted. I had no idea what to say.

He seemed to take my tongue-tied silence as some sort of ploy. "Okay, make it twelve," he said. "I'm having a lawn party tomorrow. Come on over and I'll write you a check." He abruptly stood up and walked to the door. "Thanks for the drink, sport."

I must say I hadn't a clue what to make of this strange visit. I thought the man must be deranged. He was offering me more money to write some sort of puff piece than I was getting paid to write a whole book and we'd never even met before. But, of course, this might just be a simple case of hale and hearty self-aggrandizement. He wouldn't even remember what he'd said to me by the next day. Whatever I thought though, I wasn't about to miss that party.

CHAPTER TWO

The next afternoon, Mr. Paine showed up with another pair of prospective buyers and I hid down in the carriage house wondering what to wear to Redstone's party. It couldn't possibly be formal, not in this neighborhood, so I settled on an off-white linen jacket, oxford shirt with no tie, fresh pressed Levi's, and penny loafers with no socks. I know, I know, I looked like some preppy jerk-off but at least it was safe. It had occurred to me in the past weeks, whenever I heard the sounds of revelry coming from Redstone's estate, to simply walk in and join the fun, but I didn't like the idea of being confronted with the equivalent of a surly night club bouncer demanding my credentials and so had shied away from the festivities. Now I had an actual invitation, and for reasons I didn't even understand, I felt as if I'd been elevated to a new plane, that I'd been recognized for the great talent that I think I am. Absurd? Yes, but that's how I felt at the time.

After Paine and his clients had left, I went back up to the big house and made myself a drink. I hadn't given one guilty thought to the book I was supposed to be writing all day and I wasn't about to start now. I could hear the sound of dance music wafting through the breeze from Redstone's place and decided it was time to make my way over and put in an appearance. The road to the mansion was lined with the parked cars of Redstone's guests and more were arriving every minute. I walked down the long driveway to the house entrance where a large black man in a tuxedo who did indeed look like a night club bouncer was acting as butler and greeting the party-goers as they arrived.

"Good afternoon, sir," he said to me politely. "The party's out back."

"Thank you," I replied with relief as he ushered me into this unfortunate outcross of the Taj Mahal and Disneyland. It was Ahmed Jifhraz's yacht raised to the nth power, ostentatiously thrusting all its fantastic vulgarity in your face like a Reeperbahn hooker. The ceilings soared to cathedral heights and the walls were covered with a hodge-podge of art ranging from the Renaissance to the latest offerings of the very modern Derek Schnoigel. The furnishings were positively baroque, all carved wood with gargoyle heads and serpent tails protruding from beneath the ample gold satin padding of sofas, chairs, ottomans, and what have you. Giant crystal chandeliers loomed above like flying saucers poised to target the hapless earthlings below with atomic death rays. I made my way through to a giant indoor solarium filled with every species of tropical flora imaginable that faced out on the back lawn overlooking the bay. Outside was a spacious yellow and white striped tent where a deejay was blatting out the latest musical nonsense and the guests were getting down and funky in their own unique styles. I grabbed a glass of champagne from a passing waiter and joined the Bacchanalian throng purling about on the soft under-cushion of lush green grass.

My first encounter, if you can call it that, was a handsome, middle-aged man in a white suit with no shirt and no shoes berating a willowy, slightly horse-faced blond women in a little black dress and pearls. "You silly twat," he drunkenly spat out. "I don't know why I brought you here in the first place."

The blond didn't seem at all offended. "Calm down, Pedro," she drawled. "You're drinking too much."

He didn't like her admonition at all. "Fuck you, bitch," he snarled and weaved off in the direction of the bar.

For some reason she turned to me and held out her hand. "Hello there, I'm Megan Fillywell."

I politely replied, "Pleased to meet you. Martin Seward."

She looked at me for an uncomfortable few seconds with a disconcerting smile. "Don't you know who I am? Megan Fillywell?" she prompted me.

I was blanked.

"I'm a professional television talk show guest. I represent the conservative point of view."

"I'm sorry," I phumphed, "I don't watch a lot of television."

"Well, you should," she said. "You'd see a lot more of me."

I couldn't tell if she was flirting or completely insane. "I'll try to tune in sometime," I lamely responded

"Are you a friend of Dacron's?"

"Well, no, not exactly. I'm his neighbor."

"I've never met him before. That's why I slept with Pedro. So he'd take me along to the party."

"I see," I said.

"I don't think you do. If I can hook up with Dacron Redstone, the right wing will control this country for the foreseeable future. We can fill the Supreme Court with decent, God fearing judges who will rain hellfire down on the liberal elite. We can get rid of every Communist program that the Jew Roosevelt introduced and we can prohibit the teaching of evolution and any other theory that contradicts the Holy Bible. We're in a position now to usher in the New Jerusalem."

Let me say that I am not particularly political. In fact, I've never voted in my life but I found her messianic vision disturbing enough to resolve to register and vote against any position this crackpot endorsed.

"Come," she said abruptly. "Let's take a walk around. Maybe we'll run into Dacron and you can introduce me." She clamped onto my arm and off we went. The party-goers were already turning into party animals, swilling Cristal, pushing each other in the pool, and generally carrying on like a bunch of kids at spring break. "It's so fabulous," Megan gushed. "Dacron really knows how to throw a party."

"He does," I agreed, wondering how a fervent fundamentalist could be so enthusiastic about an ur-Babylonian orgy. Perhaps it was a sign of the End Time and the Rapture was nigh, were my dour thoughts.

"Mr. Seward?"

I turned to a thuggish looking fellow unlike the butler at the door. He looked like a retired FBI agent with his cheap suit and close cropped white hair.

"Mr. Redstone would like a word with you."

"Omigod, I can't wait to meet him," said Megan.

"Just Mr. Seward, miss. Follow me." He turned on his heel and headed for the house.

"Hey, wait a minute!" Megan complained loudly. My guide paid no attention to her at all.

"Sorry," I apologized. "Gotta go." I hurried along into the house where I was ushered into a small, bird's-eye maple paneled elevator and taken to the top floor where I was conducted down a corridor lined with classical paintings in rococo gold frames to a bronze door that entered into an elaborate onyx restroom where a ceiling to floor waterfall served as the urinal. My guide turned a valve and the cascade ceased, revealing a door in the wall behind it.

"Go ahead," said my guide.

I went through the door and found myself in a bright, sunlit office where Redstone was sitting at a window looking out at his party through a telescope.

"Mr. Redstone?"

"Dack, Martin, Dack," he said without turning away from the window. "Enjoying yourself, sport?"

"Oh, yes, it's wonderful," I said.

"Well, that makes sense," he said, leaving off the telescope and turning toward me. "It's my party, after all."

"Yes, of course," I managed.

"Do you know any of those people down there?"

"Well, no," I had to admit.

"Neither do I."

"You invited them, didn't you?"

"My publicist handles that. Always good to stay in the papers, sport. Now, let's get down to business. It's also always good to be generous with the people that work for you, if you understand what I mean." He pulled out a checkbook from his pocket, filled one out, and handed it to me. The amount was twenty thousand dollars. "I'm sure we're going to have a very good working relationship, sport."

"Shouldn't we have a contract or something?"

He looked puzzled. "Why? It would only be to your disadvantage."

"I'm not sure what I'm supposed to do,"

"Don't worry about that. We'll talk tomorrow. Now go back out and enjoy the party."

"You're not coming down?"

"I don't think so. Just make sure that Reynolds turns back on the waterfall when you leave."

This peculiar encounter with my host and erstwhile employer set my mind racing. What was Redstone up to? Why on earth did he want to buy a nobody like me? I rejoined the party and was immediately accosted by the Fillywell woman.

"Did you see him? Did you speak with him?" she said with such fervor you would have thought I'd just had an audience with the Pope.

18

"Tell me everything," she demanded.

"Well, it's a private matter actually," I allowed uncomfortably.

"Don't be coy," she scolded. "Just tell me what happened."

"Look, I really don't know you and I don't think…"

"Well, we can fix that, can't we? You said you're his neighbor. Where's your house?"

"Just down the road there."

She grabbed me by the arm and propelled me out of the party for a little walk down the street. "I don't do this with just anyone, you know."

"Do what? I thought you wanted to see the house."

"Well, of course I do," she giggled. "We don't want to camp out in the bushes, do we?"

I thought she was having a little fun at my expense but I was wrong. As soon as we walked in the door of the main house, she pushed me over to the couch and pulled me down on top of her, bumping and grinding and moaning and groaning. "Fuck me!" she commanded. "Fuck me till I can't stand it anymore!"

The decision I made had far less to do with passion than with a sadistic desire to punish her. The thought of ravishing this Christian fascist was actually very exciting. I got her panties off and her legs up over my shoulders. When I drove into her, she yelped like a puppy and then rhythmically chanted, "My lord, my savior, my lord, my savior, fuck me, fuck me, fuck me!" When we lay exhausted in each other's arms, she panted, "Oh, you beast with seven heads and ten horns! You have turned me into the Whore of Babylon!" Then she pushed me off of her with such force that I rolled over onto the floor. She leapt off the couch and stood over me. "Now, let's go back to the party."

"I don't think I'm going back," I said.

She glowered at me from above, her damp, blond twat, as the gentleman at the party had called it, dribbling smegma and pussy juice down her long legs. "But you said you were going to introduce me to Dacron."

"I didn't say that," I protested. "Besides, he won't even be there. He told me he wasn't coming down."

"What?!" she exploded in a fury. "You've taken advantage of me! You've degraded me with sin!" With that, she kicked me and stormed out of the house without her panties. I decided to skip any future Redstone parties, a resolution I would, of course, not keep.

That evening with, from what I could hear, the party next door still in full swing, I left the house and drove into town for a lobster roll at Cyrano's. Culinary purists scoff at this simple pleasure as a crime against crustacean cuisine but I am addicted to the combination of lobster meat and mayonnaise on indifferent Italian bread offered by several of the dives in the immediate vicinity. The owner, Cyrano Sandwort, a heavy-set, older British colonial gentleman with a bright red nose, was holding court at the bar as usual and greeted me with a hearty, "Bollocks!"

"Good evening," I replied.

"You don't look so good, lad," he said. "You've been working too hard and not getting anywhere. What you need is inspiration! Get this young man a drink!" he called out to the bartender.

I was immediately served up with one of the specialties of the house, a lethal concoction of rum and God knows what.

"Look at this," said Cyrano holding up a newspaper. The headline read: PRESIDENT DECLARES VICTORY. "Rubbish!" said Cyrano. "Have you read Cicero?"

I had to admit I hadn't. Not recently anyway.

"The result of the President's passionate desire for excessive wealth and unendurable tyranny is the most horrible and repulsive thing imaginable," he spouted theatrically. "The perverted intelligences of men who are animated by such feelings are able to understand the material rewards, but not the penalties. Not the penalties established by law, mind you, for these they often escape. I mean the most terrible of all punishments: their own degradation!"

"Hear, hear!" the rest of the barflies cheered.

"That's Cicero talking. Not me! I stand one hundred percent behind degradation!"

The bar cheered again and I decided to take a table rather than join them. I walked into the back of the saloon and ran smack dab into Alicia.

"What are you doing here, Martin?" she asked as if I had walked into some sort of off-limits area.

"I guess about the same as you."

"I have to go to the ladies but you must join us, You see Wick over there in the corner?"

I did. I walked over to the table and said hello. He looked up at me as if he'd forgotten his glasses, trying to focus on a blur. The only thing that was clear from his distorted point of view was that he didn't recognize me at all even though we'd just spent an afternoon together.

"You're, you're...," he fished.

"Martin. Martin Seward. Alicia's cousin."

"Oh, yes, sure. Sit down if you like. Alicia's somewhere around."

"Yes, I just saw her."

I sat down at the table and neither one of us knew what to say. Offenfusser broke the ice. "So you're out for the season, Mark?"

"Actually, I'm working."

"Working? Good, good. Idle hands, Devil's workshop and all that. Ah, here's Alicia."

My cousin joined us and immediately made an awkward situation even more so. "My cousin is Danica's new boyfriend, Wick."

Before I could mouth a word in protest, Offenfusser was on me. "You must watch out for that one, Mark. She's very unstable. I wouldn't have anything to do with her if I were you."

"But you're not, Wick," Alicia pointed out. "I'm sure Martin and Danica will get along famously."

"Who's Martin?"

"You know, Wick," Alicia replied acidly, "if you ever listened to anything you might hear something."

I had suddenly lost my appetite. "Listen, I just dropped by for a drink. I've got to go home and get back to work."

"You must come by the foundation for lunch tomorrow," said Alicia.

"Yes, of course. I'll call you."

"Don't say I didn't warn you about that woman, Mark!" Offenfusser called out as I took my leave. Cyrano was surprised by my hasty departure.

"Where are you going?" he demanded. "Have we offended you in our own small way?"

"No, no," I said.

"I think you're becoming a bit of a snob, Martin. I think you're beginning to look down your nose at this humble establishment. Just remember, look on my works, ye mighty, and despair!"

"I can use that line," I needled him as I left. "Write it down."

"Impertinent young whippersnapper!" he called after me. I was still hungry but there was no place I wanted to go. I wound up at the Seven Eleven on the highway and bought a frozen chicken pot pie. When I got back to the house, the party next door was still going and I was very briefly tempted to drop back in but what I thought was wisely decided against it and a wise decision it was indeed.

The next morning I went into the village and found out from the newspaper that a Mexican migrant laborer working as a catering assistant had been hit on his bicycle by a speeding car late at night on the very road that ran by my house. He was not expected to live. The police were looking for a white SUV with a dented fender that had apparently left a fair amount of paint behind in the collision. There was no mention of Redstone or the party so I assumed it must have happened some distance away. I later learned that this was not the case. The poor devil had been run over not fifty yards from the Redstone estate.

"I hope I didn't offend you last night," said Alicia when I answered the phone after I'd got back to the house.

"Then why are you calling me Danica's boyfriend?"

"Well, you could be if you play your cards right."

"Play your cards right. Isn't that what you mean?"

"Don't be a bore," she dismissed me. "You are coming over for lunch, aren't you?"

"I'll come if you behave. Fuzzwick didn't seem too happy about your little announcement last night."

"Is that why you left? Stop being petulant, Martin. It doesn't suit you."

And so I went. The grounds of the foundation were abuzz with activity. Flatbed trucks were lined up at a large, corrugated iron shed that served as a warehouse and workers were loading them up with large wooden crates transported on rolling overhead cranes. It seemed more like some milling operation than a sanctuary for the arts. I drove up to the main house where Alicia was outside gathering flowers from the surrounding beds.

"So there you are," she said. "I was afraid you were cross with me."

"Why would you think that?" I said with as much irony as I could muster.

"I have some good news for you," she said.

"And what might that be?"

"Barrington Stoat, the literary agent, is joining us for lunch. You be nice and you'll get into the agency."

"I already have an agent, Alicia." But not a renowned one like Barrington Stoat, I thought, the biggest deal maker in the book business. I'd dump my own guy in a flat second to get in with BSL.

"Loyalty is a character flaw, Martin. Get rid of him."

When she'd picked enough flowers we went into the house and she arranged them in a vase in the kitchen. I could see Offenfusser sitting outside on the terrace smoking a cigar and reading a magazine.

"Go talk to Wick," Alicia commanded. "I'll get you a drink,"

I cautiously ventured outside. "Hello, Fuzzwick."

He looked up from the magazine and blinked in the sun. I thought he wasn't going to recognize me again but he smiled broadly. "Hello, there," he said. "Good to see you. Sit down, make yourself comfortable."

I took seat at the table across from him and looked out at the bay. "You certainly have a great view," I tried to small talk. Redstone's estate was clearly visible in the distance.

"We do, don't we? I'm so used to it I really don't appreciate it anymore. I was just reading a review of a movie we saw the other night at the festival. I can't figure out for the life of me why this guy is raving about it. 'Brilliant! Groundbreaking!'"

"What movie was that?"

"I can't remember the name." He squinted at the magazine. "Here it is. 'Purple Midnight.' It's about this Chinese guy who lives in Hong Kong and hangs out at sleazy bars and hotels where he gets involved with all these women who seem to be prostitutes. I thought it was just a sort of soft core porn soap opera but I forgot my glasses when I went and I couldn't really read the subtitles so maybe there was more going on than I thought. It just seemed terribly long and boring."

Alicia came out with two tall pinkish drinks on a tray.

"I was just telling your friend..."

"Cousin, Wick," Alicia interrupted pointedly.

"Really?" he said. "You're Alicia's cousin? Well, how about that. Anyway I was just telling him about that Chinese movie we saw last week."

"Oh yes, I loved it. So erotic."

"I don't know about that," said Offenfusser dubiously. "I was just confused."

"It's your natural state of mind," she teased him has the doorbell chimed inside the kitchen. "That must be Barrington," she said and went off to open the door,

Offenfusser gazed off across the placid waters of the bay where the coming and going boats looked like toys in a bathtub. "Do you go boating?"

"When I get a chance."

"Eases the mind. I'll take you out one day."

Alicia returned with Barrington Stoat and made introductions.

"I'm glad to meet you," I said to this short, highly coiffed, impeccably outfitted woman of a certain age. She looked like she had walked in right from one of those pictures in the back of the newspaper of charity benefits and horse shows. Her blond hair, which resembled a helmet, literally glittered in the bright sunlight from the surfeit of fixative her hairdresser had applied.

"Likewise I'm sure," she drawled in a bottled in bond posh accent that might have been completely faux or absolutely genuine. "Hello there, Fuzzwick."

"Please sit down, Bunny," Alicia prodded the Stoat woman. "Lunch will be ready in a minute or two. I'll get you a drink."

Sometime later, after some idle chit-chat over shrimp cocktails and champagne, Bunny asked me what I did. I got the feeling that Alicia had programmed her to do so.

"I'm a writer," I said.

"Really? How interesting," she said. "I fully expected her next question would be "What have you written?" or "What are you working on?" or something like that but instead she said. "I think you'd look great on a dust jacket. Young women like handsome young writers. Only natural. Do you read well? In public I mean."

The only public reading I'd ever done was at a coffee house.

"I think I can help you out," she said, studying me as if I were a piece of furniture she was about to reupholster. "When you get into the city we'll do some pictures with the photographer the agency uses. He's very hot right now."

"Do you mean you want to represent me?" I wondered.

Her eyes opened wide. "But of course. I suppose you've been to the Iowa Writers' Workshop and all that. We'll need it for the press release. By the way, do you know any young women writers, preferably southern, who look like real hotties?"

I didn't actually but I assured I'd put the word out to my vast network of contacts of whom I had absolutely none.

After lunch when Alicia had seen Bunny out, she crowed to me, "See? What did I tell you? You're going to be a famous author, Martin."

"She hasn't read a word I've written," I protested. "She didn't even ask to see anything."

"Of course not. Do you actually think she'd lower herself to read some manuscript?" Alicia scoffed. "It's not important anyway. Talent doesn't matter. It's all about publicity. Bunny's a saleswoman, not a critic. She looked you over and you got the part. It's as simple as that."

"Not quite," I said with ruffled feathers. "I don't want to be some new product with a shelf life determined by gossip columnists and paparazzi. I don't want to be the new flavor of the moment."

Alicia laughed. "Methinks the scrivener doth protest too much. Believe me, Martin, you'll get used to it."

"Well, I suppose I should thank you," I sulked.

"I think you should. For lunch anyway. Now go home and write."

Driving back to my humble domain, I really began to understand Alicia. The woman was a complete control freak. Here she was manipulating my professional and love lives in a matter of mere days. What next? Poor Offenfusser. He didn't stand a chance against her.

I had my own future to think about though and I had to admit I was tantalized by the prospect of a big time agent with the power to promote my work even if she had no idea what it was. Maybe Alicia was right. It was better not to know. I even had an idea for a novel in mind - the one you're reading right now.

I parked the car in front of the house, got out, and was startled by a hearty, "Hello there, sport." It was Redstone coming out of the trees. "Hope I'm not catching you at a bad moment."

"No, no," I assured him. "Come in."

"If you have the time, maybe we could discuss our little project."

For twenty thousand dollars, I wanted to say, I have all the time in the world. "Of course," I said.

We went into the house and sat down at the dining room table.

"Would you like something to drink?" I asked.

"Just water. You should get a pad of paper and jot down some notes." When I sat back down he wondered, "What do you know about the bond market?"

"Not very much. Actually nothing," I admitted.

"Good, good, we need a fresh point of view. You don't have to worry about the details but I'll give you a general idea how it works. Bonds are fiscal instruments that trade on the open market at floating interest rates that can fluctuate daily. When stock prices fall, investors park their assets in bonds as a safety measure. When stock market prices rise, they sell their bonds to buy equities. Do you follow me?"

"Sort of."

"Well it's not important that you understand the workings of the market. What I want you to write is that we're in for a rough go for the next few years and the situation will be quite volatile for the foreseeable future."

"That sounds like a bad thing."

He laughed. "On the contrary. The more the instability, the more buyers and sellers are out there and Moloch and Feeney makes a commission on every transaction. Do you follow me?"

"I think so."

"I want you to promote me on that basis."

Now I didn't understand. "Don't you want to talk about your background, your credentials?" I asked him.

He laughed again. "I don't think that will be necessary."

We talked awhile longer and I sketched out an outline for the piece which was not to exceed a thousand words. The shorter and more concise, the better.

"They don't really read these things. It's just pro forma," he explained.

It was time to be blunt. "Then why are you paying me so much to do it?"

He seemed completely baffled. "So much? Isn't that your going rate?"

I laughed. "I'd like to think so."

"Don't ever underestimate yourself, sport" he said seriously. "If you do, then everybody else will."

They always have, I thought.

"So, did you enjoy the party?"

"It was very interesting."

"My parties always are. That's why I don't go," he said and chuckled. "Well, sport, see what you can up with and let's talk tomorrow."

With that he was gone. Not two minutes later, I heard the phone ringing down at my own housing, and, of course, being unable to answer the call, was subjected by answering machine to: "Martin, I have a whole new idea. Instead of Buddha, why don't we make it Jesus? Call me back and tell me what you think."

What did I think indeed? How was I going to handle this assignment now? I could just call her back and tell her to find someone else, return the pittance she'd fronted me, and forget about the whole thing. After all, I was now Dacron Redstone's hack rather than hers and the pay was a whole lot better. Not to mention I could do the whole Redstone thing overnight. But you know what? Sitting there poring over my copious two pages of notes on the bond market, I could no more lift fingertips to laptop keyboard than I could with the Buddha book. I drove over to Cyrano's for a drink.

As usual, the good publican Sandwort was holding court at the bar and I immediately cut him off at the pass by ordering a simple vodka rather than one of his exotic concoctions which probably would have been free. "Young Martin!" he called out. "Have you met our local sacred monster, Pedro Barbez?" It was none other than the man who had called Megan Fillywell a twat at Redstone's party. He was also dressed in exactly the same clothes and looked like he hadn't slept in three days. He eyed me blearily and said, "Have we met somewhere before?"

I couldn't help myself. "Yes, at Dacron Redstone's party."

"That twit," he grumbled and burped.

"Pedro's just finished his new picture book on Patagonian wildlife."

"It's not a picture book," said Barbez petulantly. "It's an illustrated historical allegory."

"Oh, excuse me," Cyrano mocked him. "I thank you for correcting my ignorant assessment of your work. We should all stand corrected every now and then." He turned his attention to me. "So, young Martin, what on earth was a lowly sort such as yourself doing at the exalted Redstone's party. Pedro here I can understand. He's sort of the pet infant terrible of the obscenely wealthy, but you...?"

"He's my neighbor," I explained. "I'm staying next door to his place."

"My, my, I had no idea what circles you ran in," said Cyrano. "I thought you were the real thing, not some trust fund poseur like Pedro."

Barbez didn't take kindly to that remark. "Why, you limey bastard..."

"I know, I know," Cyrano held up his hands as if in protest. "It's the old problem. Do you tell the patient he's terminal or let him live on for the short time he has left in a fantasy of all the good times ahead? As the philosopher said, nothing is true but everything is permitted. Except smoking at the bar for which we give thanks to our right honorable governor."

"He's right, you know," Barbez addressed me directly. "I'm rich and I always have been but does that make me a bad person? What am I supposed to do? Eat humble pie and pretend I'm not the arrogant aristocrat that I am? Cyrano here is just envious of my birthright."

Cyrano guffawed. "You're nothing but a peasant, Pedro, and no amount of money can wash away your country bumpkin, hayseed soul."

"At least I'm not a complete parvenu like Redstone," Barbez shot back. "Have you seen that place he lives in?"

"Can't say that I have. Is it all that Pedro cracks it up to be, young Martin?"

This question put me in a quandary. I agreed with Barbez that the house was an architectural travesty but I didn't want to bite the hand that was currently feeding me and word does get around. "Let's just say I don't share Redstone's aesthetic," I tried to squirm out of it.

Barbez roared with laughter. "Well, that's putting it politely!" he sputtered. "The fucking place is more like a Las Vegas casino than a house. All he has to do is put in a few slots and a craps table to complete the effect."

"I say," said Cyrano. "Sounds like quite the diversion. He's never invited me to any of his parties, but then I've never met the man."

"You don't have to know him," said Barbez. "All you've got to do is go. You won't meet him there either. He never shows up."

"Wonderful! Then I don't even have to pretend to be polite."

"No one else does," said Barbez. "Especially me."

Later, the silly, barroom banter exhausted, I went back home and watched the silly news on TV where I learned all sorts of things about celebrities in rehab, celebrities at a golf tournament, celebrities on a USO tour, and celebrities getting divorced. As I'm sure you're well aware, this is what passes for journalism these days.

The doorbell rang and, assuming it was Mr. Paine with some more potential buyers, I quietly let myself out the back and headed down to my own modest dwelling.

"You!" I heard a shout behind me. I turned and there was Megan Fillywell looking somewhere between sheepish and reproachful. "I forgot my underwear," she said.

Now, I'm no pervert and I hadn't saved her panties for the purpose of sniffing or wearing on my head, though the thought may have occurred to me, but rather deposited them in the trash.

"I, uh..," I stammered. Then I had an idea. "Right down here," I said and conducted her down to the garbage bin. "I'm sorry, but I didn't know you were coming back so I..."

She bowed her head in contrition. "Don't worry, I have plenty more."

"No, no, I'll dig them out." And I did.

"I'm sorry I kicked you. It wasn't the Christian thing to do."

"How did you get here?" I said. I didn't see any car in the driveway.

"A friend dropped me off. I'll call a cab."

I took her back up to the main house where she didn't exactly jump for the phone. "Listen, I'd really like to make it up to you for the way I behaved yesterday. You must think I'm frightfully fickle."

I had no idea what to say and just stood there as if I were weighing her words.

"If you got to know me a little, I think you'd understand that I'm actually a rather stable individual."

"Oh yes," I quickly agreed. "I'm sure you are."

"Do you have anything to drink? I'm parched."

"Well, I have water and I think there's a little lemonade left."

"No alcohol?" she said as if she couldn't quite believe what I'd just offered her.

"Oh yes, of course."

"Any gin?"

"Yes, I think so. How would you like it?"

"I'd like a martini if you could manage it. Make one for yourself."

Well, why not? I mixed a couple martinis and sat down with her in the living room.

"So, what do you hear from Dacron?" she said, as if he were an old friend that neither of us had seen in a while.

I was faced with two options and the truth wasn't one of them. I could either tell her nothing or ruthlessly put her on. I decided on the latter. "I saw him this morning," I said. "He told me had a vision last night."

This disclosure greatly agitated Miss Fillywell. "I knew it!" she said breathlessly. "My mere presence at the party was enough!"

"Could be," I allowed. "He said that an attractive, young woman had taken him by the hand and led him through a scene of horrible carnage, all his party guests maimed and dismembered, to a high plateau where the sun shined eternally."

She was transfixed. I began to think I was hanging out at Cyrano's too much.

"Is that all?" she demanded.

"Well, he said there was more but he really couldn't remember."

"Come here," she all but commanded.

I was puzzled. "I am here," I replied.

"No, right here with me. I know the meaning of Dacron's vision."

I got up and I was expecting her to whisper something in my ear but instead she grabbed me by the belt and pulled down my zipper.

"I want you to think of my mouth as your heart and your cock as our lord and savior, Jesus Christ almighty. I want you to let him into your heart." With that she pulled out my penis and began sucking for all she was worth. I soon ejaculated in her mouth and she swallowed my fine substance with the sort of relish usually reserved for caviar. "So yummy," she moaned. "Now, my darling," she cooed, "take me over to Dacron's so I can interpret his vision."

But, of course. "Listen, Megan, I can't do that."

She became livid. "I should have just bit that damn thing off," she huffed and puffed and steamed right out the door

"Don't forget your panties!" I called after her but she was gone. She must have been my muse however. I went back to my place, sat down, and wrote Redstone's thousand words in about an hour.

CHAPTER THREE

I woke from a dream the next morning where I was being led by Megan Fillywell through a battlefield that looked something like Matthew Brady's photographs of Gettysburg or Bull Run except in color. Among the mangled dead were Dacron Redstone, Pedro Barbez, and Fuzzwick Offenfusser. Megan led me out of this scene of carnage up a hill to a high plateau with eternal sunshine and pushed me over the edge of the cliff. I woke in a cold sweat just before I hit the rocks below. Only kidding. Actually, I slept like a baby and I don't think I dreamed anything at all.

Of course, I couldn't call Redstone to tell him his piece was finished. I'd have to wait at least a week so it wouldn't look like I was completely ripping him off. Now that I was solvent beyond all expectations, my dilemma was whether or not to continue with my other onerous chore. Buddha was bad enough, but Jesus? Well, Jesus! I am a procrastinator by nature and decided to let things lie awhile and, for the moment at least, avoid some unpleasant confrontation with my patroness.

I drove into town and bought the newspaper and a corn muffin. Having nothing to do and not even having to feel guilty about not writing I decided to go for a drive out to the point. There was nobody there but a few surfcasters working the rocky beach beneath the lighthouse. I sat down on a bench overlooking the ocean and watched the few sailboats bobbing around in the morning sunlight. There was virtually no wind so they weren't making much progress. Suddenly, a candy apple red speedboat roared into view heading east. The driver paid no attention whatsoever to the sailboats, violating their right of way with impunity and sending up a rooster tail of spume as he sped off into the distance.

I returned to my house a little while later and turned on the answering machine. "Martin, it's Alicia. Please call me when you get this message." Now, frankly, I didn't want to speak to my cousin right at that moment. Her demands on my time, though not yet excessive, showed every sign of becoming tiresome.

The next message was from the far more urgent Sheridan March. "Really, Martin you must call me right away. We have so much to discuss." I suppose we did. I reluctantly picked up the phone and dialed her number in the city.

"Oh, there you are," she said excitedly when she answered the phone. "Did you get my message about changing Buddha to Jesus?"

"Ah, yes, I did…"

"Well, forget it. Back to plan A."

"Don't you mean plan B?" I joked. She didn't get it.

"No, I mean back to Buddha. I just had a long meeting with a very important Tibetan rimpoche who was very enlightening. He told me the Buddha had this sort of twelve step program to achieve your financial goals and he agreed to reveal the secret if I was willing to make a donation to the Dalai Lama. Isn't that fabulous?"

I had to admit it was, but not the way she meant it. "Listen, Sheridan, I'm not sure I'm really the guy for this job…"

"Of course you are! You're just having a crisis of faith in your own abilities," she admonished me. "You just have to empty your mind of all the conflicts you're having and let the Buddha be your guide to success and security. I don't mean to interfere, but you've got to listen to a little bit of my Mother Bear wisdom! All you need is to get motivated! What's the problem, Martin? Money?"

"Not exactly."

"I knew it!" she brayed triumphantly. "I'll tell you what I'm going to do. I'm going to give you incentive! I'm going to give you another five thousand dollars! But you've got to deliver, Martin. I want to see pages, I want to see progress! I know you won't let me down."

I was at a complete loss for words but it didn't matter. She had already hung up. I would have to submit my resignation by mail. But then, maybe I'd just go ahead and do the silly woman's bidding. I could use an extra five thousand bucks. I went outside and walked up to the main house where I could see the Sulema steaming into the harbor and heading for her berth at the marina. I wondered if Harry Poon were on board.

"Ahoy there, mate!" Redstone called out from the woods. He had a way of sneaking up behind you and making you jump.

"Hello there," I said.

"Why don't you come over for lunch and we can shoot the

breeze," he jovially suggested.

Why not? I was soon seated at the long table in the main room where the all too recognizable work of Derek Schnoigel towered to the ceiling, all pieces of broken glass and rocks affixed to a huge canvas and painted over with abstract abandon.

"What would you like to eat?" said Redstone. "We have lobster, soft shell crabs, steak, whatever you like."

It's not often that someone invites you to lunch and hands you a menu. "How about the soft shell crabs?" I said.

"Excellent choice. I think I'll have them myself. Perhaps you'd like a very dry white wine with that. I bottle it myself at my vineyard in California."

Now let me tell you something about Redstone's tone of voice. Everything he says, no matter how insignificant, comes off as the boasting of someone not quite sure of himself, possessing an unfathomable sense of displacement which must be covered up with proud bluster.

"So, what's new, sport?"

I thought he was talking about his report to the bond firm. "Well, I've only just started working on…"

"No, no, that can wait for another day," he said. "What I want to know is what's up in your life? I suppose you have friends out here."

"Not really," I said. "Well, there's my cousin, of course."

"Good, good, great to have family around you. Don't have any myself."

I didn't know whether to commiserate or tell him how lucky he was.

"But I don't let it get me down," he continued, "because my dreams are actually more important to me than real people."

I was curious. "So what do you dream about?"

"Oh, all kinds of things. Mostly the future."

A Mexican servant in full livery brought out the crabs on gold plates. He poured our wine and placed the bottle in a silver ice bucket.

"Thank you, Guillermo," said Redstone. "Hard to get good help out here but Guillermo's the best."

I was sure he was. Actually, I was getting bored. What was I doing there anyway? I ate the soft shelled crabs on my plate quickly and was already making excuses for my exit when something happened. There was a crash behind me and I turned around to a pile of multi-colored rocks and broken glass that had detached themselves from a patch of Schnoigel's painting.

Redstone was irritated. "Don't worry, it happens all the time," he muttered. Guillermo, who was apparently used to the drill, rushed back in and swept up the mess. "I never should have listened to that goddam art advisor," Redstone complained. "The first time this happened I called up Schnoigel and asked him to repair it. You know what he said? 'The painting, like all of us, exists in an entropic universe. Everything is disintegrating. Even you.' And that was that. He refused to do anything about the damage and now I can't even put it up for auction."

"Can't you get someone else to restore it?"

"I'm sick of throwing money at the thing. It's the biggest white elephant in my collection."

His cell phone played "Rule Britannia." "Pardon me," he said, taking the call. "Hello there, good to hear from you," he said into the receiver. "I've got a guest right now but I can meet you in an hour." He hung up. "Now where were we?"

"Listen, if you're busy..."

"I've got a few minutes. Tell me about your cousin."

"Well, I don't see her all that often," which was true except under my present circumstances. "She lives across the bay."

"Really, I'd like to meet her some time," There was a sharp insistence in his tone that was completely out of place.

"Well, yeah, maybe. We'll see."

"Introduce me," he said fixing me with blowtorch eyes and almost spooky fervor. "As a personal favor."

This conversation, if you could call it that, was getting too weird. I walked away with the impression he knew exactly who she was and I was being set up for some sort of embarrassing confrontation. I decided to ask Alicia what she knew about Redstone.

"Who?" she answered when I called her. "Never heard of him."

"He's a Wall Street guy."

"Not exactly my crowd," she snorted. "How's the Buddha book going?"

"Don't ask."

"Bunny called and she wants you to come into the city for a

photo session. She's also going to set you up with a publicist."

"In case I didn't make it clear, I don't have anything to publicize."

"But you will, Martin. I'm sure of it."

I should have been completely exasperated by her annoying persistence but the whole scenario did have a certain surreal appeal. Perhaps I could get an advance without writing a word and run away to Mexico where they would never find me.

"I'm driving into the city myself tomorrow. I can run you in," she offered.

I still don't know why I went. How bored could I have been to meet Barrington Stoat at her office in midtown and have her herd me from 59th Street to a lower Broadway photo studio to lunch with a public relations wizard on Park Avenue South?

"It's so good to see you again, Martin," she greeted me in her tastefully decorated aerie overlooking the park. "I'd ask you to sit down but we have a busy day ahead so we might as well just get going."

In the cab downtown I asked her if she'd like to see some of my work. A short story perhaps. She wasn't interested.

"We'll get to that later," she said. "I'm quite sure you're going to work out very well."

The studio was located in a loft building just south of Prince Street where she introduced me to my photographer - fat, scraggly haired Ponce de Souza, who looked me over dubiously and called over his stylist to do my make-up. When she was finished, he sat me on a stool and had me strike various poses as he snapped away.

"Look directly into the camera at the top of the lens," he ordered me. "Can't you look more intense? Pretend you're trying to pick up a girl or a boy or whatever. I need those bedroom eyes."

I felt like a fool but I tried my best which apparently wasn't good enough. De Souza shook his head and reassured Bunny, "Don't worry. We can fix him on the computer."

Next it was off to a French bistro to meet with legendary press agent Sparky Goldflugel, the wizened old wizard of the Great White Way. His attitude was avuncular. "Come, come," he said putting his hand on my shoulder and shepherding me over to a table in the corner. "Bunny's told me all about you. She tells me you're going to be the next big thing in the book world."

"All we have to do is let people know about him," said Bunny.

"Do you have a girlfriend?" Goldflugel wanted to know.

"Nobody special."

"Good, good, we'll find you one. Take a look at this list. These are all models, actresses, society girls, and other young ladies that I represent. Just pick one out and the next thing you know you two will be canoodling with the best of them at the hottest clubs in town. Just make sure you only go out with girls on the list. Understand? You'll be in the papers three, maybe four times a week. Then you do the talk show rounds. By the way, what's the name of your book?"

"Babyland," I replied dryly.

He was impressed. "Great title."

I ate a bowl of mussels while Goldflugel and my new agent talked shop. When it was time to go, he gave me a hug. "You make me feel like a midwife, kid."

"Well, everything's all set then," Bunny said on our way to the train station. "You'll be hearing from me in a few days once I've set up your schedule. You're not doing anything else, are you?"

"I'm writing."

"Forget about that for the time being. We've got more important things to attend to."

Riding back on the train, I reflected on the utter absurdity of the whole day. It was like a dream, and not particularly a good one. It couldn't be happening but it seemed to be moving along, with or without my consent. Now I was supposed to be grateful to Alicia but I didn't feel any gratitude at all. Ingrate! I chuckled to myself. One thing was for certain. Bunny Stoat's "schedule" was out of the question. I wasn't about to humiliate myself on some tour of the cocktail party, schmoozerama circuit. I looked down the list Goldflugel had handed me and, lo and behold, there was Megan Fillywell. I don't know why I was surprised.

As the train pitched gently back and forth down the track, I looked out the window at the real relics of civilization hidden from the cities and the people in their cars on the parkways; the slag heaps, the piles of gravel and sand, the rusted water tanks, the broken windows of abandoned factories. That's why I always took the train rather than the bus. It was like peeling back the cosmetic veneer of the ugly truth of wealth and commerce. Here in this wasteland lay all the dirty little secrets, all the disappointments, and all the decay that are the hallmarks and the unspoken basis of our despair. It was like a skid row bum sitting in a broken down lawn chair under a relentless, blazing sun. Curiously, this bleak panorama always cheered me. I can't say why and, if I could, I know I would be truly lost.

The train slowed and we pulled into one of those rinky-dink stations that line the track where a group of boisterous teenagers boarded my car. There were boys and girls and they looked Hispanic though they spoke perfect yo boy English. They immediately set to bounding around the car insulting each other, slap fighting, shrieking, and giggling. The boys referred to the girls as "bitches" and the girls retorted with such epithets as "dirty dog" and "midget dick." Needless to say, this exuberantly foul mouthed banter did not go over very well with the rest of the passengers, particularly a pair of elderly ladies who, after a few minutes, could take it no longer and berated the youngsters for their profanity.

"You should have your mouth washed out with soap!" one of them barked at a young man who had just run off a particularly long string of expletives.

This, of course, was like throwing gasoline on a fire. The teenagers whooped and hollered and graciously permitted the old woman to enter into their badinage.

"Whynchu shut up, you old douche bag," one of the young women shot back.

"Now you see here..!" the older woman's companion began to complain.

"That goes for you too, you fat lezbo," the young woman snapped and her friends all hooted with glee.

The conversation went on in this comic vein for another few minutes until the conductor appeared and spoiled all the fun. He ejected the teenagers from the car and things quickly settled down.

Now, you well may wonder why I'm relating all these mundane details of my train ride home, but while I was being pleasantly amused by the vicissitudes of rail transit, black clouds of smoke were gathering just over the horizon. You see, my house was burning down. Literally. By the time I got there all that was left were charred beams and wet soot. Two engine companies were still there and firemen milled around the steaming ruin. The trees around the house were only slightly scorched and the main house hadn't been touched. A lot of difference that made to me. Everything I had was gone; my clothes, my laptop, the few books I'd brought out. I was so stunned I just stood there in a daze staring at the disaster. One of the firemen came over.

"You know who lives here?" he asked.

"Me."

"That's pretty shitty. Looks like the propane tank blew. You're lucky you weren't in there." He must have noticed my distraction. "You all right?"

And that's when Redstone appeared from out of the trees. "Terrible thing, sport," he said. "I saw the smoke and called the fire department right away but it was too late."

There was an awkward silence. No one knew what to say.

"Well," said Redstone, "come on over to my place and I'll set you up."

I didn't know exactly what he meant by that and I begged off. "I've got call my landlord," said. "I'll be over in awhile."

"Whenever you like. Mi casa es suya, sport."

I went up to the main house and called Mr. Wilberforce. He didn't take the news well. "What have you been doing out there? Throwing wild parties?" he sputtered angrily.

"No, sir," I said nervously. "I was in the city when it happened. The firemen said the propane tank exploded. They said I was lucky not to be there."

His attitude flipped a hundred and eighty degrees. If there was anything Mr. Wilberforce could smell, it was a lawsuit in the offing. "Well, I'm glad you're all right. Really, I am. Just stay in the house until you can get yourself settled somewhere else. I guess I'll have to come out there and take a look. I'll call Paine and tell him to stop showing the property for the time being."

"Thank you." I didn't know what else to say. I also didn't know what to do. The things I didn't want to do were stay in the house with the acrid smell of the burnt building wafting through the windows, call Alicia, go over to Redstone's, or get drunk at Cyrano's. The latter, of course, was the least disagreeable of the possible prospects and I was soon on my way.

"Understand you had a spot of bother, Martin," said Cyrano when I walked in. News travels fast in a town where no one has anything to do but drink and gossip. "Everything's on me," he graciously offered. "By the way, there's a young lady here who's been looking for you." The young lady in question was Megan Fillywell.

"Oh, Martin, I'm so sorry," she gushed with the best imitation of sincerity she could manage. "If there's anything I can do..."

"Everything's all right," I reassured her.

"We have to talk," she said. "Privately."

Before I could even object, she grabbed my arm and dragged me outside.

"Sparky Goldflugel called and told me you're the new guy on the list. Kiss me." She pulled me to her and gave me a big smooch. There was a flash of light off to the side and, when I turned, I saw it was a photographer who immediately hurried off.

"All right," she said. "That's done. We can go back inside now. I'm supposed to meet Pedro."

When we went back in, she dumped me like a hot potato and went back to her table which was just fine with me. I hunkered down at the end of the bar for some serious thinking and drinking. I was reviewing my options when Harry Poon walked in with a comely young bimbo on his arm. They had clearly been doing some serious drinking themselves. They took seats right down the bar and Poon did a double take when he glanced over at me. He squinted and asked, "Don't I know you from somewhere?"

"I met you with Fuzzwick and Alicia. We had lunch on the boat."

"Right, that's right. This is my friend Gloriana," he said putting his hand on his companion's arm. "I've forgotten your name."

"Everybody does," I said. "Martin. Pleased to meet you."

Gloriana didn't reply directly to me. "Doesn't he look like Zarg?" she said to Poon.

"Yes, he does, doesn't he," Poon agreed.

I didn't know if I liked being compared to someone with a name like Zarg. It sounded like some science fiction character.

"I haven't seen Wick this time out," he said. "What's he up to?"

"I really don't know. Something to do with putting a show together."

"You're an artist too?"

"No, no," I said. "I'm a writer."

"Good," he said. "Then I don't have to be rude to you." They both laughed. "What sort of stuff do you write?"

I decided to tell the truth. "Self help books mostly. Right now I'm working on a book called *Buddha: The First Entrepreneur.* It's all about how to take the Buddha's teachings and put them towards buying real estate for no money down."

My little joke, which wasn't a joke at all, had the desired affect. They both looked at me askance.

"Well, yes," said Poon dubiously, "that sounds, ah, interesting."

"That's not all," I pressed on. "The Buddha can also make a huge difference in your love life and I do mean huge."

Gloriana giggled and Poon began to catch on. "You don't really write that crap, do you?"

"No."

They both laughed and Poon called out to the bartender, "Buy this guy whatever he wants."

"Are you out here on the boat again?" I asked.

"Uh huh. I'm just along for the ride but Gloriana's working. She tricks with A.J."

She cuffed him on the ear. "You're such an asshole, Harry."

"I've been called worse. But it's true, isn't it?"

"That you're an asshole?"

"No, that you trick with A.J."

"Let's just say that a little kindness goes a long way," Gloriana smirked. "A.J.'s been very generous with you as well and you don't have half the talent I do."

"Touché!" Poon brayed. "I'll drink to that!"

We all clinked glasses.

I was curious. "Tell me more about A.J. I never heard of him before last week."

They both looked at me as if I were from another planet. "Where have you been, dude? Hiding under a rock? I'll tell you who he is. Ahmed Jifhraz is an oily, pear-shaped, commercial traveler who happens to be the richest man in the world. He is also a patron of the arts and an insatiable pussy hound."

"Oh, come on," said Gloriana. "You're giving him too much credit. He never does anything. The girls are just decorative."

"Well, we all need a little arm candy sometime. Have I answered your question?"

I had another. "What's the richest man in the world doing here? Why isn't he in Cannes or Monaco with all the other big yachts?"

"Are you kidding? He's under indictment in every country on the Mediterranean. You don't get to be the richest man in the world without stepping on a few toes, if you know what I mean," said Poon confidentially.

"He better not step on mine," Gloriana tut-tutted. "I just got a very expensive pedicure."

"So you see," Poon continued, "A.J. prefers to stay out of the limelight in backwaters like this. He's also got a business partner who lives somewhere around here."

Just at that moment, Pedro Barbez lurched into the bar with a blond young lady in tow.

"Well, look who's here," said Poon. "The creature from the single malt lagoon."

The new arrivals passed out of sight into the dining room followed by the sound of people shouting and breaking glass.

This greatly amused Poon. "Off to an early start, don't you think?"

All the hubbub was just the prelude to Barbez racing out of the dining room with Megan Fillywell in hot pursuit.

"You crummy bastard!" she shrieked as Barbez tried to take cover in a Mexican stand-off maneuver by skittering around a table as she went after him.

"I can't even remember your name, you silly bitch!" he loudly defended himself.

"You will burn for this, Pedro!" she proclaimed with blazing eyes as she futilely chased him in circles.

"Now you see here!" Cyrano bellowed indignantly. "I will not tolerate this sort of unruly behavior in my establishment!"

This deterred Megan Fillywell not at all and she continued her pursuit with renewed vigor. "The Devil will throw you in a boiling cauldron of excrement for all eternity, Pedro! You have defiled a Christian woman!"

Cyrano and the bartender were required to intervene and

restrain the hysterical holy-roller by force. They grabbed her and pinned her against the wall where she continued to kick and flail and foam at the mouth. The crowd at the bar laughed and applauded.

"You tell him, baby!"

"The sonuvabitch had it coming!"

"Would you like to take a bow before you leave?" Cyrano growled at Megan before he and the bartender frog-marched her out of the restaurant.

Barbez shrugged at the barflies. "Can I help it if I'm irresistible?"

The crowd treated him to a round of laughter and boos and he disappeared back into the dining room.

Poon was delighted. "Break a leg!" he called out. "You can't pay for a show like that."

Gloriana was of another opinion. "I'm sorry for the girl. Men can be so callous sometimes."

"Yes," Poon needled her, "I suppose our boorish behavior is enough to occasionally drive the gentle sex to homicidal distraction. Who was that woman anyway?"

"Her name is Megan Fillywell," I informed. "She's a professional television talk show personality representing the conservative point of view."

They both laughed.

"It's true," I said. "She's also a fundamentalist Christian and a nymphomaniac."

This really cracked them up. What was the use in trying to convince them I wasn't joking? When I left later, Cyrano kindly offered me use of the back room as a transient apartment, an offer I politely declined.

I returned to the house and there was a white SUV parked in the driveway. Redstone's factotum Reynolds got out and said: "Good evening, Mr. Seward. Mr. Redstone would like you to come over."

This annoyed me. "Tell Mr. Redstone that everything is all right and I'll speak to him tomorrow."

Reynolds looked at me curiously as if I'd just said something completely incomprehensible. "You understand that Mr. Redstone will be very disappointed..." he trailed off.

I threw up my hands. "Okay, okay, let's go."

Reynolds drove me over to the estate and Redstone greeted me at the door. "Good to see you, sport. Just hope we can cheer you up after this terrible day. We've already set up a bedroom for you upstairs."

"That won't be necessary," I curtly explained. "Mr. Wilberforce said I could stay at the main house, but thanks anyway."

"Good, good," said Redstone with a lack of sincerity that measured in minus centigrade. He seemed clearly upset that I was not taking advantage of his hospitality. "Anyway, come on in and have a drink," he said.

"You know, I'm pretty loaded already. I just got back from Cyrano's and I need to lie down."

"Yes, I've heard of it. Sort of the local, isn't it? I'll have to stop in sometime."

"Yeah, well…"

"Just come in for a nightcap. I'll have you out of here in fifteen minutes."

What could I do? We went inside and Redstone made a couple of spritzers from "the finest white wine" he had in stock. It was, of course, from his vineyard.

"So what are your plans now, sport? I guess you lost just about everything."

"Including my computer. I'll have to get a new one."

"Don't worry about that," he scoffed. "They're all over the house. Just pick one out and take it with you."

"That's very kind of you," I said.

"We all have to help each other out in times of adversity. When I was in the Special Forces, we were dropped into the wrong place behind enemy lines. We had to hide out as best we could while those bastards tried to track us down. As the commanding officer, I was responsible for the lives of all my men. I told them we had to work as a team with clockwork precision. If anyone made a mistake, it would put all of us in mortal peril. They listened to me, sport, they listened to me, and when that chopper pulled us out of there we hadn't lost a man. I received a secret Medal of Honor."

"Secret? What war were you in?"

"Can't tell you that. Classified."

"I see."

"My point is we're all in this together. I'll cover your back and

I expect you to cover mine. Understand?"

I nodded my head. "I'll remember that." I'd had about enough of this nonsense and, of course, as I found out later, Redstone had never served in the military at all. "Listen, Dack, I've got to go. Thanks for everything."

"Get some sleep, Martin. We'll talk in the morning. I'll have Reynolds drive you back."

"I think I'll walk," I said. "I need some air."

"Of course. What's your cousin's name, by the way?"

"Alicia," I replied to this oddly inappropriate question.

"Hmm, very creative."

What he meant by that I didn't know. Furthermore, I didn't care. I left and went back to the house.

CHAPTER FOUR

The following morning, I drove into town and, against all my Luddite instincts, bought a cell phone. Both my phone and answering machine had been destroyed in the fire and I needed to maintain a tenuous grip on the outside world. I know very well that the microwaves put off by these infernal devices cause the brain to disintegrate into a radioactive mush and transform their users into babbling idiots. Believe me, I've seen it. But what choice did I have? I called Alicia and gave her my new number.

"This is just awful, Martin. What are you going to do?"

"Nothing. Mr. Wilberforce is letting me stay in the main house."

"Well, if you have any problems there's always room over here."

"That's very kind of you to offer but I'm sure everything's going to be all right." How many more times was I going to have to chant this litany to all these good Samaritans?

"Whatever, but you must come over to lunch," she bullied me.

I agreed to do so only because I had nothing else to do. Lunch turned out to be more than I'd bargained for. When I drove into the foundation, I was almost run over by a bulldozer that was only one of a whole fleet tearing up the grounds. As I carefully wove through these belching machines carving the land into some as yet unrevealed pattern, I spotted a man in a yellow hard hat driving around in a golf cart and yelling instructions to the big Caterpillars through a bullhorn. It was Offenfusser.

I threaded my way through this chaotic din past the radio tower as I called it to the main building where Alicia greeted me at the door.

"Sorry for all this ruckus," she apologized. "Wick just can't stop creating. It gets tiresome sometimes."

"Is he joining us for lunch?"

"No idea. He'll wear himself out eventually." Actually, he did almost immediately, joining us in a matter of minutes.

"Heard about your fire," he said. "Terrible thing. But perhaps it's all for the best. Phoenix rising from the ashes and all that. Did you lose much?"

"Not really. Just some clothes and my laptop. I can always write long hand," I joked.

Alicia, however, took me seriously. "Don't be silly," she scolded. "We have loads of computers here. Take any one you like." The day before, I had one old Toshiba. Now, through the good offices of Redstone and the Offenfusser Foundation, I had two. "Did you lose any work?" she wanted to know.

I wondered how to field a question like that. I hadn't written a single word on Buddha and the Redstone memo, which I didn't want her to know about anyway, could be reconstructed in a matter of hours. "I've got everything backed up on disc," I lied.

"Well, that must be a relief," said Offenfusser. "I'd hate to lose one of my works but I guess that would be almost impossible." We all laughed and I asked him about the bulldozers.

"I'm just trying to make something you can see from outer space," he explained. "I figure if I crosshatch the entire estate I have a shot at it."

I wondered what era he was living in. These days spy satellites could pinpoint a whisker on a cat.

"The way I see it, they'll soon have rocket ships for tourists flying around up there and I want to be able to point down from twenty thousand miles up there and say, 'That's my property'."

"But, it's not your property, Wick," Alicia pointed out. "It's the foundation's."

"Don't get technical," he replied. "Did you know Alicia and I were planning to be married, Mark?"

I avoided the question. "Really? Congratulations." Actually, according to Alicia's calculations, they should have been married already.

"Not so fast," he corrected me. "I said 'were'."

I looked at Alicia who just smiled and shook her head.

"We were supposed to do it this week," he went on, "but I got cold feet. I didn't know whether I was ready for my eighth marriage. If we went through with it, you'd be one of my in-laws, you know. Sort of."

"Was that the problem?" I mocked him back.

He broke into a broad smile. "Not at all. You see, Alicia got me drunk yesterday morning, hauled me into town, and we did it, Mark, we did it in the road."

This vivid description conjured up a vision of the two of them going at it like rutting beasts in the middle of the main street of the village with the locals cheering them on to even greater heights of connubial passion.

"That's right, Martin," Alicia concurred. "We have been pronounced man and wife by a certified justice of the peace in the state of New York. And don't you forget it, Wick," she teased.

"Please remind me whenever you feel the urge," Offenfusser replied. "It will give me good practice for ignoring everything else you have to say."

"I'm very happy for both of you," I said and offered a toast. "To a long and prosperous union."

Offenfusser winced and puckered up as if he'd just bit into something very sour. "Thank you so much," he said.

And so I lunched with the happy couple on steamers and beer and took my leave when Offenfusser went back to work on his strip mining. Alicia wanted to drive over later and view the smoking ruins but I assured her there was nothing to see and thought I had dissuaded her.

When I returned to the house, Mr. Wilberforce's car was parked in the driveway. "Hello, there, Martin," he called out. "Not as bad as thought. Just have all those ashes hauled away and no one will even know it was there."

His good cheer was contagious. "Too bad I wasn't here when it happened," I said. "Then they could haul me away and no one would even know I was there."

Mr. Wilberforce did not see the humor in my riposte. "Really, Martin, don't be morbid. I suppose you lost some things down there. I'd like to replace everything, especially your computer. Sad thing for a writer to lose."

Is this beginning to sound like a slapstick routine? All right, I thought, bring 'em on. I can open my own computer store.

"You know you're welcome to stay in the house until you find more suitable accommodations so don't feel I'm putting any pressure on you to leave. I never come out and it's better that the property not be unattended."

"Thank you, sir," said I.

"Good, then we're agreed. I'm going back to the city now so we'll just stay in touch."

He left in such a hurry you would have thought he was fleeing some kind of pestilence. Only minutes after his departure, another car appeared in the driveway and who should alight but little Danica. She walked up to me with a sultry smile and pecked me on the cheek. "I heard about your accident from Alicia. May I come in?"

"Yes, of course. Mi casa no es mi casa pero es suya."

"Stop with the schoolboy Spanish. I need something to drink."

"Did Alicia tell you she got married?" I mentioned casually as I followed her into the house.

"What?!" I couldn't tell if her surprise was genuine. "Not to Fuzzwick!"

"The very same."

"Your cousin is a fool," she spat out with surprising venom.

"Do I detect a note of jealousy?"

"Oh, really, Martin, you're such an innocent. If you knew by half you wouldn't believe it."

"Knew what?"

"That's none of your business. I don't want to say any more. Let's go to bed."

Although this suggestion was rather abrupt, I didn't find it disagreeable. However, once we got down to business, I might as well have been with an inflatable doll. She simply wasn't there and we both knew it. Then things got worse.

"Hello?" Alicia called out from the front porch.

Danica leaped out of bed and hid in the closet.

"What are you doing?" I demanded.

"Shut up!" she practically snarled. "Go get rid of her."

I pulled on my pants and went out to the porch. "Hello, there, Alicia."

"I'm sorry to bother you," she said with a significant look at Danica's car. "I just brought you over a new laptop and some groceries."

"That's very kind of you," I said, taking this booty in my arms.

"You're not going to invite me in? I've never seen the inside of this place before."

Having no choice in the matter, I ushered her into the living room and, to my surprise, Danica had emerged from hiding and was sitting on the couch wrapped in a towel.

"Hello, Alicia," she greeted her friend. "Martin tells me that you and Fuzzwick got married."

Alicia smirked at me. "Martin believes everything. We were just having him on."

"Now, why would you do that? Doesn't he have enough on his mind?"

"He's incredibly gullible. The people he hangs out with... Well you wouldn't believe it."

"About as much as I believe you," Danica retorted. "Tell Fuzzwick I wish you both all the best."

I thought that Alicia was going to withdraw in good order but instead she took a seat across from her rival. "Is that a spritzer you're drinking? I could use one myself."

"Martin," said Danica with weary languor, "could you make your cousin a drink?"

What was going on here? I was being reduced to a servant in my own home and being spoken about in the third person as if I weren't even there. Still, I did as asked.

"How is he in bed?" my cousin wanted to know.

"Who?"

"Martin."

Danica was taken aback. "Really, Alicia..."

"I know you're not too particular," Alicia pressed on.

"You ought to," Danica shot back.

To say I was in some region beyond discomfort would have been putting it mildly. Why these two were hissing at each other and drawing me into the melee was completely baffling. I was tempted to throw them both out on their asses but instead I simply grinned and bore it. Or I should say got bored by it. They carved each other up for the time it took Alicia to finish her drink and take her gracious leave. "I don't know if you're a saint or one lucky devil, Martin, but she's all yours."

Danica did not even honor this exit line with an acknowledgement.

"I thought you two were friends," I groused after Alicia was gone.

"Women don't have any friends, Martin. Only competitors and dupes."

"Where does that leave me?"

"Where do you think?" She didn't really mean it. Or did she? "I'm sorry, sweetheart," she apologized. "That woman just makes me feel so mean. I think I need a good spanking."

This suggestion turned out to be a lot more fun than our previous coupling and allowed me to vent some steam. She asked me if she could stay the night and I quickly acceded. "But I've got to go into town for awhile," she said. "I'll be back around nine."

"Where are you going?"

"Shopping." And she was gone. I waved good-bye as she backed out of the driveway and started to walk back into the house.

"Martin!" a voice called out from the bushes. Of course, it was Redstone. I wondered if he lurked out there all the time like a birdwatcher. More like a peeping Tom actually. "Why don't you come over for a drink!"

"Be right there," I called back. I didn't want to go but my sense of obligation overwhelmed my aversion to the prospect and off I went. Redstone was sitting at a table by the pool with a bottle of champagne on ice. "Should have invited your cousin," he said.

"Oh, she just left."

"I know."

I felt like confronting him directly and saying something like, "Are you spying on me?" but I held my tongue and joined him at the table where he poured me a glass of chilled wine.

"So how's our little project going? I'm not rushing you. I know this business with the fire has been pretty disruptive."

"I should have it done in a week or so," I allowed.

"Good, that's wonderful. I hope working on this thing will give you some insights you can take advantage of. Finance isn't as mysterious as some people crack it up to be. How do you see the market? I mean, how do you think it works?"

I treated his question as if it were a joke. "People buy and sell and you make commissions."

He ignored my flip attitude. "It's not quite that simple," he said. "What do you know about the Invisible Hand?"

"Sounds like a horror movie to me."

"It certainly can be for the reckless. The Invisible Hand is always present in every transaction, something like God being present in all of us. The Invisible Hand can lead you to great riches or give you a good spanking."

I couldn't believe it. Redstone was writing the Buddha book for me. His fortune cookie elocution was perfectly suited to the whole inspirational lexicon and I resolved to steal every line.

His expostulating was far from over. "If it weren't for the all-knowing, all-seeing, all-powerful Hand there would only be chaos and confusion. The temples of high finance would collapse in heaps of rubble the world over and anarchy would reign. Only with the firm guidance of the Invisible Hand can the free market survive unhindered by artificial rules and regulations designed to stop the Hand from doing its work. Do you understand what I'm saying?"

How do you answer a question like that? Carefully, if you're in my position. "I'm just a novice, Dack, but I think what you're saying makes sense."

"You see. I told you that finance isn't so complicated as some people make it out to be"

"It's all sort of one big hand job. Right?"

Redstone chuckled. "You are a card, Martin. A real card." It was hard to say what he really thought of my willfully obtuse mockery of his analysis of the market economy. Was he insulted or amused? Did I care?

"So, Martin, when are you going to introduce me to this cousin of yours?"

"Any time it's convenient. I think she just got married."

Redstone visibly started but quickly recovered his composure. "What do you mean, 'think'?"

"Oh, nothing. I'm pretty sure she did."

Redstone was clearly confused. "It's really none of my business, sport, but I don't understand. Do you mean she might not be married?"

"Well, I wasn't there. I just have to take her word for it."

"I see," he mulled as if he had just made a profound discovery.

Back at the house, I decided to rewrite Redstone's piece as quickly as possible just to get him out of my hair. I was beginning to think he didn't have any friends at all and I was being paid to perform a part I didn't really want to play. How quickly I'd forgotten that when people hand over large sums of money, they always want more than the initial agreement called for. And why on earth was he so interested in Alicia anyway?

I nodded off in front of the television set and woke to a late night talk show. Danica wasn't there and she didn't show up that night at all.

CHAPTER FIVE

In the morning, I drove into town and bought a copy of the Flash at the little coffee shop on the main street. I ordered a poached egg on an English muffin and perused what pass for current events in the tabloid universe. There had been a car accident on the expressway resulting in the deaths of two teenagers, a crazy man had escaped from the state loony bin and menaced an old woman until he was brought down by a Taser and reincarcerated, a school teacher had been arrested for taking liberties of a sexual nature with one of his students, and a helicopter had been shot down in one of the several foreign wars the government was lately promoting. So much for the hard news. On to the juicy stuff. I turned to the first of many photo-illustrated gossip columns and was forced into an immediate double-take. There was Megan Fillywell giving me a big smooch in the bright glow of the flash. The caption read: "Political commentator Megan Fillywell and *Babyland* author Martin Seward seem to be the Item on the Island. And you thought we weren't watching!"

Seeing this photograph in print left me with a most peculiar sensation. My stomach went into free fall, I felt dizzy, and there was a roaring sound in my ears as if I were about to be hit by a wave. It was a very disagreeable feeling that abated only slowly as it was replaced by something else altogether, a rush of wonder and elation at being accorded the status of celebrity Lothario by the press, no matter how tawdry the publication. There were problems, however, that went with the territory. First, *Babyland* didn't exist. Second, I didn't really want to be romantically associated with a fascist Christian even if I had fucked her. The third reason for my discomfiture walked into the café and took the seat across the table.

"Sorry I didn't make it back last night," said Danica, "but I see you were pretty busy yourself." She tapped the picture with her finger.

"Actually, that was the previous evening, right after my house burned down."

"I see. You really do get around, don't you."

I decided to level with her. Sort of. "I barely know Megan

Fillywell. The picture was posed by my press agent. So where were you?"

"I went to a party on a boat. I ran into Harry Poon, the artist, and he took me to this Arab guy's yacht."

"Yes, the Sulema."

She was surprised. "You know it?"

"I've been there."

"Isn't it the tackiest? Anyway, I got drunk at the party and passed out. I woke up on a pile of cushions. Everyone else was asleep so I just kind of snuck out. That's about it. Can I take a shower at your place?"

So we went back to the house and whiled away the rest of the morning in casual carnal embrace. Around noon, I got a phone call from Sparky Goldflugel.

"Hey there, kid. You see your picture in the paper?"

"Yes I did."

"So now you got to come into town for your coming out party, promote your stuff."

"Mr. Goldflugel..."

"Sparky. Call me Sparky."

"All right, Sparky, you see, I don't have any stuff to promote."

"Not to worry. Bunny's handling all that. She'll have a book for you in no time."

"What do mean by that?" I demanded.

He seemed puzzled. "Well, you're not writing it yourself, are you?"

"Listen, I've got to think about this."

"Grab it while you're hot, kid. Seize the moment!"

"Yes, well, let me get back to you."

The irony was not lost on me; ghost writer gets ghosted. I had to call Barrington Stoat and put a stop to that right away. Before I could punch in the number, however, the phone rang.

"Martin, I had no idea you were doing a fruitcake like Megan Fillywell," said Alicia. "Congratulations, by the way."

"For what?"

"You're launched, Martin. Don't you see? You're going to be a real literary lion."

"And I owe it all to you."

"Don't be snarky. It's all for your own good. By the way, Wick and I are doing the reception this afternoon. You must come over."

"Kind of short notice, isn't it?"

"You have something better to do?"

I would take my revenge by bringing Danica as my date. The only problem was she adamantly refused to go. It took a couple drinks and a full half hour of cajoling to get her to acquiesce.

"I'm warning you," she threatened. "I'm going to make a scene."

"Fine with me. Go for it."

She did nothing of the kind. Not right away, at least. What she did do was make the Offenfussers so uncomfortable by acting as if she barely knew them, they were afraid to go near her. Personally, I had a pretty good time even though the guest list was sparse to say the least. Harry Poon was there with Gloriana, avant-garde artist Kow Lekwaski, who I soon learned had organized the afternoon's entertainment, was there with his wife, Marie-Claude and that was about it.

"And I thought you'd bring along Megan Fillywell," Alicia acidly asided to me. "Really, Martin."

"At least I brought someone," I retorted. "Don't you and Wick have any other friends?"

"I hope not."

A huge screen had been erected on the carved up grounds in front of the house and a back projected movie suddenly started playing on it. Offenfusser stood in front of the flickering film and held his glass up in a toast. "I just want to thank Kow and Marie-Claude for this wonderful wedding gift!"

The moving image on the screen behind him was something I'd seen before, a scene from an egregiously silly Hollywood movie set at a crooked lawyer's coastal vacation home lawn party filled with gangsters and their molls committing all sorts of indecencies under the noonday sun, a sort of sinister Redstone party realized. The way the piece had been designed ingeniously melded the screen party into our own foreground festivities. It looked like you could just walk up and grab a drink from one of the uniformed waiters catering to the gangsters on screen. Or maybe you didn't want to mess with that crowd.

"Throw a party and they will come!" Offenfusser hollered and broke down in a laughing fit.

Danica rejoined me and, solely to head off Alicia, insisted on introducing me to the Lekwaskis who, it turned out, were a quite singular couple.

"I like the idea of having two parties going on at once," I complimented. Levity was completely lost on them.

"It was the least we could do for Fuzzwick," said Marie-Claude seriously. "He is, after all, the second foremost conceptualist in the world, right behind Kow and myself."

Danica giggled and Marie-Claude turned on her in perfect deadpan. "What is so funny? You do not agree with me?"

"I didn't realize it was a competition," Danica fired back.

"There is only room for one foremost conceptualist. There is not enough financial support for two."

I thought that was pretty clear logic, whatever my taste in concepts.

"What do you think, Kow?" Danica wanted to know.

He was not allowed to answer. "He doesn't have to think," said Marie-Claude. "Only to create."

I could see Harry Poon and Gloriana talking with Offenfusser across the lawn but Alicia had disappeared. I left Danica with the Lekwaskis and walked back up to the house to get another drink. Alicia was in the kitchen tending to a platter of hors d'oeuvre.

"Great party," I said.

"What did you expect?" she said defensively. "Wick doesn't like a lot of people around. The only party he goes to is the annual foundation fundraiser and that's only because he has to."

"In that case, I feel honored to be here."

"You should. Could you take this tray out on the terrace for me?"

I did as I was told and looked out across the bay to Redstone's estate which, of course, dwarfed everything around it. I tried to imagine him sitting at his table out on the lawn but no image at all presented itself. It was as if Redstone were a black hole, absorbing everything around him but completely invisible to anyone without a radio telescope. Alicia came out of the kitchen with another tray and set it on the table.

"Do you know I went to school with Megan Fillywell? She flunked out."

"I don't think of her as a towering intellect," I said dryly.

"She's a complete idiot. From a woman's point of view, that is. Men must look at her differently."

All right, I thought, you want to play this game? I couldn't resist. "Let's just put it this way. I loathe and despise her political and religious agendas but there's a certain thing we share in common."

Her eyebrows arched. "What might that be?"

"Bodily fluids."

She cuffed me. "You are such a pervert. What does our little Danica have to say about all this?"

"Bodily fluids?"

The conversation was fortunately terminated by the arrival of the rest of the party on the terrace.

"Show's over. Kow's projector broke down," Offenfusser announced with a bit too much glee.

Marie-Claude sternly subscribed to another opinion. "I believe someone has tampered with it."

The second foremost conceptualist in the world? But I was more concerned with Danica, or Baby D as I'd taken to calling her. I joined her at the railing where she was watching the boats sailing in and out of the harbor.

"Glad you came?"

"Don't give me a straight line for a dirty joke. Of course I am."

"Why? The Offenfussers won't even talk to you."

"You think I care?"

Harry Poon stood up and held his champagne glass in the air. "A toast to the newlyweds! What is this, Fuzzwick? The eleventh?"

"Marriage is a wonderful thing, Harry," said Alicia. "You ought to try it."

"There is no natural disaster that compares with marriage in terms of its ferocity and aftermath, but you're absolutely right, Alicia" said Poon. "I recently put a personals ad on the internet. 'Hopeless reprobate seeking rich, nymphomaniac, liquor store owner with late model car.' I can't wait to get home and open up the computer."

"Hear, hear," said Offenfusser, raising his own glass. "It's about time some woman made an honest man out of you, Harry. Just look at Kow and Marie-Claude here and you'll see how far you can go with the right life partner."

The Lekwaskis were completely non-plussed by this accolade.

"Well, you don't have to throw cold water on the whole thing," said Poon.

Danica and Gloriana burst into laughter and I might have chuckled myself if I didn't have such good manners.

Poon was on a roll. "The source of all success in America is a vast and unfathomable inferiority complex. Just look at the president. A man of no intelligence or talent who has risen to the mighty position of leader of the free world! And how did he did he do it? With that deep down sense of his own shocking inferiority, his realization that he was, in fact, a human zero. They say that one is the loneliest number but what about zero?!"

"Zero is an abstraction," Marie-Claude pointed out, "It does not exist in nature."

"Neither does the word 'no' but we use it all the time."

"Dogs seem to understand it," said Marie-Claude, "besides which, the president has commissioned one of Kow's projects for the White House lawn."

There was a sudden silence, as if a storm cloud had appeared overhead, blotting out the sun.

Danica was the first to speak. "You're going to work for that prick?"

"It is not a temporary installation, such as the president, but a monument for posterity."

"Well, at least we'll all be dead so we won't have to look at it," said Poon. "Now that we've disposed of politics, what'll it be? Sex or religion?"

"Sex!" Danica piped up.

"Ah, yes," said Poon, "the reproductive act in all its glory. Just think, everyone here evolved from a few cells in the primordial soup of this miserable planet, struck by lightning thousands of times a second. Just where do you think the orgasm comes from? A simple electrical discharge caused by two clouds running into each other and transmitting all that energy to something even more primitive than the amoeba! To a double helix of amino acids rubbing up against each other and producing... life!"

"That's not the way the thing happened at all, Harry," Offenfusser objected. "God did the whole thing in six days and then he went to his weekend house in the country. Anybody knows that."

"Yes, of course," Poon agreed, "but the theory of evolution makes a pretty good story, don't you think? As a metaphor, I mean."

"What is this nonsense you are talking?" Marie-Claude complained. "The young lady wants to discuss sex, not creationism."

I must say I was impressed by the foremost conceptualist's complete dearth of mirth.

Poon looked around. "Well, does anyone know anything about the subject?"

"Ask Martin," said Alicia. "He's been getting around lately."

Danica let this slide with admirable forbearance and so did I. "I don't know much about sex, but I know what I like," I wisecracked.

"If only Pedro Barbez were here," said Poon. "He could probably tell us more about it than we want to know."

Then Marie-Claude set herself up as a punching bag. "I don't understand. Don't any of you know anything about sex?"

Only Offenfusser put on the gloves. "This was a convent, you know," he pointed out, "and the exaltation of celibacy once practiced here appears to have rubbed off on all of us. Perhaps you could enlighten us on the subject."

"You don't think we have convents in France? You are all Americans. You come from a tradition that makes it impossible for you to understand such things. Your whole culture is descended from the worst of the English Puritans, outcasts and pariahs in a country where even the more liberal minded British people think of sex as an embarrassing nuisance. Is that not so?"

"Are you telling us that even if you did tell us all about sex we wouldn't get it?" said Offenfusser.

"Exactement. There is no use even discussing the subject."

"I say something now," said Kow.

"No you don't," Marie-Claude cut him off.

"Well," said Poon, clasping his hands together as if in prayer, "what say we move on to religion?"

"Let me get a book I was just reading," said Alicia. "It's really got the last word on the subject." She disappeared into the house.

"We can't discuss this without reading a book?" Poon wondered.

"Alicia can't do anything unless she reads it in a book," said

Danica acidly.

Offenfusser pointedly ignored that catty remark.

Alicia returned with her book and read: "Faith is a wondrous thing. It is the wellspring of hope, an impregnable fortress wherein one can dwell safe from the horrors of the world."

"Nonsense," Poon scoffed. "Faith is a delusion based solely on the fear of death and the loathing of the world and ourselves as we actually are. It's also all tied into the silly notion of progress. We may not be having such a good time here, but there are streets of gold right around the corner."

"Has anyone ever heard of the Sedgwick Circle?" said Offenfusser.

"Of course," said Alicia. "It's in Massachusetts."

"That's right. It's a large cemetery plot in Stockbridge. The whole family, including employees and pets, are buried there in concentric circles around the tomb of the patriarch and his wife. On Judgment Day, they shall arise as one and ascend to heaven where they will presumably reconstitute their earthly household."

"Cool," said Gloriana.

"It's a wonderful vision," Offenfusser agreed, "your whole dysfunctional family gathered around an eternal dinner table attended to by family retainers and panting dogs performing tricks for scraps."

"This is not religion," Marie-Claude objected. "This is like the circus or a television show."

"Let's not get into metaphysics," said Offenfusser. "My primary interest lies in the Circle itself which I intend to recreate right here on the grounds. I will bury only art dealers, critics, and curators so that future generations can come and venerate their judgment and taste."

"You forgot collectors," said Poon.

"I'm sorry. Please tell Mr. Jifhraz there is still space available."

"I don't know," said Poon dubiously. "I think he's got the Black Stone booked."

"Are you talking about Ahmed Jifhraz?" Marie-Claude wanted to know.

"Yes," said Offenfusser. "Harry just did his boat."

She turned to Poon. "He gave you money?" she demanded.

"Well, I don't work for free, you know."

"Mr. Jifhraz has always been very generous when it came to financing projects by real artists such as Kow and myself. How could he possibly..?"

"Hey, listen, you bitch..."

Alicia immediately intervened. "Please, no need for rudeness on this blessed occasion. We must celebrate."

"Hear, hear," said Offenfusser, "and, in support of my friend Harry, I personally find pornography a very high art form indeed."

"I'd like to make a toast to the newlyweds," said Danica, tapping her glass with a spoon.

Oh, oh, I thought, here we go.

"I've known the happy couple as long as anyone else here. Alicia and I were in dance class together years ago while I was fucking Fuzzwick and, since she was such a wonderful person, I decided to bring her home with me and have a three-way. Well, you can see how happily it all turned out. Salud!"

These cheerful good wishes were greeted with the silence of a vacuum, as if the medium of response had been sucked out of the atmosphere. Poon let the air back in. Some of it, anyway. "I'd just like to thank the Offenfussers for the pleasure of their company and wish them a happy union... no matter how abbreviated. Just kidding, you guys," he said pointing his finger back and forth from Alicia to Offenfusser and making a comical face as if he'd just told a joke on one of those late night celebrity puff shows.

"Well," said Offenfusser, "thanks to Harry and Danica for their kind regards." It was the first time he'd mentioned her name the entire afternoon. "Now I'd like to invite you all on a boat ride to celebrate this blessed occasion. It's not exactly the Sulema, Harry, but I think you'll find it's got a lot more punch."

With minimal cajoling, Offenfusser got everyone, with the exception of Alicia, who begged off on account of kitchen chores, to follow him down to the shore to the little, wooden boathouse where the craft was berthed. I can't say I was flabbergasted when Offenfusser emerged in the driver's seat of the candy apple red speedboat but I can say it was unexpected.

"Who can read charts?" he called out over the roar of the inboard engine.

I volunteered and took the seat next to Offenfusser at the helm.

Everyone else piled into the cramped seating behind us. Offenfusser reached into the glove compartment and handed me a wad of mangled papers which it turned out were the charts of the harbor and the sound beyond. As I tried to disentangle this crumpled mess, Offenfusser pulled the throttle and off we went at a speed far exceeding the bay speed limit.

"Just keep us out of trouble!" he called out to me. That was not to be an easy task. The first thing that Offenfusser did was quickly weave through the other outgoing boats in the harbor creating a serpentine wake that pushed what before had been an orderly procession into near collision confusion. The other boat owners were enraged but there was little they could do because Offenfusser could easily outrun any of them.

Once we had cleared the sea wall, Offenfusser throttled up and took off into the sound as if he were in drag race. It became immediately clear that he knew nothing about the water and treated it as if it were a smoothly paved highway. As the boat caromed through the thankfully minor swells, I forgot all about the charts and just tried to keep Offenfusser on a course closest to the surrounding boats in case we capsized.

"I know this great bar!" Offenfusser shouted over the din of the engine. He took off in a beeline through the current and the boat bounced off every wave. It felt like we were hitting concrete every time it came down and I had to stand up with my knees bent to avoid irreparable kidney damage. We eventually made it across the sound to the Frog's Lip Harbor inlet where Offenfusser set course for the public dock. Fortunately, the pier attendants recognized the boat and immediately scrambled to the open berth with long poles to fend him off and keep the speedboat from doing damage to the pilings.

"Here we are!" he called out to his green passengers as the dock tenders eased us into snug harbor. "Let's celebrate!"

"Alicia's not even here," Poon pointed out.

"Exactly," said Offenfusser. "I couldn't have said it better myself. Come on, Kow," he beckoned from the dock. "Get on up here and get your land legs screwed back on."

Lekwaski had other priorities. He leaned over the side of the boat and puked in the water.

"There, there, Kow," said Offenfusser, "Alicia hasn't quite mastered the culinary arts. But she will! Believe me, she will!"

"You are a sadist, Fuzzwick," Marie-Claude complained.

"I'm going to take that as a compliment," said Offenfusser. "Please, let me give you a hand."

Danica and Gloriana had leapt out of the boat like the young gazelles they were and headed for the waterfront bar with Poon in hot, if rather wobbly, pursuit.

The open-air deck of El Farolito, the eatery overlooking the former whaling port (now a marina for well-heeled boat owners), was virtually empty and we commandeered a large table without any problem. Bringing up the rear with the Lekwaskis, Offenfusser immediately ordered a magnum of local champagne for the table. Unfortunately, it turned out to be undrinkable. Offenfusser spat it out into the water lapping under the deck with great fanfare. "Swill!" he loudly proclaimed. "May the wineries out here all be struck by the noble rot!"

"And just as I was about to propose a toast," said Poon.

"Not another one," Offenfusser objected. "Oh, look, there's Pamela Sturgeon with Piggy Bigwig. You always see celebrities when you come to this place."

Everyone turned to look at the fat black chef who was talking to the hostess, neither of whom even vaguely resembled the mega-celebrities Offenfusser was comparing them to.

"It's so great to be in the center of things," he exulted.

"This center cannot hold," said Poon. "What say we order a bottle of something else. On the Lekwaskis, of course."

"I beg your pardon," said Marie Claude.

"Just kidding," said Poon. "Gloriana will pick up the tab. A.J. pays her enough. How about a quart of tequila?"

"I'll buy a round," said Gloriana, "but not a bottle of tequila. People can order whatever they like."

And so they did. After they were served, a cell phone sounded out the first few bars of the "Marseillaise" from Marie-Claude's bag. She answered and excused herself from the table. "This is private," she explained.

"She must have left you here by accident," said Poon to Kow. "You are now free to speak your mind."

And speak his mind he did. "I would say few words. I want kill my wife."

Poon was delighted. "Such fine sentiments to bring to a wedding reception, Kow. How do you intend to do it?"

Offenfusser chimed in, "The method doesn't matter. Just do it soon!"

"You guys are such assholes," said Gloriana.

"No knife, no gun. I make look like accident," said Kow without the slightest glimmer of irony. He leaned forward conspiratorially. "Maybe boat accident."

"Now, there I can help you out. You just have Harry take you over to the yacht he's staying on and I bet anything can happen."

"What's wrong with your boat?" Poon objected.

"Too many witnesses. Besides, A.J. can afford to pay off the authorities."

"I am glad you think me serious," said Kow.

"Well, it's definitely a concept," said Offenfusser.

Marie-Claude returned from her phone call. "We must go, Kow. The Humanitas Foundation has just agreed to fund our project in Ulan Bator."

"You can't leave now," Offenfusser objected. "We were just planning to kill you."

"Next time perhaps," said Marie-Claude. "Now we must go. Come, Kow." And off they went to the cab stand down the wharf.

"What are you doing for the Humanitas Foundation?!" Offenfusser called after them.

"Read about it on my blog!" Marie-Claude called back.

"Her what?" proto-Luddite Offenfusser wondered. "Is that something sexual?"

"You better believe it," said Poon. "Mama's got a brand new blog!"

"No, really," said Offenfusser.

"It certainly can be sexual," Gloriana volunteered. "It's sort of like the combination of a personal website and a chat room."

"These days," said Poon, "it's sort of like an opinion or an asshole. Everybody has one. Don't any of you?"

The only answer was murmured negatives and shaking heads.

"Well, at least I'm not alone," said Offenfusser. "What I want to know is why the Humanitas Foundation rejected my entry for the Ulan Bator project in favor of the Lekwaskis."

"Let's face it, Fuzzwick," said Poon, "your day in the sun is over. Perhaps you should go into one of those government retraining programs. You might find great satisfaction in a new career."

I was the first to notice the Sulema easing through the Frog's Lip inlet into the harbor. The yacht was so much bigger than any of the other boats, it looked like Cleopatra's barge floating down the Nile through a bunch of papyrus canoes. "I think we have company," I said. Everyone turned and watched the steaming yacht moor offshore. They were all strangely quiet about this unexpected appearance. A launch was lowered off the taffrail, cleared the Sulema, and headed toward the dock. The pilot was a swarthy fellow in a captain's hat. To my curious surprise, his companion was none other than my next door neighbor.

"Well, I'll be damned," I said. "That's Dacron Redstone."

"Excuse me," Danica whispered in my ear. "I've got to go. I'll meet you later at the house." She got up and hurriedly walked out without even giving me time to complain. But then, it wasn't the first time she'd behaved erratically.

The launch eased into a slip and Poon called out, "Ship ahoy, A.J.!"

The swarthy man in the captain's hat waved back and clambered onto the pier with Redstone. When they joined us at the table there was an undercurrent of discomfort which I first thought was mine alone.

"Hello there, sport," said Redstone giving me a hearty slap on the back. "Good to see you."

Ahmed Jifhraz, who looked pretty much as Poon had described him at Cyrano's; oily, pear-shaped, and obviously very well-to-do, seemed rather ill at ease. He was quite clearly uncomfortable running into Poon and Gloriana at this out of the way place but he did his best to hide it. "Harry, Gloriana, what a surprise. Please allow me to buy you and your friends a drink."

"No way, sport," said hearty Redstone. "Drinks are on me."

"I think some introductions are in order," said Poon. "Ahmed Jifhraz, this is the second foremost conceptualist in the world, Fuzzwick Offenfusser, and this is his new cousin-in-law, Martin — what's your last name?"

"Seward."

"The Chowderhead Bay Sewards," said Redstone proudly.

"Me and Martin, we're old buddies."

"I'm glad to make your acquaintance," said Jifhraz with strained cordiality.

"You just missed Kow Lekwaski and his charming wife."

Jifhraz was puzzled. "I'm sorry, who?"

"It's not important. So who's this guy?" Poon wanted to know.

"This is my associate, Mr. Redstone. Now, if you'll excuse us, we have some business to discuss."

As Jifhraz herded him away from our table, Redstone leaned over and whispered, "Where's your cousin, sport?"

"She couldn't make it."

He shook his head. "That's a shame. Just remember our deal." And off he went with Jifhraz.

Now, let me explain once again that my own or anyone else's likely initial impression of Redstone is that he is the most hollow, boring man in the world and, to give him credit, he knows it. On the other hand, his desperate need to prove his importance and initiate some sort of human contact is so pathetic that it elicits a quiet sympathy of the sort reserved for the crippled and maimed which Redstone is most definitely not. Or is he? Am I making myself clear? Anyway I once again resolved to finish his report to Moloch and Feeney as soon as possible and get him out of my hair.

"We are but barnacles glommed onto the hull of a treasure ship," Offenfusser waxed philosophical. "We hold on as best we can until we are abruptly scraped off." He looked around the table. "Where's Danica?"

"She scraped herself off and took a cab."

"Is that so, Mark? Was it something I said?"

"I don't think so."

"That's good. I hate to give offense. Even to a cunning little minx. What say we head back?"

Once again, we boarded the speedboat and took off across the water with a breakneck burst of acceleration. As we sped through the Frog's Lip inlet, Offenfusser belted out a jarring, off key version of "Barnacle Bill the Sailor" which was mercifully all but lost in the roar of the engine. After another kidney shattering voyage across the sound, we puttered into the foundation boathouse and disembarked.

"We must give a prayer of thanks for our safe return to terra firma," said Offenfusser. "Isn't that Alicia I see up there on the widow's walk? I'm afraid I've disappointed her again."

"I suggest we drink to a successful voyage in life for the Offenfussers," Poon proposed as we made our way up the hill to the house, "with many happy returns."

"I don't know what you're talking about, Harry," said Offenfusser, "but I like the drink part."

We gained the terrace where Alicia greeted us. "Only three overboard?"

"We left them for the Coast Guard to deal with," said Poon. "What say we crack another bottle of champagne for Auld Lang Syne?"

I excused myself rather early in this second round of festivities and drove back to the other side of the bay where I found Danica waiting for me at the house.

"What was that all about?" I wanted to know.

"How do you know Dacron Redstone?" she demanded.

"He's my neighbor. He's got the place right next door."

Her eyes widened.

"Actually, I'm doing a little writing job for him."

"Don't have anything to do with him," she spat out with such vehemence you would have thought it was a life or death situation. "He destroys everything he touches."

"That's what Offenfusser says about you."

"He's joking; I'm not."

"All right, all right. Redstone's beginning to give me the creeps anyway. I'll just finish up his piece and that will be that. But, come on, you make him sound like a horror movie monster."

"Do you remember in the original Frankenstein movie when Dr. Frankenstein's assistant mistakenly takes the "abnormal brain" from the medical school and that's what causes all the problems when he transplants it into the monster? Dacron Redstone is the monster with no brain at all."

I was amused. "Really? I never thought he was that interesting."

"He's not. That's the whole point."

With her overcooked words of warning percolating in my own addled brain, I suggested we send out for Chinese and that's what we did.

CHAPTER SIX

I hadn't even bothered to ask Baby D how she knew Redstone. It just seemed par for the course that everyone knew everybody else out here. When she left in the morning and went wherever she goes, I sat down and cranked out his piece for the brokerage, saved it on three separate CDs, and wondered whether to call him or not. Not. Instead, I decided to drive into town and get a paper and some beer. It seemed to make more sense than getting involved in some inane conversation with the famous self-made man that early in the day. As I drove through the poor, white trash section, Bonefish Lane with its trailers clustered along a single stretch of road on the outskirts of the village, I passed the rundown Pentecostal church where the sign out front announced the subject of the weekly sermon. "You catch 'em, I'll clean 'em!" it read, the gospel according to St. Matthew proudly rendered in pure, redneck patois. For some reason this exuberant, vernacular inter-pretation of the Lord's comforting words, greatly cheered me. It was only appropriate to what had once been a renowned fishing port. "Getcher ass out there and be a fisher of men!" was probably next week's holy text.

I arrived in town to find some sort of rinky-dink carnival in progress. The lawn in front of the town hall had been turned into an outdoor dining area where middle-aged women scurried to and fro serving pancakes to benefit the volunteer fire department. This was clearly not an event you would find the snooty summer people attend-ing but there was Pedro Barbez standing by a miniature ferris wheel that had been erected in the parking lot adjoining the lawn. He had a plastic cup of beer in one hand and a hotdog in the other. I passed by the festivities and found a parking space near the town delicatessen. After purchasing a newspaper and a six-pack, I turned around and headed back past the town hall where I had to slow down because there were two police cars with roof lights whirling in a light show of blue and red pulled up in the parking lot. Two policemen were questioning Pedro Barbez while two others were fending off an obese, bald fellow who was howling epithets and trying to attack him.

"You ever touch my daughter again, I swear I'll kill you!!" the fat man roared. The fact that Barbez was laughing at him did nothing to soothe his would-be assailant. "You're dead, Barbez, dead!! You hear?!" It looked like something off the Jerry Springer show. Eventually, the police put Barbez in the back of one of the cars and drove off with him. That was enough for the rubberneckers and, with traffic resuming its normal pace, I was soon back at the house. I had little time to reflect on the peculiar incident I had just witnessed because the phone rang as I walked in the door. It was Redstone.

"Good morning, sport. What's going on?"

"Well, I finished your piece for Moloch and Feeney."

"Great, that's wonderful. Why don't you run it over here and we'll have some breakfast."

Well, why not get it over with? I printed out a copy and set out for Redstone's. He was sitting outside at a table overlooking the bay reading the Financial Times in his bathrobe.

"Ahoy there, mate!" he waved me over. "How're they hanging?!"

Low, I thought. I walked over and took a seat at the table. I handed him the manila envelope with the report inside but he didn't seem interested.

"So, what's going on?" he said, setting the envelope aside.

"I was just in town and I saw Pedro Barbez being arrested."

"Who's Pedro Barbez?"

"You don't know? I met him here at your party."

"Oh well, I hardly know anyone at my parties. It was great seeing you yesterday."

I decided to play dumb. I asked him, "Who was that guy you were with? The one with the yacht?"

"Oh, Ahmed Jifhraz, a great guy and a very close friend of mine, one of my real pals."

Redstone had a way of deflecting all questions back to self-aggrandizing clichés without saying anything at all. I decided to press it. "I mean, what does he do?"

Redstone looked out across the bay at the red beacon on top of the Offenfusser tower which glowed and blinked brightly even in broad daylight. His guffaw was overly hearty. "Do? Nothing if he doesn't feel like it!"

I smiled but he could see I was not satisfied with his little joke for an answer.

"Seriously, sport, he's in finance. Have you ever heard of the Wizard of Oz?"

"Of course."

"Well, you know when they pull back the curtain and discover he's just a guy with a P.A. system? What they forget to do is to pull back the curtain behind the curtain. If they did, they'd find A.J. running the Wizard. You catch my drift? He's one helluva mover and shaker."

I decided to take another tack. "Well, he's certainly got an impressive boat."

"The Sulema? The finest yacht in the world. Only the very best for A.J. You should see the interior. It's like a floating palace."

"So I've heard. Harry Poon, one of the people I was sitting with yesterday, did all the sculpture on the boat."

This comment greatly amused Redstone. "Did he? Well, you have to see it to believe it." Guillermo appeared in full waiter mufti. "So what'll be?" said Redstone. "How about eggs Benedict and a bottle of champagne?"

"Sounds fine to me."

"It better," Redstone chuckled. "It's already done."

And so it was. Guillermo returned in minutes with the tray and champagne bucket and set them down on the table.

"Good boy, Guillermo," said Redstone as if he were praising a dog. "You know what makes this country great, Martin? All that Constitution and Declaration of Independence stuff has nothing to do with it. Just pieces of paper. What makes this country great? Go ahead and guess."

"Uh..."

"No clue? Well, I'll tell you. The Work Ethic." I'm only capitalizing the words because that's the way he said them. He made it sound as if the phrase should be accompanied by a trumpet fanfare. "That's right, Martin, the Work Ethic."

I wondered if I was getting set up for some more "Invisible Hand" nonsense. I didn't care. Just more Buddha book material.

"Hard work is the key to America's greatness," said Redstone.

"Look at Guillermo. He used to be some sort of peon in Mexico. Now look where he is. He's here in the land of opportunity where anything can happen for someone who wants to get ahead. Guillermo's learning that being a lazy, tequila besotted Mexican wasn't such a good thing after all because he's discovered... the Work Ethic! And the Work Ethic is setting him free!"

Redstone's evangelical fervor seemed more appropriate to a TV preacher than a pillar of the business community. What could I say? Hallelujah?

"You know why that is, Martin? We live in an entropic world." (Was he stealing lines from Derek Schnoigel?) "Everything is wearing down and the only way to fight back is... work! Work against decay and deterioration! Work against slacking off and throwing in the towel! You really can have it all if you just put your shoulder to the grindstone and keep pushing! You know that old song, 'Keep on pushing, like your leaders tell you to...' and then there's, 'Push, push, in the bush...'"

That was about enough for me. Redstone babbling was one thing; singing was out of the question. I looked at my watch. "Excuse me, Dack, but I've got an appointment..."

"Hey, wait a minute! We haven't even talked about your cousin."

"Let's do that tomorrow, all right? Really I've got to go."

"I'll have Reynolds drive you."

"No, that's all right. I need the exercise. Thanks for breakfast."

"Anytime, sport, anytime."

As I walked back to the house, I passed Reynolds on the fringe of the great lawn smoking a cigarette. He looked at me impassively as if I were a passerby on the street, a complete stranger. And, you know, I was.

When I walked out of the woods, there was Mr. Wilberforce surveying the charred remains of my former dwelling with another short, squat man in a suit with a clipboard.

"Ah, there you are, Martin," he greeted me. "This is Mr. Ames, the insurance adjustor." The short, squat man didn't look up from his clipboard where he was busily making notes. "I'll walk you up to the house."

As the gravel ground under our shoes, Wilberforce looked at

me curiously. "I saw your picture in the paper the other day. I had no idea how well you're doing. I mean, that woman is really quite a looker."

"Just a friend," I said uncomfortably.

"And this new book of yours, I'm not much of a reader but I'd like to see a copy."

"Well, it's not really out yet. Publishers don't move all that quickly, you know."

"Yes, of course. Now I must go back and attend to Mr. Ames. Nice seeing you."

The net effect of this short conversation was not pleasant and things were just about to get worse. As soon as I walked in the door, the phone rang. It was Barrington Stoat.

"Martin, you must come back into town right away to rehearse for your first reading at Marymount."

"I don't understand. Reading what?"

"Oh, didn't I tell you? The book's done. The publisher's already sent it to the printer."

"What do you mean it's done?" I demanded.

"I had this lovely young woman from the Columbia creative writing department do it for a flat fee. It's from the male point of view, of course."

"Uh, what's it about?"

"No idea. I haven't read it myself but one of my readers told me it captures the very essence of being young and ambitious in New York."

It was time to put my foot down. "Now listen, I know you mean all the best but I can't go along with this."

"Go along with what?"

"I mean, I didn't write the book. I haven't even seen it."

She was completely baffled. "You want to see it? I suppose I could messenger a copy but why don't you wait until you get into town and work over the lines with Dimitri."

"Who's Dimitri?"

"Dimitri Bobokoff is the finest acting coach in New York. We have to work on your presentation skills."

"I don't have any," I muttered.

"Exactly. Try to get into town by one and we'll go over everything."

Frankly, I was curious to take a look at this book I'd written. It was sort of like being a hack politician who gets handed a speech by his writers and simply reads it to the rubes. Who cares what it says? Such were my bitter thoughts as I reluctantly drove over to the train station. On the clattering ride into the city, it occurred to me that I was being forced to tramp the well-worn path first blazed by the late artist who actually reveled in being reduced to a name brand commodity. I should be so lucky. I dozed off and had a dream. I can't remember most of it but at the end I was standing on a narrow rock shelf of a cliff overlooking a vast sea of pink fog punctuated by mountain top islands in the distance. I don't like heights so I flattened myself against the cliff wall as far away from the edge of the shelf as I could. I didn't dare move. Suddenly the rock beneath me gave way and I plummeted down toward the fluffy, cotton candy cloud below. I can't describe the excruciation of my panic, but, to my great surprise and relief, I hit the fog and bounced back up as if I were on a trampoline. Up and down I went, performing a graceful gymnastic routine of twisting flips. But then the fog gave way and I plunged toward the earth like a skydiver whose parachute has failed to open. I woke in a cold sweat just before I hit the ground and the train pulled into the station.

I took a cab to Barrington Stoat's office where, among many other things hanging on the walls of the reception area, there was a poster featuring the cover of *Babyland*. The artwork was a cartoonish representation of a crowded night club; the title and my name were embossed in gold. "Martin Seward takes us as far as we thought we were going and then way further!" was the enthusiastic blurb beneath the book jacket.

"It's so good to see you, Martin," Barrington Stoat gushed as she came out to greet me. She gestured at the poster. "What do you think? Isn't it fabulous?" I had to admit it was. "Come into the office and I'll show you a review copy so you can go over it before we meet Dimitri."

We went into the office and she retrieved a copy of the book from a tightly packed shelf. She handed it to me and I looked at my photograph on the back cover. It had been retouched to the point I was almost unrecognizable. My eyes looked like I was wearing mascara. My mouth had been conformed into a pouty smirk.

"It's the disaffected, ironically detached young man look," she said. "The English publishers have been doing it for the last few years and it's worked out very successfully for them. Just bring it along and we'll go meet Dimitri."

As we cabbed down to Dimitri Bobokoff's acting studio, Barrington chattered away incessantly, giving me no chance to even glance at the book. "After were finished with Dimitri, Sparky has arranged a small press conference for you at the Estuary Hotel. No press, really, just publicists and press agents, the important people. That woman you were in the paper with, she'll be there too."

"What?" I demanded.

"You're a couple now. At least for the next two weeks."

I put my foot down. "I won't do that. I can't stand her."

"That's fine. You can break up with her right there in public. Next week, we'll have you out at the clubs with some equally famous young woman where your ex can make a scene and throw a drink in your face. Great for all three of you, don't you think?"

Now I ask, what would you have done? Gotten out of the taxi at the first stop light and fled? Believe me, I thought about it. But my morbid curiosity got the better of me and I went along for the ride as if I were ascending the first giant hump of a roller coaster that would soon plunge me into white knuckled panic.

The Bobokoff Studio was located in a third floor loft on West 49th St. and, when Barrington Stoat and I arrived, there was a class in session. Dimitri Bobokoff, an imposing, bald, fat man in a caftan presided over a room full of his students who were barking, squawking, growling, screeching and making other animal sounds as they crawled around on the floor.

"Ah, Bunny, it is so good to see you," he greeted us. "This must be your young man." He looked me up and down with a frank leer and simpered. "Please, let us adjourn to my boudoir."

"Enough with the Nathan Lane impression, Dimitri," Barrington admonished. "We don't have much time."

Bobokoff led the way into a smaller room at the rear of the studio and closed the door behind us. "Please sit down," he said graciously and we did. "Now, young man, I understand that you need a little help presenting yourself in public. Not to worry. By the time we're finished, you'll be able to emcee the New Year's show in Times Square.

Do you wear glasses?"

"Pardon me?"

"Here, try these on. It makes you look more serious. Like a writer, you know." He handed me a pair of wire rimmed glasses with no lenses and I put them on. "Fabulous," he said. "Now, you see that eye chart on the wall? Read it to me from the top down."

I looked over at an eye chart of the sort used by opticians and read off the letters as far as I could.

"All right," he said, "now I want you to read those letters like you mean it! I want you to read them with gusto!"

"I'm sorry, I don't understand..."

"Read them like your delivering a speech, like your giving the State of the Union address!"

I had no idea what to make of these peculiar instructions, but I did the best I could to give a more animated reading of the letters on the wall.

"Much better," Bobokoff praised me. "Now I want you to make the letters on top sound as big as they are and the letters on the bottom to sound as small as they are."

I gave it another shot and he pursed his lips. "I can see we're going to need a little work together. I want you here every Wednesday afternoon at four."

"Is that all?" said Barrington, looking at her watch. "We really must be off."

"I won't keep you," said Bobokoff and escorted us back through the studio where his students were still behaving like animals.

"What are they doing?" I wanted to know.

"That's a character armor shedding exercise. Only for the advanced class. They're about to go out into the real world of auditions and cattle calls and such so they have to get used to debasing and humiliating themselves."

And so would I, so would I, for the real world awaited me at the press conference Sparky Goldflugel had arranged in a meeting room at the ultra-chic Estuary Hotel. Barrington schooled me in public relations etiquette as we wove through midtown traffic. "Ignore any question that can't be answered with a joke. Never stop smiling. Any time that Sparky interrupts you, just shut up and let him do the talking. Let me take the book. We need them to see the cover." With these words of wisdom tossing about in my fevered brain like pickles in a brine barrel, she escorted me into the hotel where what I thought were my fifteen minutes of fame awaited me.

Sparky Goldflugel greeted us in the lobby and grabbed me by the arm. "Wonderful to see you, Martin. Always a privilege to be in the presence of literary genius," he chuckled and nudged me in the side as if he'd just told a real knee-slapper. He ushered us into the elevator where we took a short ride to the mezzanine floor and walked down an attention grabbing, abstract carpet to the suite where my fate as a public person awaited me. I entered into a room temporarily inhabited by a few bored looking paparazzi raiding the minimal buffet, a gaggle of rather plain, young women in suits murmuring on their cell phones, and Megan Fillywell who gave a little wave and beamed at me with patently false admiration.

"Hello, hello there," Goldflugel greeted this small gathering, "glad you could all make it. Why don't you do the honors, Bunny."

Barrington Stoat held up her hands as if to silence the barely audible, dull roar of her audience. "Thank you all for being here today. I'm quite sure you won't be disappointed. It's not every day that I have the pleasure to introduce the sort of precocious talent that only comes along once in a blue moon, an author who exemplifies the very best that our country has to offer the world of literature, Mr. Martin Seward." She pulled me to her side and the paparazzi flashed away. Some of the young women in suits held up miniature tape recorders. I grinned lamely. "Martin's new book, *Babyland*, is being printed as we speak and it's going to cause quite the sensation, I assure you."

Then Goldflugel took over. "You've all got your press kits, right? I can't tell you what it's like to make a discovery like this young man. It's like a once in a lifetime thing, a real epiphany. And now you can discover him yourselves. Step up to bat, Martin. Any questions?" he asked the audience.

"Mr. Seward? What inspired you to write your book?" one of the earnest, young women wanted to know.

Thankfully, Goldflugel immediately cut off my stammered, "Uh, well…"

"Martin is inspired by everything he sees every day… and every night," he leered. "Come on over here, Megan." He guided me over to a small table and sat me down as Megan Fillywell joined us and

Barrington Stoat set down the copy of *Babyland* in front of me with an expensive fountain pen clipped to the jacket. "Go ahead, sign," Goldflugel urged me on. "I bet that Megan can't wait to get her copy."

I did as I was told as the photographers flashed away and the professional television talk show personality displayed the cover to the cameras.

"Okay, that's a wrap, folks," said Goldflugel and the room quickly cleared out. Megan Fillywell, book in hand, was in as much of a hurry as anybody else to get out of there and left with, "I'll call you later, Sparky," as her parting words. She and I had not spoken at all.

"You did just great, kid," Goldflugel congratulated me. "Now I've got to run," and he was gone.

"I thought you were going to break up with her," said Barrington Stoat. "That would have really got some attention. Remember, there is no such thing as bad publicity."

"Listen," I timidly complained, "I don't even have a copy of the book now."

"What do you need one for?" She seemed genuinely puzzled. "As soon as they're out of the printers, I'll send you a whole crate. By the way, here's your advance check." She handed me an envelope. "What you've got to concentrate on now is your public image. I think we can do something about that hair. You agree?"

I was so weirded out that all I could manage was an, "Uh, yeah," before she put me in a cab and sent me off to the station. "You must stay in touch, Martin." she commanded as taxi pulled away into traffic.

Stay in touch with what? On the train back out, I ruminated on this question as well as a few others. Actually, my so-called thoughts were all over the place and I found it difficult to focus on any one of them, but whatever was racing through my head always wound up in the same place: "Why me?" Why had some malign, practical joker god singled me out to make sport of. What could I do to palliate this cruel, cynical demiurge? Prayer, burnt offerings, human sacrifice?

When I got off the train I was still in a daze and immediately headed to Cyrano's where the good publican Sandwort greeted me from behind the bar.

"You look like shit," was his considered opinion.

It was a difficult observation to ignore and I immediately set about sedating myself with a martini.

"You know, Martin," said Sandwort, "when I was I young man – you may not believe that, but I was! – life seemed full of hope and promise. However, as I aged and mellowed, gradually and gracefully as a fine red wine or a pungent Stilton cheese, I began to realize that the whole thing wasn't all it's cracked up to be. I have never found any solace in religion, although it does provide a certain comfort to those who can't read the writing on the wall or, for that matter, read anything at all. Politics were dreary, endlessly repetitive, and only offered a silly vision of the perfection of human kind. Sex I reveled in until I woke up the next morning and found myself in the clutches of a being quite like me but so infinitely different, any attempt at communication was an impossible and probably undesirable dream. And so, here I am ministering to the likes of romantic fools such as yourself, waiting like a troll under the bridge for you to slip and plunge into the only fate that can possibly await you – utter despair! You take my meaning?"

"Hear, hear," I muttered sourly as Sandwort mixed me another drink.

"I knew you'd see it my way," he said cheerfully. "Have you heard that our friend Pedro Barbez has been incarcerated for offending the delicate sensibilities of a minor young lady?"

"I saw him being arrested this morning. He was laughing."

"Really? I thought he'd never let them take him alive but rather go down in a hail of gunfire from our local constabulary. I can just imagine his arrest report: 'Suspect was cheerful.'"

As if conjured by Sandwort's ruminations, who should walk in to the bar but Pedro Barbez himself looking none the worse for wear.

"A hearty and boon welcome to our favorite local child molester!" Sandwort greeted him and poured a double bourbon on the rocks.

"Shut up, you limey bastard," Barbez growled. "How did I know she was only twelve?"

"What did you think she was? Thirteen?" Sandwort genially retorted.

"I assure you, she is very mature for her age," Barbez allowed, "but she's still Daddy's little girl. She simply couldn't wait to reveal all the lurid details of my tossed off wisecrack to her troglodyte father."

Sandwort laughed. "That will teach you to keep your big mouth shut. You wouldn't want to share your witticism with us, would you?"

"The young lady is rather steatopigeous and I merely asked if I could set down my beer on her ass while I squirted some mustard on my hot dog."

"A quite reasonable request," Sandwort concurred, "but one that, unfortunately, might be misconstrued."

"Is it my fault she has no sense of humor?" Barbez whined and downed his bourbon in a single gulp. "The problem with this society is that it's all pussied out."

"You may have a point there but, you know, young women who have only recently bloomed from sleek and slender children into more curvaceous beings are often very sensitive about the width and breadth of their sometimes ample posteriors and you may have touched a nerve," Sandwort opined.

"Not the one I wanted to! That's for sure."

"So tell us, Pedro, given the gravity of your crime, why are you still walking around? Did you escape from jail?"

"Jail? Have you taken leave of your senses, Sandwort? You think those cops are going to risk getting blackballed from my Labor Day weenie roast?"

"What a threat to hang over their heads, the poor bastards," said Sandwort, sadly shaking his head.

"I know how to take charge when I have to," Barbez snapped.

I stayed another half hour or so listening to their idiot savant repartee and then went on my way back to the house where Danica's car was parked in the driveway.

"Where have you been?" she demanded as I walked in, as if she had taken over the place and I was an intruder.

"Not that it's any of your business, but I had to go into the city today."

"You're drunk."

"So I'm drunk and you're a pushy little pest," I growled. "I can go to sleep and wake up sober. What are you going to do?"

She chuckled. "I'm going to push you right into bed and when you wake up I'm going to pester you to death." And she did.

CHAPTER SEVEN

No sooner had I stumbled out of bed the next morning than Baby D started badgering me before I could even rinse the accumulated goo out of my eyes.

"I ran into Alicia yesterday. We had a little talk."

"I thought you two weren't speaking."

"We're not. Not in front of you anyway."

"How very kind of you. I guess I wouldn't want to hear what you had to say."

"But I think you would. What's all this business about you having a book published? You told me you hadn't written a word."

"Oh, you mean the Buddha book," I phumphed. "Well, that's true. I haven't really gotten into it yet."

Her eyes narrowed. "Alicia didn't say anything about any Buddha book. She told me you were having a novel published."

"Oh, that. Just something I wrote a while back."

"What's it about?"

"Well, I guess you could say it's about being young and ambitious in New York."

She stamped her foot. "You're lying, Martin, and you're not very good at it! What do you think you're doing letting someone else write your book for you?"

I didn't know how to respond. "I really don't know," I said sheepishly. "It just sort of happened."

"It's bound to get out," she said angrily.

I'd already thought this possibility over. "Whatever gets out will just be a rumor. My publicist will immediately spin it as the backstabbing envy of other writers less successful than my own worthy self," I said with weary resignation.

"How on earth did you get yourself into this mess? As if I didn't know. Dacron Redstone did this, didn't he?"

Talk about being wide of the mark. "Redstone had nothing to do with it. Didn't Alicia tell you?"

"Tell me what?"

"Well, you see, it's like this...," and I poured out the whole, fantastic, mortifying story as if I were confessing to the cops after a painful third degree. Her reaction was strangely disconcerting; her accusatory anger had turned to into a dismissive sigh of relief.

"I guess that's all right. I mean people do it all the time, don't they? You really had me worried, Martin."

Now it was my turn to get pissed off. "What do you mean it's all right? I feel like a complete fool."

"There's nothing I can do about that," she said brusquely. "Would you like some tea?"

I followed her into the kitchen. "Don't you see what this means?" I complained. "I've prostituted myself to the whole public relations machine. They've soaked my ass up like a sponge."

"You should be so lucky," she retorted. "Do you know how many people out there are standing in line to get co-opted?"

"That's not the point!" I protested. "I'm not one of them!"

"Please, don't get all bent out of shape. You've got nothing to worry about as long as you're not involved with Dacron Redstone."

"What does Redstone have to do with any of this bullshit?" I blustered in complete exasperation. "What's the deal between you and him?"

"You don't want to know."

"Yes I do."

Just on cue, as if we were actors in some lame, bedroom farce at the local little theatre, there was a knock at the door. It wasn't Redstone, however. "Who is it?" I demanded without opening the door.

"Mr. Seward?" a high pitched voice called out. "My name is Mrs. Bradley from down the road."

I opened up to an older woman with her ash blond hair pulled back in a chignon dressed in casual khaki pants, a white blouse, and penny loafers. She was carrying a clipboard. "I'm Mr. Seward," I said.

"Yes, I'm pleased to meet you. I'm your neighbor from just down there." She pointed in the opposite direction from Redstone's property. "Mr. Wilberforce suggested I talk to you."

"Please come in," I said. "This is my friend Danica."

"Nice to meet you," said Mrs. Bradley.

"I was just on my way out," Danica apologized. "I'll see you later, Martin," and she was gone.

"Mr. Seward, I'll come right to the point. We are circulating a petition to take to the village council and we'd very much appreciate it if you'd sign."

"What's this all about?"

"Surely you're aware that man down the road, Mr. Redstone, is having a very disruptive effect on the neighborhood with all his parties and the attendant traffic. A poor man on a bicycle was even killed the other day by one of Mr. Redstone's guests."

"Yes, I heard something about that," I said without mentioning that I'd actually attended the party.

"What we want to do is ban parking on the street which would greatly alleviate the congestion caused by Mr. Redstone's gatherings."

"Yes, I see, but I don't really live here. Why doesn't Mr. Wilberforce sign the petition? It's his property."

"Mr. Wilberforce intends to. We just thought that tenants might join us in our effort." There was something vaguely threatening in her tone, a sort of unspoken, "or else." What to do?

"I'll tell you what," I said. "Let me think it over and get back to you."

This response obviously did not please Mrs. Bradley who looked like the sort who was accustomed to getting her own way right away. "Well," she said icily, "you do that."

In this world of woe, I should not have been surprised by another unpleasant complication walking in from out of the blue. Why had Wilberforce "suggested" this woman talk to me? Was my staying in the house contingent on my signing the petition? Why would Wilberforce even care about Redstone? He was never there himself. Maybe he was just trying to get this old battle axe out of his hair.

Well, signing was pretty much out of the question. Even though I owed Redstone nothing I could not engage in this sort of backstabbing. The only positive thing that could come out of it was that he would never speak to me again was my wry thought. But I had other things to think about than neighborhood parking problems. I called Alicia.

"Why did you tell Danica I didn't write the book?" I demanded.

"I thought she'd be amused," she replied blandly. "You're not really annoyed, are you? I mean, it's not like it's a big secret, is it?"

"You're the one who got me into this, Alicia, and now you're trying to sabotage me?" I said angrily.

"Oh, come on, Martin. You haven't even read the book yourself. No one else will either, except desperate young college girls. That's your audience."

Her logic was indisputable. I was forced to retire from the field with my tail between my legs. "I wish I never had to read it," I muttered.

"I know," she sighed, "it's an unpleasant chore, but just think of all the adulation you're going to get from those nubile young things on the book reading circuit."

"What do you think I am?" I complained. "Some sort of child molester?"

"Oh, I'm sorry, Martin," she purred. "I know you prefer more…mature women… like Danica. You don't have to get involved with any of your ardent fans. Just nod and smile and sell them books."

That was about enough for me but not quite enough for Alicia.

"Speaking of child molesters, did you hear about your friend, Pedro Barbez?"

"What makes you think he's my friend? I barely know him."

"Well, it seems…"

"Yes, yes, I heard all about it," I cut her off. "It's the talk of the town."

"Well, I thought it was interesting," she said archly.

I couldn't resist. "No, no, haven't you heard? It was all just a misunderstanding. Pedro asked the young lady in question if he could set his beer down on the shelf of her protruding rear end while he ate a hotdog. Apparently, she took his innocent request the wrong way."

There was silence at the other end of the line.

"That's all that happened," I pressed on. "I mean, he wasn't charged with anything."

And that was quite enough for Alicia. No sooner had I got off the phone with her than Sheridan March called. "Martin, congratulations!" she brayed. "I had no idea! Now that you're a big name, I have to give you co-credit on the Buddha book!"

"Thanks, but I don't think that will be necessary, Sheridan."

"But I insist! Don't you see how good this is for both of us? Did you get my last check? I'll send you another five thousand so you can chain yourself to the desk and concentrate. Now I've got to run, so get to work! Tata!"

Her bubbly mood was anything but contagious. In fact, I suddenly felt as if something had grabbed me by the back of my neck and was going to throttle me within an inch of my life. Wave after wave of anxiety rolled over me until the tide finally receded and I was left standing there in a confused and shaken funk. I had embarked on a voyage that only promised sailing off the end of a flat earth as a destination. I was suddenly awash in money for which I had done nothing whatsoever and confronted with leaving all my real hopes and aspirations behind in favor of utterly bogus notoriety and a fortune founded on a series of hoaxes. Which reminded me of the envelope Barrington Stoat had handed over that I'd almost forgotten. I found it in my coat pocket, tore it open, pulled out a check for fifteen thousand dollars, and realized I was beyond redemption. It was if I'd been granted membership in a country club to which I'd never applied. Now I would be expected to make nice with the other members and pretend I was one of them. To some, the people whose opinions I despise, I would be an object of envy; to others, the ones I respect, I would be just another craven sell-out, pandering to the bonehead, lowest common denominator of the whiz heads. And that's when I realized, to my own disgust, that I wasn't going to give the money back and tread the lonely, difficult path of the true artist. I was going to become a middlebrow household name, immersed in creature comforts and lingering self doubts. Later on, when the creative juices had all but dried up, I would write the book I'd always meant to, resulting in a pathetic, barren travesty of everything I might have accomplished. However, my somber, maudlin thoughts soon gave way to something more compelling than my unearned self pity. There was a little man inside my head was trying to kick his way out which required the intervention of a couple aspirin washed down with a beer. I lay down on the couch but I was too restless to stay still. I got up and decided to do something I rarely even think of anymore. I got in the car, drove through the village, and headed for the other side of the island where the forest gave way to open spaces, fields and farms and rather bleak luxury housing developments.

This was a more desirable neighborhood than mine because of its proximity to the ocean with its endless white sand beach and other amenities such as manicured golf courses and polo grounds. I did not tarry long in this haut bourgeois idyll but headed east to a place where the summer people and the tourists rarely, if ever, set foot. An unmarked road forking off the highway away from the ocean meandered through decrepit, abandoned buildings left over from a once thriving canning industry that had been fished out long ago. The road abruptly ended on the shore of a large shallow inlet where the only other creatures in sight were seabirds and the occasional amateur clammer feeling out the bottom by foot. As I walked along the gravel shoreline, I felt my many cares slowly dissolve into the glinting, unroiled water and the wispy, nacreous clouds floating lazily overhead. This was a peaceful place in the midst of all the surrounding holiday clamor and glamour and I soaked up its calm beauty like the dried up sponge I was until I was saturated with warmth and good feeling. Sounds great, doesn't it? But don't ask me where it is because I'm not telling.

As I looked out over the water, I spotted something a ways offshore that looked like a floating log. Then it suddenly disappeared beneath the surface and re-emerged with its head held high out of the water as a seal with a fish in its mouth. I was close enough to see its whiskers. Now, I've seen small islands covered with seals on the west coast but I had never seen one in these waters. Was it a sign, an omen? I would have to consult someone more oracular than myself to decipher the meaning of this odd visitation. Perhaps Sheridan March. I found an old tennis ball in the gravel, possibly an abandoned dog toy, and threw it out to the seal. No dice. What did I think it was going to do anyway? Balance the ball on its nose like a circus act? All the vain expectations we harbor.

I returned to the car curiously refreshed and drove back to what passes for civilization. It was too early to go to Cyrano's. Or was it?

Of course, that's where I wound up with a couple old daytime regulars nursing their beers and pawing through the tabloids. I waited for Cyrano to crawl out of wherever he was coming from and ordered a martini.

"Starting rather early, aren't we?" he chided me. "But then, young Martin, a big time celebrity such as yourself can do pretty much what he pleases, n'est-ce pas? Do we have a quorum, gentlemen?!" he called down the bar. "Turn to page six of the Flash, which is actually page twelve, and feast your eyes on Mr. Seward here charming yet another sweet young thing out of her panties."

I had no idea what he was talking about but I soon found out. After a flurry of page turning, the gentlemen down the bar broke into laughter and squinted at me as if to confirm my actual presence among them. Cyrano picked up one of the papers and laid it down open in front of me.

"Good likeness," he said. "Isn't that the young lady I had to eject from the bar the other night?"

There I was handing Megan Fillywell her signed copy of the book. Her face was turned to the camera and her deranged eyes were all aglow. She fairly exploded off the page in a pyrotechnic display of glittering, if theatrical, charm. I, on the other hand, looked considerably less luminous and faded into the background like a dissipating puff of smoke. The caption below the picture read: "Ultra hot Martin Seward and his very own ultra hottie Megan Fillywell celebrate the publication of his new book, *Babyland*, which has a first printing of 500,000 copies." The half million figure was so absurd I could only assume it was a misprint or that Sparky Goldflugel had so far exceeded the level of decent expectations as to render anything he had to say completely ridiculous. But then, isn't it the function of public relations to invest the ridiculous with the status of myth?

"You've come so far up in the world, Martin," Sandwort crowed. "Who would ever think we might have the privilege of sitting in your exalted presence and soaking up the drippings from your magisterial aura?"

"Lay off, Cyrano," I whined as the other patrons hooted with laughter. "This is not my fault. What are you reading this trash for anyway?"

"Trash? The Flash?" Sandwort recoiled in mock horror. "You are talking about one of the shining lights of American journalism. To paraphrase the Bard of Baltimore, a successful tabloid newspaper must always be irritable and bellicose. It must never defend anyone or anything unless it is forced to, and then, only by denouncing someone or something else. So don't be so self-effacing," he scolded. "You are one of the lucky few to be offered a free ride. Lay claim to your grand eminence in this sorry world of ours, a world where the ignoble, the corrupt, and the craven usually reign over natural aristocrats such as yourself. Take advantage of the situation and only remember: false modesty is a far worse sin than honest arrogance. You have now graduated from the city that never sleeps to the city in a coma!"

"Here, here!" voices rang out from down the bar.

"Why are you trying to make me feel like shit?" I complained.

"I do it out of unalloyed envy and a certain sense of schaden-freude" said Sandwort cheerfully. "I think you need another martini."

The barflies quickly tired of their sport at my expense and left me in relative peace to peruse the rest of the newspaper where I learned something interesting in the financial pages. Dacron Redstone had indeed been selected for the board at Moloch and Feeney. Maybe I had-n't charged him enough.

When I got back to the house, there was something waiting for me on the front porch — a yellow floral wreath on an easel in the shape of a dollar sign that would have been more appropriate to a funeral par-lor. The attached card said: "Thanks a million! Call me! Dack." I immediately picked the damn thing up, took it down the road, and chucked it in the dumpster. But I was still obliged to make a congratu-latory phone call and that I did.

"Hello there, sport!" he answered exuberantly. "All good things on the same day! You must join me for lunch. I'll send Reynolds over to fetch you."

I didn't want to go but why spoil his good mood? "That's all right, Dack. I'll walk but I only have time for a drink." I walked through the woods out onto the expansive lawn where Redstone was waiting for me at his glass and wrought iron table. He greeted me in his bathrobe with a broad smile and a hearty handshake. Then he hugged me close, kissed me on both cheeks, and growled, "I couldn't have done it without you, baby." Needless to say, this weird display of affection made me distinctly uncomfortable, but I did my best not to obviously recoil from his fervid camaraderie. I felt as if I were in some silly Mafia movie and had just received the kiss of death. "Sit down," he com-manded. "Sit down and have yourself a glass of the very finest cham-pagne in the world."

"From your own vineyard, of course," I cracked wise.

He guffawed. "I wish! Salud!" He raised his glass in a toast. "To my new job and your new book."

If he knew how phony the book was he might not be so enthu-siastic about the job, I thought as we clinked glasses.

"Who's that hot babe you're with in the paper, sport?" He leered and winked like a burlesque top banana from an old movie.

"You don't know? I met her at your party."

"Really? Maybe I ought to show up next time. I'd like to get me some of that."

Offering to make the introduction was almost irresistible, but I controlled myself. Instead I changed the subject. "Speaking of parties, there's some old bat down the road circulating a petition to stop your guests from parking on the street."

"You're kidding."

"No, she came by my place this morning. I didn't sign, of course."

Redstone laughed. "Why not? It's people like me who bring down property values in the neighborhood. Find out what her favorite charity is and we'll fix things up."

"You find out what her favorite charity is. I'm not part of the landed gentry out here."

"You've got a point, sport. I guess I better get to her soon because I'm having a party on Saturday. Do me a favor and bring your cousin and her husband."

"I'll see if they're interested. Anyway, I've got to go. I'll see you later."

"You make sure they're interested, Martin. Believe me, I'll make it worth their while."

I had no idea what Redstone was talking about and I didn't much care. Offenfusser would never go and Alicia probably wouldn't either. Maybe I'd bag it myself, I thought as I walked back into the woods towards the house. It had already been a long morning and it was time to put everything aside and tuck the fevered brain in bed. I popped open a V-8 juice, sat back in a deck chair on the porch, and focused on the beacon that crowned the Offenfusser tower flashing dimly red in the hazy distance across the bay. Unfortunately, the light put me in mind of my cousin who I sourly considered had gone to some lengths to get me into my current predicament. All with the best intentions, of course, she had tossed me into a process whose outcome could only be guessed at and was bound to yield a few unpleasant surprises. But that's ambiguity for you. All the certainties I had clung to in my late impoverishment and anonymity had dissolved away into a random sequence where any meaningful result was irrelevant. I could no longer coolly observe the absurdity of the world; I was the absurdity. Ironic detachment was a thing of the past. I had foolishly become engaged.

As I lounged there in the late morning sun, I began to expand and inflate like a balloon because hot air was all I was riding on at the moment. I contemplated the plus side of my peculiar situation and found it alluring enough to keep me afloat for awhile. Visions of money and fame, fancy houses and hot babes, all the treasures due commoditized celebrity danced through my head in a moving panorama of the garden of earthly delights that awaited me. I wanted to want it as badly as everyone else does. I wanted absolution in an orgy of confectionary consumer dreams but my interest in that bright future was unfortunately wanting and, as my enthusiasm ebbed, the hot air cooled and I began to slowly deflate. Soon I was just a limp exoskeleton of my former self. I know what you're thinking. You're just snickering at my lame attempt to excuse my new bought-in status with a self-flagellating mea culpa as if I were asking you to pardon my sins. But that's not really the case. I didn't have enough interest in the horns of my own dilemma to even try and forgive myself, much less expect others to do so.

But enough about me. The wind was dusting up whitecaps on the bay and the close, warm air was thick with moisture. In a matter of minutes, I heard the first clap of thunder in the distant west and the sky began to rapidly cloud over. Soon it had darkened to a twilight tone and the first heavy drops of rain were beginning to come down. I went inside and watched the storm from the window. Suddenly, a lightning bolt snaked out of the sky and arced with Offenfusser's tower across the bay, followed immediately by the gunshot snap and billowing roar of the loudest thunder I'd ever heard. I peered out toward the foundation estate but I couldn't see anything through the soupy mist and driving rain. When I tried to call Alicia, all I got was static.

The storm passed over quickly and the bay was bathed in bright sunlight once again. I could see the silhouette of the tower still standing in the distance but the red light on top was no longer flashing. I decided to make a run over to the foundation and see what had happened.

When I got there, Offenfusser was up on a cherry picker near the top of his piece, which had frozen into a tableau of running molten steel.

"Hallo there!" I called up. He looked down and waved. Then he went back to doing whatever he was doing. I went into the house and found Alicia in the kitchen.

"How are you? I watched the fireworks over here from across the bay."

"I'm glad someone saw it," she chuckled. "I just got the flash and the boom. It shook the whole house."

"That must have been frightening."

"Not at all. I love thunder and lightning and this is as close as I've ever been to a direct hit. It was really quite exhilarating." She paused as she dried a plate. "I hope you're not still mad at me."

"I have a serious anger management problem that doesn't allow me to be mad at anyone nearly as long as I should be."

"Really?" she said. "I can hold a grudge forever. I'll teach you how."

"Thanks. That's very kind of you to offer."

"So, is there anything else on your mind but morbid voyeurism?

"I tried to call you but I didn't get any answer. I just came over to make sure you were all right. But there is something else. Dacron Redstone is having a party this weekend and he wanted me to invite you and Fuzzwick."

"Who is Dacron Redstone?" she said. "Do I know him?"

"He's my millionaire next door neighbor. He's also a big time art collector."

Alicia was suddenly all ears. "Oh yes," she said, "the Wall Street guy you were talking about the other day. The one who thinks he knows me."

"The very same."

"Tell him we'd be delighted to attend. At least I would. I don't know if I can drag Wick along. You know how he feels about parties."

Just at that moment, Offenfusser walked into the kitchen and went to the sink to wash his hands. "Hello there, Mark," he greeted me. "Pretty exciting around here today."

"Yes," I agreed. "I saw your tower get hit from across the bay. It was quite spectacular."

"Damn," he said, "I wish I'd seen it myself. I heard it. That's for sure. Now I've got to put a new beacon up there before the aviation people slap me with a fine."

"Martin's invited us to a party this weekend at that estate across the bay," said Alicia.

"Well, I think I'm going to be pretty busy…"

"The owner is a major art collector. He really wants to meet you."

Offenfusser's response was to get off topic as quickly as possible. "I know someone who lives a little farther out on that side of the bay. Grady Schick."

"Who's that?"

Offenfusser chuckled. "He's an artist. Sort of. He used to change movements like his underwear. He was always on the cutting edge of every new thing that came along – Neo-Feo, Straight Line, Intuitionalism, Post Ersatz – you name it, Grady was right there in the thick of things."

"How come I never heard of him?" Alicia wanted to know.

"Before your time, young lady. Grady disappeared from the scene years ago and lives as a hermit on a sand spit out there by the sound. A hermit with a wife."

Alicia laughed. "I didn't know hermits were allowed to have wives."

"She's never there. She lives in the city. She's very social."

"How convenient for both of them."

"Rumor has it that this self-same wife has him chained to a tree on the property and fed twice a day by a catering company in the village."

"He must be pretty wet after this storm today."

"I'm sure she has provided him with a comfortable dog house where he can take shelter from the elements."

"I'm sure that's all very interesting, Wick, but what about this party Martin's invited us to?"

"Major art collector, you say?" Offenfusser chewed this over for a few seconds. "I'll see if I can make time in my schedule."

"He was the fellow with Ahmed Jifhraz out in Frog's Lip Harbor," I offered helpfully. "He bought us a round of drinks."

"Yes, yes, I can almost remember him," said Offenfusser. "Now I really must attend to my lighting problem." And off he went.

"He seems like he might go," I said. "Not that I care. I was thinking of skipping it myself but, if you're going to show up, I'll be there."

"Wait a minute, Martin. You're inviting us to a party that you don't want to go to? Sounds like great fun but I don't understand."

"I'm just kidding. I'm sure you'll have a great time," I reassured. "Redstone really lays it on when he throws one of these things. He's even got the neighbors up in arms."

"Well, if people are complaining, it can't be all that bad," she concurred. "We'll be there."

CHAPTER EIGHT

What happened in the few days between my leaving the estate and Redstone's party is of little interest. Baby D adamantly refused to go and urged me to do likewise. I explained that I was merely chaperoning for the Offenfussers.

"Fuzzwick won't even show up," she scoffed.

But he did. The newlyweds showed up in my driveway at three o'clock in the afternoon when the party next door was already in full swing. Offenfusser was wearing a paisley velour suit with bell bottoms and a green satin ribbon around his neck. He looked as if he'd just walked out of a time capsule from 1968. Alicia, on the other hand, was all in art dealer regulation black

"Damn good thing you've got someplace to park," said Offenfusser. "There are cars out there lined up for miles."

He was, of course, exaggerating, but the road was pretty clogged up and I imagine Mrs. Bradley was not pleased. We decided to waste no time at my place and immediately headed off toward the musical hubbub beyond the trees.

There were scores of revelers streaming through the house out to the back lawn and we joined this throng of fun loving pilgrims on their journey to this tent show shrine to Dionysius where many delectable victuals and untold cases of champagne would be sacrificed that afternoon.

"Quite a place he's got here," Offenfusser observed. "Sort of a bad acid trip rendered in brick and mortar."

"If that's what you think it looks like, you certainly fit right in," said Alicia, doubtless commenting on his party clothes.

We proceeded through the indoor tropical garden with the others and soon passed out of the house to the main locus of the festivities, the swimming pool and two covered pavilions on the surrounding lawn. The casually dressed guests mixed and mingled in a swirl of sociability that whisked the new arrivals into a world far removed from care, a world where you could make a complete ass of yourself without fear of censure or repercussion. The opportunities to do so would, of course, become more pronounced as time passed and good cheer and substance abuse combined to encourage all manner of hyper-liberated behavior among the party-goers.

A band floating on a raft in the middle of the pool dispensed covers of the latest dance tunes but the crowd was not yet liquored up enough to get down and funky, preferring for the moment to chatter with their friends, acquaintances, and complete strangers on the sidelines.

"So where's our host?" Alicia wanted to know. "Why don't you introduce him to us."

"I don't see him but he must be somewhere around," I allowed. I hadn't mentioned that he was unlikely to even put in a brief appearance. However, I was mistaken on that point. No sooner had we wondered about his whereabouts than Redstone showed up at my elbow wearing a rubber monster mask and a fright wig.

"It's me, sport," he said sotto voce. "Don't let anyone else know."

"I won't," I agreed.

"When your cousin arrives, bring her up to my office. You know how to get there."

"But she's right here," I said. Alicia and Offenfusser, however, had wandered a little ways off into the party. "I'll fetch her."

"No rush," said Redstone. "Let her take a good look around before you bring her up." With that, he was off. I found the Offenfussers at the bar where Fuzzwick had run into someone he knew.

"This really is a coincidence, Grady," he said to a gaunt looking, ill-kempt, sallow faced man with a goatee. "We were just talking about you the other day."

"I wish you wouldn't do that," said Schick flatly.

"Well, of course not. I'll watch myself in the future. What are you doing out anyway? I heard that Rhoda had you chained to a tree. How did you escape? Does she know you're here?"

"I see no reason to leave the property," Schick replied without rising to the bait. "Being alone concentrates my thoughts."

"Oh, you're still doing thought," said Offenfusser. "I thought that was last year. By the way, this is my wife Alicia and her cousin Mark."

Schick nodded to both of us but said nothing.

"So, Grady, what are you doing here? This place hardly seems conducive to solitary meditation."

"Mr. Redstone bought one of my pieces which unfortunately obligated me to attend. I certainly wouldn't be here otherwise. Now, if you'll excuse me, I've put in my appearance and I'm leaving." Schick put down his empty glass and hurried off toward the house.

"Peculiar man," said Alicia.

"You have no idea," Offenfusser snorted. "I wonder what sort of piece he sold."

It was time to proffer Redstone's invitation. "I just saw our host a moment ago and he invited us all upstairs to his office."

"Well, let's go," said Alicia.

So we walked back up to the mansion and I led them to the elevator where Reynolds stood like St. Peter at the pearly gates adjudging sinners and good souls alike to determine their fitness for an audience with Redstone. We were not found wanting.

"Good afternoon, sir," said Reynolds as politely as a thug in a suit can. "Mr. Redstone is waiting for you." He ushered us into the cramped elevator and we ascended to the top floor where he conducted us down the hallway past the numerous old master paintings.

"These are fakes, right?" said Offenfusser. He couldn't believe they were real and I can't say I did either.

We passed through the bronze door into the onyx lavatory and Reynolds turned off the urinal. He opened the door and gestured for us to continue into Redstone's aerie. The Offenfussers were temporarily rendered speechless by this bizarre ingress and silently followed me into the spacious, sunlit office where Redstone was hunkered down with his telescope viewing the ebullient proceedings on the lawn below. He had doffed his mask and wig and donned a satin Sulka dressing gown over silk pajamas in his best Hugh Hefner impersonation. He turned away from his peeping when we walked in and greeted us.

"So, there you are at last, sport. Who's this you've brought along with you?"

"This is my cousin Alicia and her husband Fuzzwick Offenfusser."

"Dacron Redstone," he said, enthusiastically pumping Offenfusser's hand. "Pleased to meet you." Then he turned his attention to Alicia. "But you're not really Martin's cousin, are you? I guess this is his idea of a little joke."

"I beg your pardon," said Alicia.

I fully expected Redstone to spring some strained compliment like, "How could anyone so lovely be related to a guy who looks as if he's been whupped upside the head with an ugly stick?" but this was not the case. Instead, he turned to me and said, "Always the practical joker. Just make sure you get it right next time, sport."

First, I am not a practical joker by any stretch of the imagination. Second, I didn't have the slightest idea what he was talking about. There was nothing to do but protest my innocence. "But she is my cousin, Dack. My one and only."

"Of course, of course," he patronized me. "Now, would you all like something to drink? I've got the very finest kickapoo joy juice in the world right here on ice."

He poured us all glasses of champagne which we used to toast the glorious afternoon. Then Offenfusser got right down to business, immediately turning the nascent conversation to the arts.

"I ran into Grady Schick downstairs. I understand you bought a piece from him."

"I did indeed, Fuzzwick. In fact, that's it right over there in the corner."

We all looked over at a three foot tall, Ionic column of the sort used to decorate lawns in certain neighborhoods in New Jersey. There was a sign hanging from the top that read: SUBSTANCE.

"You see," Redstone continued, "the piece itself is actually invisible. That's just the pedestal holding it up."

"Curious," said Offenfusser. "Can I touch it?"

"Touch what?"

"The piece."

"Of course," said Redstone with a smile and a wink. "Just don't knock it over."

When Offenfusser went over to the pedestal and tried to pass his hand over it, he ran into unexpected resistance as if there actually were something solid there. I thought he was having us on but when he knocked on thin air and it made a clanking sound, I realized there must be something more to the thing than met the eye.

"All right, how do you do that?" said Offenfusser as if he were asking a magician to explain one of his illusions.

"I don't do anything," said Redstone. "I told you. It's invisible."

After that, we all had to try it and I can vouch for the existence of something material in that impermeable void.

"Grady made the piece invisible to call attention to the pedestal," Redstone explained. "He says we don't pay enough attention to what things stand on. That's what substance means."

"It's an interesting idea," Offenfusser had to admit, "but it sort of renders art criticism obsolete, doesn't it?"

"Well, there's always pedestal criticism," said Alicia.

The conversation continued on in this pleasantly casual vein until it was time for us to leave Redstone to his voyeurism and return to the party. But not before the second foremost conceptualist and the financial wizard had agreed to meet again with an eye toward a commission for the lawn.

"Really," said Offenfusser in parting, "you must come by the foundation and let me show you what we're up to."

"Love to, sport," Redstone replied. "I'll make it over as soon as I can." Before I passed out the door, he pulled me aside and whispered, "Just make sure you bring your real cousin by next time," along with a meaningful look.

"Of course," I said as if we were sharing a joke. Actually, I was beginning to think Redstone had a screw loose.

Once back outside, we almost immediately ran into the threesome of Ahmed Jifhraz, Harry Poon, and Gloriana.

"Jesus, Wick," said Poon, "how did they get you out of the house? And where did you get that costume?"

"It's the new me, Harry. Fuzzwick Offenfusser, party animal."

Jifhraz clearly seemed at loose ends. He nodded and smiled uncomfortably until he was mercifully saved by Reynolds who joined us just at that moment and obsequiously informed, "Mr. Jifhraz, Mr. Redstone is waiting for you upstairs."

"Yes, yes," said Jifhraz and turned to us apologetically. "Please excuse me."

As he walked away with Reynolds, Gloriana purred, "Isn't A.J. cute? So shy."

"Where's the booze?" said Poon. "I'm parched."

So we all adjourned to the bar. "Why didn't you bring little Danica?" Alicia asked me as we walked toward the pavilion. "Afraid she'd run off with one of these swells?"

"I did invite her, but, as you well know, Alicia, Danica does what she damn well pleases."

"She didn't want to come?"

"Correct."

"Strange. She's such a party girl."

When we had all procured whatever we were drinking, Poon raised his glass in a toast. "To you, Fuzzwick, in your new incarnation as a cross between an aficionado of the Grateful Dead and a rodeo clown. Cheers!"

"Mr. Redstone is going to commission a piece from Wick," Alicia couldn't help blurt out in defense of her man.

"Well, there's nothing set. It's all very preliminary," said Offenfusser modestly.

Poon was having none of that. "You sonuvabitch," he said. "And I thought you were here to meet new friends."

"Only one," said Alicia archly.

"Omigod!" said Gloriana. "It's Piggy Bigwig. The real Piggy Bigwig."

And so it was. The enormously obese hip hop star was waddling along the side of the pool sporting a baby blue satin suit and a trailing, thuggish looking entourage, one of whom held up an umbrella to shield Piggy from the sun.

"Do you suppose we could get his autograph?" Offenfusser wondered.

"No way," said Poon. "He's completely illiterate, a true artiste naïf."

"I've just got to introduce myself," gushed Gloriana who had gone gaga in the presence of such a luminary. She made a beeline for the star and tried to tell him what a great fan she was but one of Piggy's posse intervened and shooed her away at gunpoint.

This greatly amused Poon who gleefully called out, "Shoot the bitch!"

Gloriana returned without honor and complained, "All I wanted to do was show my appreciation."

"Is that what you call it? Try taking off your clothes next

time," Poon suggested, "and show him some tits and ass. Then, who knows? Maybe you'd be in a position to move on to appreciation. But not the missionary position for obvious reasons."

"You are such an asshole, Harry," Gloriana sighed.

"He is, isn't he?" said Alicia brightly.

"You," said Poon, pointing at me. "I saw your picture in the newspaper the other day."

"Ah, that wasn't me. Apparently I've got a doppelganger."

"It was too," said Alicia. "Martin's going to be almost as famous as Piggy Bigwig."

"You dog, you," said Poon, wagging his finger. "Have you actually been doing that blond fruitcake?"

"It's an arranged marriage presided over by my publicist."

"Hey, don't get me wrong," said Poon. "I get hot just thinking about it."

"Who's the dog now?" said Gloriana.

"Woof woof," said Poon.

"Do you know who I saw here earlier?" said Offenfusser. "Grady Schick."

"Really?" said Poon "I thought he was dead."

"Well, he is in a manner of speaking but he just sold a piece to our host."

"You're kidding. What kind of stuff is he doing lately?"

"Invisible stuff."

"Oh, yes," said Poon. "I can't see it, but I can feel it all around me, a colorless, odorless, possibly poisonous gas. Hang it at the Modern, I say."

Just then, some of the now thoroughly inebriated celebrants decided it was time for a swim. That is, it was time for the people they were pushing into the pool to swim. With much whooping and hollering, those in the water splashed around with such exuberance the spray they kicked up shorted out the amp on the raft which spat out a shower of sparks followed by a plume of white smoke.

"Oh, look," said Offenfusser. "They've finally chosen a new Pope."

I was only waiting for the raft to founder, dump all its electronic gear in the water and eliminate the aquatic contingent via electrocution. I knew, however, that my apocalyptic vision would not be realized since I am acquainted with a manic-depressive young woman who tried to end it all by plunging a plugged-in radio into the bathtub. What happened was not what she expected. Rather than jolt her into oblivion, the charge in the water built up slowly until it got so uncomfortable she had to get out. So much for best laid plans.

I didn't see much point in hanging out any longer and I informed the rest of the crew that I was fanning the breeze.

"You can't go now," Alicia complained. "The party's just beginning."

"Yes, I can see that," I said, which was precisely the reason I was leaving. "Please stay and enjoy yourselves if you like. I've got some things to do."

And so I left the party and returned to my considerably humbler abode where I found Baby D curled up on the couch watching figure skating on TV. She was surprised to see me.

"What's the matter? Was it that bad?"

"No, it was just fine. Alicia and Fuzzwick seemed to be having a good time."

"I can't believe she got him to go. Why did you leave?"

"I caught your sweet scent in the air and it drove me to distraction. They begged me to stay but nothing could dissuade me from putting my nose to the ground and tracking you down to your little nest."

She giggled. "Oh Marts, you're so romantic. Come snuggle up with me."

I accepted her invitation without reservation and we were soon engaged in the heaviest sort of petting.

"Oh my little bloodhound," she crooned. "Do me doggy style."

I happily obliged her and we were going at it with the sweetest abandon when someone rapped sharply on the door and all but spoiled a sublime moment in the annals of bestial carnality.

"Just a minute!" I called out. Then I hurriedly pulled on my pants and went to the door. "Who is it?" I demanded.

"It's Thelma Bradley!" I opened up and there she was with her clipboard. "I'm sorry to bother you, Mr. Seward, but really, you must sign the petition. Just listen to all that racket. I don't understand how you can stand it."

"You know," I said, "I spoke to Mr. Redstone the other day

and he told me he was willing to make a sizeable donation to the charity of your choice."

"Oh my goodness," she said as if she didn't believe what she was hearing. "Does that... that fool have the idea he can bribe me? What sort of person thinks he can just buy off anyone?"

Danica joined us at the door. "It's none of my business," she said, "but, if I were you, I'd march right over there and give him hell. Catch him right now."

Mrs. Bradley considered this suggestion and apparently found it sound. "You know, that's exactly what I'm going to do," she said with flinty resolve and off she went.

"Don't shoot until you see the whites of his eyes!" Danica called after her.

I was mildly irritated by Baby D's enthusiasm for harassing my neighbor even if she did bear ill feeling against him. "Thank you very much, Madame Defarge," I said. "You should have stopped right after, 'It's none of my business.'"

Her eyes widened in mock surprise. "It's just a good natured practical joke, Martin."

"At my expense. Why don't you just tell me why you've got it in for Redstone."

"Can't do it," she said. "Better you don't know." She kissed me. "Now where were we?"

This time we retired to the bedroom to continue our sport and the afternoon blurred into what even today is a highly pleasant, vividly visceral memory.

CHAPTER NINE

Speaking of memories, you might have thought I didn't have any. I mean, I don't think I've mentioned anything at all about my past in the preceding pages. I do have memories, though; lot's of them, mostly fragmentary or unpleasant which is a pretty good reason in itself not to consign them to paper as reminders of things best forgotten. However, is that fair to you, the reader, to remain a human cipher who appears with no baggage whatsoever like Athena popping directly from the head of Zeus?

Probably not, but I've always found autobiography to be either self-serving solipsism or bogus self-deprecation. Little Me keeps cropping up in the narrative with drearily predictable monotony, immune to any attempt keep it at a decent distance. However, I do think you deserve a general outline no matter how sketchy and dispassionate and this I shall try to provide.

I was born on the shores of Chowderhead Bay during the reign of Richard Nixon whom I knew nothing about until long after his awkward departure from the White House. I grew up in a stolidly bourgeois suburb which has since been swallowed up by the ceaselessly expanding Northeast corridor megalopolis. My parents were a study in contrasts. My father was a taciturn, staunch Republican estate attorney who would eat no fat; my mother an affable, overweight, motor mouth busybody whose politics leaned towards radical socialism. I could never understand how they got together in the first place but I could hardly complain being the sole issue of their union. Their quiet stalemate lasted through my youth and only gave way to open hostilities when I left the nest and they felt free to get divorced. I went to so-called "good" schools and I did well enough to be accepted into a well-known university where my academic career took a turn for the worse. I had this romantic notion that I wanted to be a writer and I had to experience the world directly rather than study it in books. So I did in my cautious, even timid manner. I saw a few things and managed to skirt a number of dangerous situations and entanglements. I even kept a journal from which I culled the material for my novice short stories which I look back on now and cringe in embarrassment. I kept my writing habit afloat with a series of odd jobs peculiar to the young and foolishly ambitious until I could actually eke out a marginal existence writing magazine articles and advertising copy. All this led to one progressively better paid assignment after the other, while the desire to write a well received novel still smoldered in my breast. Now I have, sort of. My future is assured without writing a word. I mean, how post modern can you get?

Most of the above is, of course, confabulated. The so-called real details of my earthly sojourn are even duller than I've made them out to be and I won't belabor you further with my C.V.

After Baby D had left in the morning to go do whatever she does, I called Alicia to ask her how she had liked the party.

"It was wonderful if you have a particularly morbid sense of humor," she said. "Your friend Pedro Barbez showed up after you left..."

"He's not my friend."

"Whatever. He and Harry Poon certainly seem to know each other. Anyway, Mr. Barbez was completely snockered and proceeded to sit down in Ariel Sumner's lap and undulate."

"Who's Ariel Sumner?"

"The famous fashion editor. I would have thought she'd be horrified but she just laughed and gave him twenty dollars."

"I guess that's what a lap dance costs these days. Is Fuzzwick really going to do a piece for Redstone?"

"No idea. You know how Wick is. You can never tell whether he's serious or just having a little fun at Mr. Redstone's expense."

"I'm sure it would be worth his while. Redstone's pretty free handed."

"It's not a matter of the money. Not entirely anyway. It's more like a, 'Would I want to hang on that wall?' sort of thing.

"It's not the Met," I agreed.

"Mr. Redstone certainly does make up for his surplus of money with a consummate lack of taste," she laughed.

"Ah, yes, what's the ancient saying? 'The desire to decorate one's nest is always poignant no matter how disastrous the results.' Something like that."

"Speaking of disastrous results, have you spoken to Bunny

Stoat about your book?"

"What do you mean 'disastrous results'?" I defended myself. Well, not myself exactly. "For all I know it might be good."

"It better not be if you want to make the best seller list."

She had a point, but it didn't boost my spirits any. After I got off the phone, it was time to drive into the village and pick up the newspaper and some sandwich stuff. There I ran into Cyrano Sandwort playing the lottery in the delicatessen.

"Hello, Martin. There was a young lady in asking after you last night," he said as he scratched away at one of his tickets.

"Yeah? Anyone we know?"

"Never saw her before in my life. Asian, not very good looking. She wanted your address but I kept my mouth shut."

My curiosity was piqued. Who could this be? A reporter after an interview? Did I already have groupies? "Do me a favor, Cyrano. If anyone asks, you don't know me."

"Right. I don't know you, you don't know you, nobody knows you," he said with mock gravitas. Then suddenly: "Begab! I just won four dollars." He held the ticket up for all to see. "Pay up!" he demanded of the bored counterman.

I took leave of the lucky publican with my meager purchases and retreated back into the woods. As I was driving up the road to the house a tow truck pulling what looked like Redstone's white SUV and a village police car passed me going in the opposite direction. Was that Reynolds in the back seat? As soon as I got back to the house I gave Redstone a call. He was not a happy camper.

"They're just doing this because that woman complained about the party," he said angrily.

"Doing what?"

"They told me they think it was my car that hit that man on the road after the last party so they've taken it in to be inspected. I sent Reynolds along to drive it back when they're done. The whole thing is ridiculous. I know it's all that goddam old hag down the road's doing."

"You mean Mrs. Bradley."

"Whatever she calls herself. Apparently she was here yesterday trying to see me."

"She's quite persistent. I thought you were going to talk to her before the party."

"Completely slipped my mind. After this, she can take her favorite charity and shove it up her ass."

I had to chuckle at that one.

"I don't see what's so funny," he snapped. "I pay taxes in this town. Lots of taxes and they come out here and treat me like some sort of common criminal."

"Hey, calm down," I soothed. "All you have to do is swallow your pride and go make nice with the old lady."

"You're an asshole, Martin, but, unfortunately, you're right."

I was just imagining how delighted Danica would be to hear of Redstone's woes since she had, in fact, brought them down upon him.

"Bring her some flowers or candy or something," I suggested. "Turn on the charm."

"Right, and a bottle of sloe gin," he said sourly. "Why don't you come over and cheer me up? I'll crack a bottle of champagne. God knows, there's enough left over from yesterday."

To this request, I reluctantly agreed even though I didn't really care to see him. Maybe I was just a wee bit guilty about Danica's role in the affair.

I was soon seated at the table on the front lawn quaffing champagne while Redstone paced back and forth nervously in his bathrobe. "I hope you enjoyed the party," he said. It sounded more like challenge than a pleasantry. "What was the idea of trying to pass off that woman as your cousin anyway?"

No more of this nonsense, I thought. "Well, you see, Dack, my cousin was here. The thing is, she's invisible – like your new Grady Schick."

"All right," he said throwing his hands in the air. "I surrender. I'll run into her sometime or another."

"I think you've got more pressing problems than my cousin. What are you going to do about Mrs. Bradley?"

"Exactly what you suggested, Martin. I'm going to get dressed and have Guillermo collect some flowers from the garden. Then I'm going to drag my ass down the street and humbly apologize to the old bag. You know what's wrong with people like this Bradley woman? They live in an obsolete reality. They think that everything is steady state, unchanging, carved in stone, and all that crap. Then I show up with a whole new, improved reality and they freak out. Beware the stodgy Puritans, Martin."

"I'll keep my distance," I agreed and wondered how clogging up the road with parked cars had transmuted into a socio-philosophical problem.

"They simply don't understand that the engine of the universe is change, Martin, constant, unceasing change. You've got to keep moving, keep right ahead of it, or it's liable to run you over."

A lesson the poor devil on the road with the bicycle should have taken to heart.

"Anyway, duty calls," he sighed. "I've got to suit up and play the gentleman caller for the old bat."

I wished him luck and took my leave. Back at the house, I briefly weighed the idea of trying to do a little work on Sheridan March's book but I could not bring myself to give it any more thought than that. The prospect of actually sitting down and writing the damned thing was pure anathema to my slothful soul that sunny morning. Buddha would just have to wait for the spirit to move me, a possibility that seemed to recede further into the distance with each passing day. Did I feel a twinge of guilt, a nagging sense that I was not living up my responsibilities? Later for that. I opened a beer and went out onto the veranda where a surprised squirrel skittered away along the railing and leapt off the porch into an adjoining tree. Down below I could see a plover walking along the water's edge. There were not many boats out at that hour and the harbor seemed a bit empty and forlorn. Out across the bay, I noted that Offenfusser's beacon had been repaired and was once again flashing red from the top of the tower. My phoned rang and I went back inside to answer it.

"Where have you been?" Barrington Stoat demanded. "You missed your acting class yesterday."

I thought fast. "Look, Bunny, there's an acting coach out here that I can go to. It's much easier than coming into the city."

"What's his name?"

"Uh, Harry Poon."

"Never heard of him. I suppose he'll do for the time being. You have to start taking your image more seriously, Martin," she tut-tutted.

"I'm working on it, believe me."

"As you know, the book goes into the stores in six weeks. We already have advance sales of over five thousand so you better be ready to go on tour."

When she hung up, I considered this unwelcome news. It was no longer good enough to simply write a book or, in my case, not write a book. You had to get out there and flog it to Mr. and Mrs. John Q. Semiliterate Public. You had to appear on inane talk shows and make nice with the harebrained host. You had to have opinions about everything and everybody, you had to subjugate yourself to your audience's rapacious appetite to share in all the details of your glamorous life. Did you pick your nose? Who was your favorite ingénue chanteuse? What horse were you betting on the Kentucky Derby? Did you like to do it doggy style? So many questions to be answered as you signed copies for the clamoring hordes of book lovers basking in the dazzling brilliance of your scintillating presence. It was enough to give any reasonable person a sick headache and the onerous day of reckoning was almost upon me. Would they eat me up or boo and jeer at my lettered performances? Would I care?

Such were my thoughts as I contemplated being transported from one bookstore or college gathering to another in a whirlwind tour of the boonies. If Alicia was not mistaken, I would soon be fending off or maybe not fending off aggressive young women with something more than my signature on their hormone besotted minds. Did I like to do it doggy style indeed?

My reverie was interrupted by what sounded like an explosion in the distance. I went back out on the veranda and spotted a cloud of black smoke billowing into the air above the Sulema. Like most people, I am magnetically attracted to disaster scenes, and I hurried out to the car for a little ambulance chasing. When I got to the marina where the Sulema was berthed, the yacht was listing to one side and had apparently settled on the shallow floor of the basin. A.J.'s stock traders and crew stood on the dock scratching their heads and chattered away in a cacophony of Asian languages. Harry Poon and Gloriana hovered nearby holding cocktails in their hands. They waved me over.

"Ahoy there, mate," said Harry. "I'd have you aboard but the place is a mess and the cleaning lady doesn't come until tomorrow."

"What happened?"

"Don't know. Big bang down below and the thing sank like a rock. Not very far, as you can see."

"Is anybody hurt? Where's A.J.?"

"No idea. We got off in a hurry."

A police car, a fire truck, and an ambulance turned into the marina with their sirens wailing. The firemen hurried toward the yacht with fire extinguishers but there was no more smoke to be seen. A moment later, a black BMW pulled up alongside the police car and Ahmed Jifhraz got out and surveyed the situation. For a split second, he looked stunned. Then he frowned and started cursing in Arabic. Poon rushed over to comfort him.

"Hey. come on, A.J., it's only money. You'll be able to get that baby up and running in no time."

"Why don't you shut up, Harry," Gloriana suggested.

Jifhraz ignored his guests and went over to his crew to find out what had happened. Nobody knew it at the time, but they would shortly find out that the Sulema was the victim of an underwater mine attached to her side by persons unknown. I felt a little awkward just gawking and, since I was on this side of the bay, I decided to drop in on the Offenfusser's and tell them the news. I told Poon and Gloriana where I was going and left the disposition of the distressed vessel to the proper authorities.

There was nobody at work on the outdoor artwork when I arrived, no Offenfusser, no crew, no nobody, but the Chevy Nomad was parked in front of the house and I assumed correctly that they were in.

"Didn't you hear the explosion?" I wondered as I joined them in the kitchen.

"I hear explosions all the time," said Offenfusser, "but the doctor tells me that they're just auditory hallucinations, one of the hallmarks of paranoid schizophrenia."

"What are you talking about?" said Alicia. Apparently they hadn't heard anything.

"The Sulema must have had some sort of boiler explosion that ripped a hole in the bulkhead."

"What's the Sulema?" Offenfusser wanted to know.

"It's Ahmed Jifhraz's yacht," said Alicia impatiently. "Are you just making this up, Martin?"

"If you don't believe me, go down to the marina and see for yourself. They're all down there at the dock next to the wreckage. Not wreckage exactly. The boat just settled to the bottom."

"Well, I'll be damned," said Offenfusser. "Is there anything we can do?"

"I don't think so. I told Harry and Gloriana that I was coming over here and they said they'd join us."

This disturbed Offenfusser. "They're not staying here. That's for sure," he muttered.

"For God's sake, Fuzzwick," Alicia scolded him. "What kind of attitude is that?"

"A bad one," Offenfusser countered, "and it's all mine. Self-preservation, you know."

Poon and Gloriana did show up within the hour and their mood was strangely upbeat for someone who's just been dispossessed.

"Harry, Gloriana, I'm so sorry," Alicia sympathized.

"Relax," said Poon. "A.J.'s got it all figured out. All the power is below the water line so he's going to rig up a generator upstairs. Then he's going to patch the hole from the inside, pump out the water, and refloat the mother."

"Patch it?" said Offenfusser. "That won't last long."

"It only has to hold up for a little run across the sound to a dry-dock in Connecticut."

"Well, if you two aren't worried, I won't bother myself," said Alicia. "Would you like something to drink?"

"We certainly would," said Poon. "A.J.'s wine cellar on the lower deck is currently under water."

So we all adjourned to the terrace outside the kitchen and made ourselves comfortable while Alicia tended to the bar.

"Something like this happened to me once before," said Offenfusser. "I was giving a talk at a small college and I opened with a joke. The room suddenly went as quiet as the tomb. There audience just sat there staring at me as if I'd made some unforgivable gaffe and I experienced this awful sinking feeling, as if I'd sprung a leak and was going down, down, down to the bottom of the sea."

"You don't have to make fun of it," Gloriana huffed.

"I don't suppose I do but it's just my nature," Offenfusser suavely replied.

"You wouldn't have been laughing if you'd been there," said Poon. "Boom! The whole thing shook like a koochie dancer."

"My goodness. I hope none of your pieces was dislodged from

its pedestal and came to harm. What a blow that would be to art history," Offenfusser deadpanned.

"Who gives a shit? They're all insured."

"Such a philistine you are, Harry."

Alicia came out of the kitchen with a tray of some kind of cloudy rum drinks.

"What are those?" Poon demanded and scowled. "They look like they were dredged up from a swamp."

"Dark rum and grapefruit juice. It's got a name but I can't remember."

"So Harry," said Offenfusser, "is this the end of your country sojourn?"

"By no means," said Poon. "A.J. has graciously invited us to stay on board and oversee the repair crew while he's in Dubai."

"What do you mean 'oversee'? What do you know about ship repairs?" Offenfusser scoffed.

"Very little. I think he just wants to make sure no one steals anything. Who knows what sort of twisted, depraved perverts take up underwater welding as a career?"

"I see your point."

"Speaking of welding, what happened to the top of your tower? It looks like a steel ice cream cone."

"With a cherry on top," said Offenfusser.

"You're not the only ones with things exploding around you," said Alicia. "The tower was struck by lightning."

"And a very successful direct hit it was," said Offenfusser proudly. "I have become the Benjamin Franklin of my age."

The conversation soon turned to the Redstone party and the entertaining shenanigans of Pedro Barbez in particular.

"The man is absolutely shameless," said Poon. "He makes me look like a rank amateur when it comes to public misbehavior."

"I wouldn't give him that much credit," Gloriana pooh-poohed. "He's just a rich buffoon while you, Harry, bring the creative dimension to making an ass of yourself."

"Well said, Gloriana," Offenfusser agreed. "No one does it quite like Harry. Who is this Barbez anyway?"

"He does illustrated historical allegories," I said helpfully.

"Uh...?"

"Don't you wish you'd thought up a name like that for coffee table books?" said Poon. "The man is brilliant in his own peculiar way."

"I understand he's quite the ladies' man," said Alicia.

"Among his other fine qualities," said Poon. "He certainly was getting down and dirty with that anorexic woman yesterday. I thought he was going to crush her."

"At least she wasn't twelve years old," said Gloriana.

"You shouldn't call attention to Pedro's alleged pedophilia," Poon admonished her. "He hasn't been forced to register as a sex offender yet."

"I heard he was arrested recently for groping a young girl," said Alicia.

"Well, you know the police out here. No sense of humor. Besides, as a certifiable bon vivant, Pedro is beyond the petty prejudices and injunctions that comprise the corpus of established law."

"He thinks so," Gloriana snorted, "but one day he's going to get his."

"And what a grand day that will be!" Poon exclaimed. "He shall be borne to the village green shackled in the back of a pick-up truck and from thence be tossed into a cannibal pot and boiled in front of the cheering throng."

"I don't know," said Offenfusser dubiously. "Do people really want to eat this guy?"

"Just think of a nice slice of foie de Barbez sauced off with a butter and cognac reduction from his own cirrhotic pan scrapings. Magnifique!"

"You're disgusting, Harry," Gloriana said matter-of-factly.

"It's this demon rum," said Poon, squinting at his cloudy drink. "It's brought out the beast in me."

"I don't know about eating Pedro Barbez," said Alicia, "but how about some lunch?"

And so we whiled away the rest of the afternoon in pleasant enough conversation until it was time to leave and return to our lodgings. Well, me anyway. Poon was agitating for an expedition to Cyrano's, but I opted out and drove back to the other side of the bay where I found a note tacked to the front door. It read: "Mr. Seward, my name is Nuk Nuk Noing and I would like to talk to you at your earliest convenience. Please call me at…" What on earth could this be? And what kind of name was that anyway? Was it male or female? I certainly didn't want to find out and tossed the note in the trash. Inside, on the kitchen table, there was another note from Danica informing me she'd gone into the city for a day or three. I took a can of peach nectar from the refrigerator and turned on the television where I saw an agitated woman describing a bear attack in her back yard in New Jersey. There were aerial shots of the bear making a futile attempt to elude the authorities before he was taken down by a tranquilizer dart.

CHAPTER TEN

The next morning, I woke early, too early, and managed to doze back off briefly, but, in the short time before I woke again, I had a little dreamlet. I was in a labyrinth of Greek column lined corridors crowded with people in robes pushing and shoving their way along and carrying me with them. Eventually, I was extruded onto the balcony of a great arena filled to capacity with noisy spectators where I managed to find a seat right between Megan Fillywell and Sparky Goldflugel. Their presence there did not surprise me in the least. In fact, I was relieved to see them. "Good to have you on board, kiddo," Goldflugel greeted me. "Get yourself a hotdog." I looked down at the arena where Offenfusser's tower rose from the floor in the center hard by an out-sized, inflatable reproduction of Rodin's "The Thinker". A series of trampolines radiated from the base of the statue to the edge of the field and a man, urged on by the chanting throng, was climbing the tower. "Die, motherfucker, die!" they caterwauled in unison and made "the wave" around the stadium. I looked more closely and saw that the man was none other than Pedro Barbez, which, for some reason, made perfect sense. When he got to the top, a hush settled over the crowd. "I stand guilty before you!!" he bellowed over the public address system. "I accept my fate with some reluctance but I must submit to the court's decision! Just remember! What an artist dies with me!!" With those words, he jumped off the tower and landed on one of the trampolines below which propelled him through the air to the next trampoline and so on. He bounced across the field like a jumping bean and disappeared into the grandstand to a mighty cheer from the mob. Megan Fillywell was livid with rage. "The man has escaped again!!" she howled loudly enough to really wake me up.

Overnight, dense fog had rolled in over the bay and I could barely make out the shoreline from the window. A foghorn boomed at regular intervals adding a layer of funereal nostalgia to the thick quiet of the morning. Distant train whistles have much the same affect on me, setting off ill defined memories of a faded world slipping through my tenuous grasp. I got up and made myself a cup of green tea.

Later, after I'd showered and shaved, I drove into town and bought the local newspaper where the sinking of the Sulema had roused surprisingly scant attention. In fact, it had been relegated to a back page in favor of news of the horse show, an art opening, and a zoning board meeting. This relative lack of interest surprised me because I thought both the upper and lower crustacean, old family denizens of the area would have delighted in the sinking of some rich Arab's ostentatious power yacht. That it was hardly mentioned was interesting in itself.

When I returned to the house, there was someone waiting for me on the porch, a short, young Asian woman with a very round face, thick horn rimmed glasses and a paisley scarf around her neck.

"Mr. Seward?" she asked warily.

"Yes."

"Oh, I didn't expect you to be so old."

I had certainly never thought of myself as even approaching old but that should give you an idea how very young this young lady was.

"And I didn't expect to find someone sitting on my doorstep," I replied good naturedly.

"I'm sorry," she said. "My name is Nuk Nuk Noing. I wrote your book."

To say this introduction was unexpected would be quite an understatement. I didn't know what to say. Was she some sort of spy sent to reveal me as a fraud? She was too young to have written a novel. I decided to behave as if we were both in on the joke.

"Of course you did and I thank you for it," I patronized her. "Would you like to come in?"

She accepted my invitation and we were soon seated in the living room.

"Would you like something to drink? I've got rum, whiskey, gin..," I teased.

"I don't drink," she said, "but I guess you have to for the image and all."

"What image is that?"

"You know, the hard drinking, party hearty writer."

"Well, I do try to keep up appearances, Miss Noing, Now, why don't you tell me what this is all about."

"Call me Nuk Nuk."

"Nuk Nuk," I repeated mechanically. What the hell was she? Some sort of Eskimo? "What are you doing here?"

"I told you. I wrote *Babyland* and I wanted to meet you. Mrs. Stoat wouldn't give me your phone or address. She said that was against the rules so I had to track you down by myself."

"You wouldn't mind if I give Mrs. Stoat a call?"

"I'd prefer you didn't," she said. "I'm really not supposed to be here."

"Well, you are. What did you want to see me about?"

"Money."

"Money," I repeated. "I don't understand what you're talking about."

"When Mrs. Stoat bought my manuscript…"

"Wait, wait," I interrupted. "Don't you mean commissioned the manuscript?"

"No, I mean bought. It was my creative writing thesis piece. My professor said he thought he could sell it and he did. I made some money and that was that."

I had no idea what to say. "You knew what you were doing, didn't you?"

"Yes, but I had no idea Mrs. Stoat was going to make it into a best seller."

Talking contract was neither my strength nor my department but I had to ask, "Do you have any legal claim to the book?"

She hesitated before she spoke. "My claim isn't legal; it's moral. I think I should get more money."

"How much did you get in the first place?"

"You don't know? Two thousand dollars. I'm entitled to more."

"I'm not familiar with the particulars of your contract but I'd guess you're only entitled to what's in it. If you want more you should be talking to Mrs. Stoat."

"I already talked to her and she refused."

The whole situation was beginning to give me a sick headache. What sort of quandary was this anyway? I could just show her the door, send her on her way and forget all about it. But of course I couldn't. Here I'd just received a fifteen thousand dollar advance for a book the

116

young lady had written for a pittance. I know what you're going to say and I was saying it to myself. I'd agreed to write Sheridan March's next best seller for a pittance and I had no compunction about doing that. I certainly didn't expect any more than what was offered. What right did Nuk Nuk Noing have to hit me up when I was in the same situation myself? But, you know, I could nurse this rationale all I wanted and it still wouldn't cut it. She was right to object to being ruthlessly exploited.

"How much did you have in mind," I asked cautiously.

"A reasonable percentage of your royalties."

And here I was hoping I could just hand over another couple grand and be done with it.

"Look," I said, "you're being very optimistic. What if there are no royalties? The book may be a complete flop."

"That's not going to happen," she said flatly. "I wrote it from a strict market analytical viewpoint. Its target demographic is going to eat it up."

"I'm glad you're so confident," I said with only a trace of irony. "You know, I think I'm going to conform to my image and have a drink. You want anything? Water, soda?"

She didn't and I went into the kitchen and made myself a large, very dry martini. I returned to the living room with my glass and a proposition.

"I have an idea," I said. "What say I pay you four thousand dollars and we're quits. I could give you the money right now."

"No deal," she said.

"Deal?" I sputtered. "What are you talking about? You've got no claim on me. This is out of my good will."

"I don't want your charity. I want to be paid what's rightfully mine."

I must say, I had to admire her spunk. Personally, I would have taken the money and taken a walk but then I'm not much of a negotiator. I was about to continue with my protestations when I had a sudden brainstorm, an epiphany that would light my way out of the wilderness and simultaneously kill two birds with one stone.

"So, you want to be paid, do you? What are you doing right now? I mean, are you working?"

"I'm an assistant at an art gallery in Chelsea."

Music to my ears. "So you're not making any money," I guessed correctly. "How would you like a much better paying job where you can put your real talents to work?" Of course she would. In a matter of some fifteen minutes I had convinced her to ghost Sheridan March's book (without ever mentioning the name of the famous "author"), pointing up her cultural familiarity with Buddhism (she was Vietnamese) and waving half my commission in front of her. But she still wanted a piece of the *Babyland* action.

"Exactly what do you think is reasonable?" I asked, expecting the worst. When she hesitated before responding, I thought a threat might be in order. "You know, I could just say forget about the Buddha book and give you nothing at all for *Babyland.*"

"How about two percent?" she said tentatively. She really did want to write the March book!

I pretended to turn this figure over in my mind with grave reservations and then simply conceded, "Sold American." The only condition was that she never reveal our arrangement to anyone. I handed over Sheridan's chapter heading suggestions, which were actually the only material I had, told Nuk Nuk to write it as quickly as she possibly could with a first payment of a thousand dollars as an inducement to begin, and sent her on her merry way. I could hardly believe my own cleverness and I briefly basked in the warm glow of self-congratulation, the fantasy of fools before they get the real news. Such must have been the deluded certainty, the sadly misplaced optimism of George W. Bush as he preened on the deck of that aircraft carrier in his campy flight suit. Mission accomplished! Here I had hired the girl I didn't know without having read a word she'd ever written including my own purported book and I expected everything was just hunky-dory. I wanted to celebrate but it was still early and there was nowhere to go. Just to kill some time before Cyrano's opened, I decided to drive around the harbor and see what was going on with the Sulema.

When I pulled in, there was all sorts of activity on the dock. Welders in frogman suits bobbed in the water, a huge pump was being rigged up next to the yacht, and a gasoline generator chugged along rhythmically providing light and power for the whole operation. Harry Poon waved to me from the deck and walked off onto the pier.

"I don't believe these guys," he said. "They say they're going to have the thing patched and pumped out by the end of the day." He lowered his voice. "They say the explosion didn't come from the boiler or anything. It came from the outside."

"What?" I said. "What does that mean?"

"Don't talk so loud. It means someone did it on purpose and A.J. doesn't want any publicity."

"Does he know who did it?"

"A.J.'s got more enemies than I've had hot dinners. Could be any one of them. Gloriana left as soon as she heard. Can't say that I blame her." He looked around distractedly. "I need a drink. Come on board." He led the way back through the wounded vessel to the galley and cracked a bottle of champagne. "Sauve qui peut," he said by way of a toast.

"Cheers," I said. "What happens after they pump the water out?"

"They tow her across the sound to a repair yard tomorrow but I'm not going along for that ride. No telling what might happen when you're playing with this crowd."

Poon made the whole thing sound wonderfully sinister as if he were a character in an Eric Ambler thriller. He seemed to relish playing the part of a sort of confidential agent caught up in a web of international intrigue and it made me think he was making the whole story up. I decided to call him on it. "This is all bullshit, right?"

"I wish it were," he sighed with such weary fatalism that I was immediately convinced my instincts were correct and the story was a complete fabrication.

"Then watch your back," I warned him with exaggerated urgency. "Don't get in over your head."

"I believe you're mocking me," he said with the slightest trace of indignation..

"Of course not," I mock protested.

"So what brings you out this way, Martin? On your way to the Offenfussers?"

"Actually, no," I allowed. "I'm just at loose ends until Cyrano's opens and I can go over there."

"Now that is a capital idea," said Poon. "When's post time?"

I looked at my watch. "In about ten minutes."

"Well, let's go then."

We drove into the village in separate cars and parked in the empty gravel lot in front of the place. The door was open so we walked in and sat down at the bar. There was no one else there.

"Cyrano!" Poon called out.

The good publican shortly appeared from the restaurant area and greeted us with a hearty, "Bollocks! What are you two doing here this early? I warn you - only the slippery slope into the black pit of endless morning happy hours awaits those who play with firewater before the clock in the village square strikes noon."

"Thank you very much for advising caution," said Poon. "I shall take it to heart and have a rum and soda." Cyrano knew what to make me.

"I understand you've had a spot of bother out there at the harbor," he said as he poured our drinks.

"Nothing really," said Poon. "Just a little oversight on the part of the crew."

"Really?" said Cyrano. "The crew sets explosive charges on the hull in their spare time?"

"I should have known," said Poon. "In this town, the life of rumor, the more preposterous the better, is so much richer than mundane fact."

"Does the souse protest too much?" Cyrano chuckled. "Who do you think you're kidding anyway?"

This was the moment Poon had been waiting for. "All right, Sandwort, I know there's no use in trying to pull the wool over your world weary eyes. So I'm going to tell you everything as long as you give me your word of honor as a gentleman that not a word I say leaves this bar. Agreed?"

"For chrissake," said Cyrano, shaking his head.

"I'll take that as a yes," Poon continued. "As you may know, Ahmed Jifhraz is the richest man in the world but there is another fellow, a sinister Chinese tycoon named Mr. Gum, who wishes to topple A.J. from his throne. His agents are everywhere and there is no doubt in my mind that they were responsible for the scuttling of the Sulema. Why, you may ask, would Gum waste his time with an annoying attack on another rich man's pleasure craft?" Poon lowered his voice to a stage whisper and leaned close to Sandwort with a knowing smile. "Why indeed? You see, the Sulema is far more than it seems. It is the very nerve center of an empire that stretches into outer space. An attack on the Sulema is an attack on the command and control nexus of A.J.'s television networks, his radio stations, his newspapers, his gambling and porno websites, his OTC stock exchange, his server farms, and, of course, his satellites."

Cyrano nodded sagely. "Yes, I can see where such an assault might constitute an inconvenience."

"You're telling me, brother," said Poon. "The fate of hundreds of front corporations hangs in the balance. Any interruption of the orderly flow of capital through A.J.'s various laundries threatens the very survival of tottering economies and other assorted Ponzi schemes around the world. Are you taking my point?"

"I believe I am," said Sandwort, "but then I believe all kinds of things."

"Well, believe this," said Poon with evangelical fervor. "If A.J.'s empire collapses, the streets will run with blood, the sky will darken and frogs shall rain from the heavens! Flesh eating dinosaurs shall emerge from their tar pits with ravenous appetites and devour whole nations with savage gusto! The living will envy the dead! Repent! The end is nigh!" Poon paused to wipe the sweat he had worked up from his forehead. "So you see, the sinking of the Sulema is not simply a matter of another rust bucket going down to Davey Jones' locker. It's a potential calamity of another order entirely. Now, will you please refresh my libation?"

"Yes, of course," said Sandwort, "right away. I can see that you are suffering from post traumatic stress syndrome and must be immediately medicated. Young Martin, another for you as well?"

At first I had thought that the mining of the Sulema was a complete fiction. Now I wasn't so sure. Poon's preposterous allegations were so over the top, they were more than enough to throw anyone off the scent and render any possible questions moot. If Jifhraz had ordered Poon to suppress any talk of an attack, he couldn't be doing a better job. All the sinister rumors of sabotage had devolved into a barroom joke and Poon was making damn sure that it stayed that way.

"Well, what next?" said Cyrano as he passed us our drinks. "The savages are scaling the ramparts. Soon what's left of civil society will be forced into underground bunkers to preserve its breeding stock from the taint of barbarian blood. You might be right, Poon. This attack on your filthy rich benefactor's floating palace may be only the beginning."

Sandwort's sly condescension simply proved the effectiveness of Poon's strategy. No one would believe that the Sulema had been the victim of foul play now.

"So," said Sandwort, "from one world of fiction to another. What's going on with your book, Martin?"

"How should I know? Out of my hands."

"Ah, yes, the true artist never really finishes a piece; he simply abandons it to an uncaring world, discarding the fruits of his labor like a bag of trash."

"Not me," said Poon. "Not unless they pay for it."

"Bag of trash?" I weakly objected.

"Pardon me. I had no intention of denigrating your efforts. I can hardly wait for my own signed copy," said Sandwort.

Foisting *Babyland* on the unsuspecting public was one thing. Having friends and acquaintances read and critique it was quite another, seeing as I had no idea what I'd authored myself. I should have asked Nuk Nuk Noing for a synopsis.

"It shall be very interesting to see how you handle your new-found celebrity, young Martin," said Sandwort. "Maybe you'll go insane like Poon here and become a babbling paranoid. Or perhaps you'll follow in the stumbling footsteps of Pedro Barbez and find yourself in regular imbroglios with the gendarmerie. Only time will tell."

Poon offered up another option. "He could become a portly drunk and open his own drinking establishment so he might badger the captive audience patrons at his leisure."

This buoyantly insulting jabbering would have usually cheered me but now their words just weighed on my shoulders like a yoke, causing them to droop like sagging wind socks. I was no longer a mere hack. I was a celebrated fraud. I begged off an offered next round and returned to the house where Danica's car was parked in the driveway.

"Out early," she greeted me from the deck. "Isn't that A.J.'s boat over there? I heard it blew up."

"Reports of the Sulema's demise have been somewhat exaggerated. I thought you were staying in the city."

She took mock offense. "You want me to go?"

"Of course not, but I may demand certain favors in return for your early arrival."

"Ooo, baby," she simpered, "punish me."

I ignored her tempting invitation. "I thought you'd like to know that, in no small part because of your own efforts, the police paid a visit on Redstone yesterday."

She clapped her hands and squealed with glee. "I love it! I hope they hauled him away in handcuffs."

"Not quite. They did tow away his car though."

"His car? Why?"

Knowing full well the reaction I was likely to get, I flushed discretion down the toilet. "They think he might be involved in a hit and run accident."

This astonishing news only silenced her for a split second. "Wow! That is so cool!" she burst out and did a little dance around the room.

"Don't get excited. I'm sure it's all a mistake."

"Who cares?" she exulted. "He'd buy his way out of it anyway but I wish I could have seen the look on his face when they put it to him."

My phone rang and I answered.

"Is this Martin Seward?" a voice crackled. "My name is Junius Flatmeat. I'm Sparky Goldflugel's nephew. Maybe you've seen my column in the Weekly Flush."

The Flush was a particularly tawdry publication that specialized in all sorts of slanderous innuendo and character assassination.

"Can't say that I have," was my cautious answer.

"Sparky told me you're a right guy, a real ball player."

"I don't understand what you mean. I don't play any sports."

"Ho, ho!" he laughed. "Real wise guy, are you? Listen, Marty, you and me can work together. I've done a lot of work for that squeeze of yours…"

"Excuse me, Mr…"

"Flatmeat. Junius Flatmeat."

"Mr. Flatmeat. What are you talking about?"

"The broad. Megan Fillywell. She treats me nice, I treat her nice."

"That's wonderful," I rather egged him on. "I'm glad to hear you two have such a close relationship." What could this fool possibly be up to? I soon found out.

"Ah, you, always with the jokes." I could almost see him wagging his finger at me. "What I mean is there's things I can do for you. But you got to remember, there's also things I can do to you. It's all a matter of how you want to play the game."

"What game?"

"Look, Marty, we got two kinds of publicity. Which one would you prefer?"

I was getting bored. "I'll have mine on the half shell." There was a pause at the other end.

"Okay, okay," he said with menace aforethought, "you think it over. It's like you're in or you're out and I can't be responsible for the consequences if you make the wrong choice. I'll call you back tomorrow."

"Listen, Mr. Flatmeat, please don't bother to call…" but he had already hung up.

"Who was that?" Danica snooped.

"Some idiot from the Weekly Flush."

"Oh my, you really have hit the big time," she teased. Then she leaned over the couch and picked up the paisley scarf that Nuk Nuk Noing had apparently left behind in her great haste to get started on the Buddha book. "What's this?" she demanded, dangling the scarf from her pinky finger.

I looked over. "Oh, Miss Noing must have left it."

Baby D's proprietary hackles shot up. "And just who is Miss Noing?"

I can't say I didn't enjoy this little flash of jealousy and I considered pushing it. Instead I opted for the truth. "Miss Noing is the author of my book. She was here to shake me down."

The truth did not wash. "You're really something, Martin. The moment I leave you've got another girl over here."

I couldn't resist. "I assure you that this time nothing of a sexual nature took place between us although money was exchanged for future services."

Her eyes widened. "You're going with a prostitute?"

"Only in a manner of speaking. Miss Noing has agreed to write the Buddha book for me."

"Wait a minute."

I explained everything as best I could and set her mind at ease. In fact, she looked at me with newfound respect.

"I didn't realize that you were such an operator, Martin."

Such an operator. I would find out the bad news soon enough but thanks be that day was a ways off and I could still recline on my unjustified laurels.

CHAPTER ELEVEN

We dozed through most of the afternoon between occasional bouts of languorous carnality as though we were living in some sweltering town on the shores of the Amazon though the weather was actually so temperate it seemed to demand some sort of outdoorsy activity. We, however, passed on this opportunity and only rose when the sun was already rapidly descending toward the horizon.

"I've got tickets to the show at the Frog's Lip Players Club tonight if you're interested," she informed me as she brewed some tea.

The very thought bummed me out. My reply was cautious. "What are they doing?"

"Some cabaret stuff, I think."

If there is one thing I can't stand, it's cabaret. My skin crawls when I hear a show tune and my tolerance for the artistes that perform this abysmal, saccharine bullshit is less than nil but I was bored and the fact that she'd gone to the trouble to buy tickets made me feel I ought to make nice and accommodate her. She was surprised when I agreed to go.

"Gosh, Martin," she said. "This will be our first real date. Even if I am paying for it."

"I just remembered nice girls don't do it on the first date. Let's forget it."

"Don't be such a pessimist. There's only one way to find out, isn't there?" she played it up.

And that's how I wound up on the Frog's Lip Wharf down the way from El Farolito where the Player's Club made its home. The players are not so much a theater company as a loose affiliation of actors and actresses out for the summer who like to get together and torture all the husbands whose wives drag them to the Club's performances. The tickets are exorbitant because each piece features several "names", old warhorses whose presence at their neighbors' cocktail parties and soirees is always much in demand. The price of admission, of course, went to some worthy local cause such as the Frog's Lip High School Marching Band or the Summer Solstice Clam Bake. The tickets were so coveted, I could only wonder how Danica had acquired a pair.

The wooden sidewalk in front of the little playhouse was crowded with theater goers smoking one last cigarette or nursing one last cocktail before the curtain call. The men were all middle-aged, a little paunchy, and tan from being on the water. The women in their summer dresses, who were usually darker than their mates this time of year, were considerably lighter this season because a society doctor's new book had impressed the horrors of ultra-violet radiation on them with blood-curdling tales of women their own age and social standing occasionally being mistaken for Mexican patio chairs or alligator bags. It was through this throng we pushed our way to the box office where Baby D picked up the waiting tickets.

Once inside the theater, I was much distressed to find out that our seats were located two rows back from the stage which made walking out at any point in the show before the end problematic. Why are people so decorous? Why would I be embarrassed to get up and flee some Broadway abomination performed by a sentimental old hack before the number came to a grinding halt? Less inhibited Danica laughed at my irritation and promised to support any walk-out on my part with her full approval.

"Really, Martin, what do you care what these people think? You're never going to see them again anyway. Just get up, turn your ass to the stage, fart, and leave."

This so-called logic seemed reasonable but was, of course, unworkable in anything approximating real life. Soon the house lights went down and a tall, thin, gray haired man in a seersucker suit lurched out from the wings and sat down at the baby grand on one side of the stage. I do not use the word "lurched" lightly. This guy was plastered. He also looked familiar. I thought I'd seen him before on television or at the movies but I couldn't quite place where. He was soon joined by the one and only Sylvia Sylvester, a fixture on the Great White Way for the last thirty years. She wore a black satin, floor length gown which showed off her bulging mid-section to best advantage. In the glare of the spotlight, her make-up looked as if it had been slapped on with a brick trowel. She took the microphone.

"I want to thank all of you wonderful people so much for your support. Without you, our friends and neighbors, the Player's Club would have foundered and passed beneath the waves long ago and the

Frog's Lip experience as we know it would be that much poorer."

The room reverberated with a polite smattering of self-congratulatory applause.

"Tonight we are going to pay tribute to the magic and majesty of Broadway with an homage to Richard Rogers and Oscar Hammerstein, two of the giants of the musical comedy stage." She signaled to her accompanist and he launched into the first few notes of "Bali Hai" but then something happened. Reaching for a high note, the piano player lost his balance and fell off the bench onto the floor. The audience gasped and then applauded as he got back to his feet. They didn't applaud for long.

"Fuck you!!" he drunkenly bellowed at the top of his lungs. "Fuck all of you and the whores you rode in on!! Scum!! That's what you are! Scum!!" Then he staggered off stage and apparently fell down again from the sound of it.

Sylvia Sylvester was at a complete loss. "Oh dear, I think we better take a short intermission," she apologized and broke into tears. "Why don't you all get yourselves something... to drink and come back... in fifteen minutes," she managed between sobs. The other featured performers rushed out from the wings to comfort her.

The audience surged in a wave toward the exits, jamming the aisles in their haste to escape this disturbing scene of failure and degradation, and it took Danica and myself no little time to get out of there. I noticed the people who had fled before us had mostly disappeared, leaving only a small gaggle of hardcore fans on the sidewalk waiting for the show to resume. I did not intend to be one of them.

"Great!" I said enthusiastically. "Best thing I ever saw. Now what?"

"You don't have to be so pissy, Martin."

"What do you mean by that? We're going back, aren't we?"

She did not dignify my question with an answer and instead led the way to a hotel bar down the street. I would usually not go into a place like the Fishhead Inn for two reasons; the drinks are too expensive and the kitschy colonial-nautical interior cloys in a way that makes you feel as if as if you are in some horrible theme park. But I had plenty of money and a couple of drinks in this fancy saloon might allay Baby D's disappointment in the show. It was, after all, our first date. We managed to find seats at the bar with a crowd of others who had also decided to forego the theater and I extravagantly ordered a bottle of champagne. This foolishness immediately cheered Danica.

"You are such an idiot, Martin."

"Only the best for my baby," I crooned and clinked her glass. "Cheers."

The Fishhead bar was the sort of place that Pedro Barbez would fit right into, full of fashion models, real estate moguls, poseurs of every stripe, and all the rest of summertime society; it was also the sort of place that had probably thrown him out some time ago and banished him for life. I must have surveyed the room a bit too long and Danica noticed my inattention. "What's the matter, sailor?" she teased, "I'm not enough for you?"

At that very moment, who should walk in but Megan Fillywell. She immediately spotted me at the bar and came right over.

"Fancy meeting you here," she greeted me. "Sparky didn't tell me you'd be out tonight."

Brushing that odd remark aside, I introduced them. "Danica, this is Megan Fillywell."

Danica's eyes widened. "Really? I'm a huge fan. Could I get your autograph?"

Megan was all aglow. "Of course you can." She set down her signature with great flourish on a bar napkin printed with cartoons. Danica held it up to the light as if she were examining a passport or a suspicious looking one hundred dollar bill.

"Okay," she said, "now I just need your Social Security number, your mother's maiden name and the pin number on your bank card."

Megan didn't quite know how to take this peculiar request. She had no sense of humor but she could somehow sense that it might be a joke. She decided a short titter would be appropriate and she was right. "I'm so glad you're here," she said. "I'll be right back." And off she went into the gloaming.

"That's my competition?" Danica demanded with teasing indignation.

"Now, now, simmer down. She's just my public relations cross to bear." Well, I certainly got that one right.

Megan returned with a guy with a camera and asked, "Are you ready?"

"Hey, wait a minute," I protested.

"Listen, you little slut!" a whole new Megan spat out, wagging her finger at Baby D. "You keep your hands off my man!" A flash popped and Megan turned to the photographer. "It's a take?" He gave her a thumbs up and she turned back to us with a gleaming smile "It's so good to see you guys. Don't be strangers."

Off she went leaving us to suffer the curious stares of everybody else in the room. Danica thought the whole thing was delightful. "I can see the picture in the Flash already. Hotshot author Martin Seward had to sit a little lower on his high horse last night when main squeeze Megan Fillywell caught him canoodling with another knockout blond at Frog's Lip harbor's tres chic Fishhead Inn."

"I just hope they got my good profile," I said sourly. They did and Danica had pegged the copy almost verbatim. But I wouldn't find that out until the next day.

"You were making it with that?" she demanded.

"Are you crazy? No way," I lied like a dog. "She's a concoction of my press agent. I believe we just broke up so now I've got to find another girl on the list."

"The what?"

"I can only go out with women represented by Sparky's P.R. firm."

"I guess that lets me out."

"Maybe not. If that picture makes the papers, Sparky might put you on the list with me as a sort of two for one package. You want to be famous for a limited time only?"

"I think I'm about as famous as I want to be."

"You should reconsider. Fame is the new coin of the realm, the only currency worth possessing because the more you have, the more you get. For a while, at least, until it gets forcibly removed by the fickle public and you wind up in the limbo of shopping mall ribbon cuttings, key to the city presentations, and guest appearances at fading Catskills resorts."

"You make it all sound so delicious," Baby D purred.

"I do, don't I?"

"Martin, do you know that one of your many problems is your complete lack of ambition."

"I never thought of it as a problem actually. More like an

inconvenience. What about you? Do you have ambitions?"

"I don't need any. I've got hormones."

"What's that supposed to mean?"

"I don't have to aspire to anything. What I do is determined by biochemistry. Men are confused because their programs have bugs. That's why they need things like ambitions to keep them in line."

I poured us both another glass of champagne. "To distraction, long may it reign."

"You see that woman over there?" said Danica, gesturing with a combination of her eyes, her eyebrows, and her shoulder which did me no good as there were several women off in that general direction. "She used to be a model, then she was a call girl, then she was a drug dealer. Now she's a financial analyst. She's friends with Redstone."

"I didn't know he had any friends."

"How about you?"

"I'm just a somewhat ambivalent former employee but as long as we're on the subject..."

She put her finger to my lips. "I told you I don't want to talk about that."

"Nothing to do with you. I don't know if they're friends but Redstone seems to have some sort of relationship with Ahmed Jifhraz."

A gentleman in a Madras jacket sitting to my right tapped me on the shoulder. "I'm sorry," he said, "I couldn't help overhearing you. I understand someone bombed Mr. Jifhraz's boat."

"The newspaper says it was an accident," I pointed out.

"Yes, yes, they must cover it all up I suppose, but I heard from one of the local artists that Mr. Redstone was under suspicion in the explosion."

"I'm sure he did it," Danica jumped in. "There's absolutely no doubt in my mind."

There was no doubt in my mind who the local artist was but why was Poon slandering Redstone? I looked over at our neighbor with his a sharp, angular face and pop bottle thick glasses. "I'm sorry," I said, "I don't believe we've met. I'm Martin and this is Danica."

"Oh, I know who you are," he said as if it were common knowledge. He did not reciprocate with his own name. "Bad business with these sorts bringing their sordid affairs into our community. Run the whole lot of them out of town on a rail is what I say."

"I couldn't agree with you more," my little agent provocateur egged him on. "But tar and feather them first. That's how they used to do it."

He squinted at Danica. "It's nothing to joke about," he snapped.

She feigned wide-eyed innocence. "I'm not joking," she protested. "I know it may sound a little extreme but painful problems often call for painful solutions."

He snorted and laid down a twenty dollar bill on the bar. Then he got up and left without another word.

Danica turned to me and pouted, "What did I say?"

"You really shouldn't be promoting Harry Poon's nonsense," I scolded. "People get the wrong ideas."

"You don't know who that was, do you?" she said.

"No."

"That was the township tax assessor, Chappie Wilmerding."

"How would you know something like that?" I said dubiously.

"I know more than that," she said. "He's also the brother of your neighbor, Mrs. Bradley."

"I know you're lying because no one is actually named Chappie, but it certainly would explain his distaste for Redstone," I agreed. "What say we get out of here? This place gives me the creeps." This was true. For some reason, I always get uncomfortable in the presence of the haute bourgeoisie, as if their behavior is so egregiously and transparently vulgar and self-serving that I have to turn my head away in embarrassment from their ludicrous antics. I paid for the bottle of champagne and we took what remained with us.

As we walked in the moonlight toward the end of the wharf drinking from the Styrofoam cups I'd sponged from the bar, a man in a hurry raced by us shrieking, "I've got the heebie jeebies! I've got the heebie jeebies!" It was none other than the drunken piano player from the show. He ran to the end of the dock and flopped into the water below with a great splash. A man and woman came running after him and looked over the end of the dock where the piano player was thrashing about yelling, "Let me die! Let me die!"

The man and woman were not amused by his performance. "If you make me come in after you, I'll kill you myself," the man barked. "Do you hear me, Spandex?"

"Let him drown," said the woman disgustedly and the two of them walked away back up the dock.

Almost immediately, the piano player crawled back onto the wharf with long streamers of snot running from his nose and dripping with seaweed. He yelled after them: "You scum! I thought you were my friends!" Then he spotted me and Danica. "What are you looking at?" he bellowed accusingly. "Do you know who I am?!

Danica must have been in a playful mood. "No," she answered. "Who are you?"

The sodden fellow went into a frenzy. "I'm Spandex Greenleek! That's who I am! Spandex Greenleek!"

Only then did the vaguely familiar face come into focus. Indeed he was Spandex Greenleek, a character actor who had appeared on numerous television shows as a generic, middle-aged good burgher, say a lawyer or banker, a dependable spear carrier for the principal players. Not tonight, however.

"Buy me a drink!" he demanded.

What else could I do? I held out what was left of the bottle of champagne and he eagerly guzzled it down. Then he threw the empty bottle off the pier.

"I shouldn't have done that," he said. "Now I have to go back in and get it."

I grabbed his arm dissuasively. "No need. We can get another one at the liquor store."

"Capital idea!" he said, twirling his finger in the air like a cartoon character.

Danica and I each took one of his arms and gently frog-marched him off the dock.

"I can't tell you how much I admire your work," she gushed.

He seemed to take umbrage. "If you can't tell me how much you admire me, what's the point in saying anything at all," he huffed. Then he reconsidered. "No, let's talk about me."

Without going into the details of the besotted rant that followed, let's just say it was a magnificent, if self serving, exercise in braggadocio and maudlin incoherence. When we got to the liquor store I handed the great thespian a ten dollar bill, wished him well, and sent him on his way into the shop. Of course, he was summarily ejected but Danica and I were already a half block down the street and hurriedly fled his wails and lamentations back to the car.

"Some first date," Danica pouted as we sped out of Frog's Lip Harbor.

"You want me to take you home?" I offered. "Your parents must be worried you're out so late."

"Forget about them. They don't understand me. Let's find a lover's lane and do a little heavy petting."

"I'm sorry, miss, but the rumble seat is out of order."

"You're the one that's out of order."

Then we actually had to decide what to do.

"Does it really make any difference?" she said.

"Is that an existential question?"

"No, just an awkward one."

Now, from what I've told you so far, you might think with some justification that I'm a mere pussy hound who couldn't be bothered to ask Danica any questions at all about her past, her present circumstances, or her prospective future. You would not be entirely correct. Getting a straight answer out of the woman was often a thankless task but I had persisted to the point where I knew (or thought I knew) a thing or two. Talking about her apparent entanglement and ensuing disenchantment with Redstone was useless but I had managed to piece together a fractured scenario from fragments I had gleaned. Danica was a dancer, that is to say she had lived for quite some time on the largess of various arts foundations created for the purpose of funneling funds from baffled, moneyed parents to their lazy, ur-Bohemian daughters until such time as the young ladies came to their senses and acquired suitable mates, an iffy, often quixotic proposition at best. Now, at the tender age (and I'm guessing on this) of twenty-eight, she had retired or been forced to retire from the fray and was living a gypsy existence on a mysterious source (or lack) of funding. Clearly, she'd been around the block a few times but was she really looking for a parking place? In her own words: "You know, Martin, you're different from all these people."

"What people?"

"You know, Fuzzwick, Harry Poon, Dacron."

I had to chuckle at that one. "Yes, they have more money," I agreed solemnly.

"Don't patronize me," she scolded and continued, "What I mean is there's a certain denseness to you."

Before I could even ponder the question of whether I was opaquely complex or merely stupid, she had the answer.

"You're completely clueless. In a good way. That's what I like about you. Those other guys, they're just different channels on the same TV set. You, on the other hand, are workable, like dough. Do you understand?"

I had to admit I didn't.

"You see?" she said. "Look, Martin, all a woman really wants is one man she can totally control. That's why you're my guy."

Of course I knew and appreciated that this sort of rude and offensive honesty was part of Danica's charm. Except when it applied to me, that is. "Hey, wait a minute..." I started to object.

"That's why I'm jealous," she cut me off. "It's not like me, you know." Something caught her eye out the window. "What is that?"

I had more or less somnambulated on automatic pilot back toward the house with no real intention of doing so and we were now just a short way up the road from the driveway. The object of Danica's attention was a peculiar little cement or plaster structure set back a foot or two from the shoulder.

"Stop," she demanded and I did with my headlights shining on what looked like a weird shrine with a white cross affixed to the roof of a small, powder blue model of a house. Plastic flowers and fruit were strewn at the base. "What on earth is that?"

"It's Mexican," I said. "They put them up at the scene of fatal road accidents."

"That's spooky."

We got out of the car to look at the thing more closely. There was a small oval photograph of a swarthy man I took to be the recent sideswipe victim attached to the center of the cross.

"This is why they're investigating Redstone's car," I guessed. "It must be the spot where the poor bugger was run down."

"You're joking."

"I'm not and I don't think the neighbors are going to take kindly to this little memorial. A bit jarring, don't you think?"

"I don't know," she said. "It's very original. It might become sort of a tourist attraction like Lourdes. I can see hundreds of Mexicans crawling up the street on their hands and knees to pay homage to their late friend. The neighbors might not like it but what can they do? It's hallowed ground."

This vision of a procession of *penitentes* ecstatically flagellating themselves as they marched up the road to the shrine with Mrs. Bradley and the local branch of the White Citizens' Council frantically trying to hold them at bay greatly cheered me. The good lady would forget all about Redstone's parties and become a royal pain in the ass for the immigration police with her incessant complaints and demands. Local property values would plummet and all that deluxe housing would be forced to give way to shanty towns of fervent pilgrims. Redstone's lawn would be reduced to a squalid refugee camp with bloated, starving children playing in open sewers running into the bay. Such were my happy thoughts as Baby D and I got back in the car and continued the short way back to the house.

CHAPTER TWELVE

Two days later, I was obliged to go into the city and be brushed and groomed for the upcoming (too upcoming) kickoff of my book tour. I arrived at Barrington Stoat's office promptly at ten in the morning and was almost immediately whirled into the frantic world of New York publishing.

"Martin, it's so good to see you," she gushed, "but aren't you an hour early?"

"I thought you said ten."

"Well, one of us is wrong and it's not going to be me. Why don't you go down to the restaurant across the street and order anything you like on my account. Here, you can take this with you." She handed me a copy of my now hardbound book. The back of the dust jacket was filled with enthusiastic blurbs.

"We gasp in recognition as Seward leads his young heroine down the garden path of earthly delights to a climax of fiery intensity." – Sindra Rabitz

"The most interesting, complex female character to emerge from the world of letters since Monsieur Flaubert reached down from on high and gave breath to Madame Bovary." – Brandade Puissant

"Splendoriferous!" – Alan Jones

These accolades were all from authors Barrington represented who had apparently graciously agreed to have their arms twisted into flattering my humble self. "This is sort of over the top," I modestly protested. "I mean, don't you represent all these people?"

"Of course. Do you think I'd promote someone I had no interest in? I expect you to do the same for them once you're famous. Now, shoo. I'll see you in an hour."

I took the book down to the Starlight Deli, a ridiculously overblown amusement park set which specialized in large hot dogs and enormous pastrami sandwiches. It was hard to imagine Barrington Stoat dining in such an exuberantly crass and vulgar place and I'm sure she never did. It was just her way of humiliating her stable of artists when they needed something to eat. The glorified diner was largely empty and I took a seat in front near the window. I ordered 1 cup of tea from the disinterested waitress and looked around this cavernous space with its framed photographs of huge, meaty sandwiches which had certain perversely erotic overtones. I noticed a woman sitting a couple of tables away gazing absently out the window. It was the former pop diva, Landa Lucey, who had been a big deal twenty years earlier. She was, of course, older and somewhat the worse for wear, which she tried to conceal with too much make-up, but she was still possessed of an attractive, Betty Boopish magnetism that commanded some attention. I kept glancing at her after the waitress brought my tea and noted that she was completely immobile like a mannequin or a wax figure. I had the curious desire to go over and poke her. A cruel joke even came to mind. I would say, "Aren't you..? Aren't you..?" and then guess another name entirely. My strange musings were interrupted when she suddenly turned her head and stared straight at me. I averted my eyes but when I glanced back her way, she was still staring at me. Then she got up and walked over to my table.

"Would you mind if I join you?" she said. "I don't like to sit alone. People might get the wrong idea."

I wasn't sure what "wrong idea" she had in mind. "Please, sit down," I offered graciously.

"Thank you. I hope I'm not intruding."

"Not at all."

She sat down and introduced herself. "My name is Landa Lucey."

"I knew that," I said. "I'm Martin Seward."

"I'm surprised you recognize me. I haven't made a record in twenty years. You know how it goes. When you're young they say, "Landa who?" When you've made it they get all excited and say, "Oh my, it's Landa Lucey!" When you get to be my age they say, "Landa who?""

I uncomfortably remembered my own idea of a little joke from a few moments beforehand and wondered if she read minds.

"Anyway, enough about me. What have you been writing lately?"

This startling question caught me completely off guard. How could she possibly know that I was a writer?

"You're wondering how I know about you. I do read the

papers."

The power of the tabloid press was truly awesome. A nobody like me who had never done anything was now recognized by total, formerly celebrated strangers.

She continued. "I'm glad you got rid of that Fillywell woman. Can't see what you saw in her in the first place."

To have my so-called personal life discussed in this manner was more than disconcerting. It was downright bizarre. I had to put a stop to this impertinent probing. "Well," I chuckled lamely, "don't believe everything you read in the papers."

"Oh I don't. For all I know she's just a beard. Maybe you don't even like girls."

"Excuse me, Miss Lucey…"

"There's nothing to be ashamed of. I was a beard myself once for a very well known actor. I won't mention his name but everyone knows he's queer except his silly fans. I hope I'm not making you uncomfortable."

"Uh…"

"It's my medical condition. I have logorrhea. I can't stop talking. And the things I say." She rolled her eyes. "My doctor tells me I shouldn't talk to anybody. Not even him. But I get so lonely." She broke into tears and buried her head in her hands on the table. All I wanted to do was flee in horror but I was rooted to my chair as if an invisible force were pressing me down in place. I felt like Henry in "Eraserhead" being accosted by his girlfriend's mother.

"Is everything all right here?" the waitress, who had quickly come over, wanted to know.

"No! Everything is not all right!" Landa Lucey wailed. "Everything is shit!"

The waitress put her hand on my shoulder. "You're going to have to get her out of here."

"But I don't even know her!" I protested as we were joined by the manager, a short, bald man in a suit.

"All right, you two. Time to take a walk."

There was no point in objecting. In fact, I was very much relieved to be eighty-sixed. I got up and headed for the door forgetting to pick up the book in my haste to get out of there

"Hey, you!" the manager barked. "Aren't you forgetting something? I told you to get her out of here."

I had two choices. I could either make a run for it or escort Landa Lucey at least as far as the door. Out of a twisted, misplaced sense of compassion and common decency, I opted for the latter. I came back and leaned over the table. "Miss Lucey, we've got to go," I said gently.

After her outburst, she was surprisingly tractable. "Yes, I suppose you're right. Please take my arm."

I helped her to her feet and guided her toward the door.

"Don't come back until you learn how to behave!" the manager called after us.

Outside on the sidewalk, Landa Lucey wouldn't let go of my arm. "I want to thank you so much for what you did for me in there. If there's anything I can do for you..."

No, no, that's all right..," I assured her trying to disengage myself from her grasp as she pulled me closer.

"I'm an experienced woman," she said urgently. "There are things that I could do for you. Why don't you let me suck your cock? You can come in my mouth if you like. I love the taste of fresh sperm."

Just at that moment, Barrington Stoat walked out of her building and waved to me from across the street.

"How do you know that woman?" Landa Lucey demanded. "Is she your mother?"

Barrington joined us. "Landa," she said. "would you please let go of that young man. He's a client of mine."

"I'm sorry, Bunny," Landa blubbered. "I just couldn't help myself."

"Now just run along and take your medication, Landa. Come with me, Martin."

Barrington took me by the arm and guided me away from the mad woman. "These performing artists," she tut-tutted. "So sensitive. She just needs all that attention she doesn't get anymore. Sad, isn't it? Did she try to get you into bed? She always does that with good looking young men."

I decided that discretion was indeed the better part of valor. "No, no, nothing like that. What now?"

"There's someone that Sparky wants you to meet. His name is Junius Flatmeat and I personally think he's the most repulsive, obnoxious pig in New York but he can do you wonders in terms of constant

140

exposure, especially during the first weeks of your tour."

I decided not to mention that Flatmeat had already called me and the conversation had not been congenial. We arrived at Goldflugel's office which covered an entire floor of the building and were ushered by the receptionist down a corridor lined with paintings by Derek Schnoigel's principal commercial art competitor, LeeRay Mezcal, to the inner sanctum where Goldflugel greeted me warmly and bade us sit down.

"Junius will be here any minute. He's got your whole tour mapped out for you. I see you're done with the Fillywell girl. That's fine. I wanted her to move on to that hockey player anyway. But who's the other girl with you? No one I know. Just make sure your next one's on the list. Understand?"

"I don't understand why Junius is doing the campaign," said Barrington. "Who's paying him?"

"You let me worry about the compensation. He's really excited about getting out of that sewer he works for and classing up his act."

Then he was upon us. Junius Flatmeat blew through the door with the gale force of a seasoned hard sell huckster and immediately turned his gusting attention on me. "So we meet in person, Mr. Comedian! No hard feelings. I love a good laugh." He shook my hand heartily and took a seat which was a problematic undertaking for a four hundred pound greaseball.

"All right, Junius, let's show these people what you've got," said Goldflugel enthusiastically.

Flatmeat whipped out a folder and tossed it in my lap. "That's your complete itinerary. I want you to read it like the Bible and follow every commandment."

I picked out a commandment at random and read it out loud. "Chicago, September 29th. Narrowly escape a gun battle in a hip hop night club."

"I thought it was better if you get arrested with a smoking gun," said Junius, "but my uncle said no."

Goldflugel shook his head and tut-tutted, "That's going too far, Junius."

Flatmeat winked at me. "These old geezers, they just don't understand modern P.R. Take a look at the rest."

My head began to spin as I scanned this litany of public squabbles with women, fistfights with men, confrontations with all sorts of authorities from the police to nightclub bouncers, incessant substance abuse, mouthing off bizarre opinions on everything from politics to game show hosts, well, you get the drift.

"It doesn't sound like this schedule gives me much time for promoting the book," I said acidly.

"Are you kidding?!" Flatmeat hooted. "You're not going to just be famous! You're going to be notorious! Those books will be flying off the shelves!"

I shook my head. "I don't know. It sounds pretty exhausting."

"Hey, you don't really have to do any of this stuff," Flatmeat protested. "We're just building an image. Creating a brand."

"My nephew's right," said Goldflugel. "You don't want to be some kind of namby-pamby guy with a tweed jacket. You want to be like an arrogant little prick movie star."

"I guarantee you'll get more column space every day than any politician, pop tart, serial murderer, or what have you," Flatmeat proclaimed. "You'll be so famous all the top clubs and restaurants will throw out the other stars to give you a table. You'll have your own posse of down and dirty dogs. The babes will be swarming around you like flies on shit... er, well, what do you say?"

"I don't know if I want to be compared to a turd," I complained.

"Martin's one thousand percent right," Goldflugel defended me. "You should watch your language when you're talking to a client, Junius"

"It's just an expression," Flatmeat whined. "Hey, Marty, I'm sorry, but you know what I mean. We can put you right up there on top of the steaming heap!"

"Listen, Sparky," said Barrington. "Why don't you let me discuss this with Martin over lunch. I'm sure we can come to an agreement." She looked at her watch. "Hate to run off so quickly, but Martin's got to meet with his stylist."

"That's my Bunny," said Goldflugel affectionately. "He's a good looking kid but there's always room for improvement. Just make sure you deliver me the finished merchandise."

"Have I ever let you down?" she said, bussing him on both cheeks and holding out her hand to Flatmeat as if she expected him to kiss it. He struggled to his feet and gave her a one pump handshake. "Always great to see you, Mrs. Stoat."

When we were descending in the elevator, Barrington confided, "I loathe and despise Junius but he does seem to have his big fat finger on the pulse of the younger demographic. I think we should take his advice to heart... with a few provisos, naturally"

Now, you may well ask, why was I allowing myself to be herded around by this crew of noodle brains? Rapacious greed? Maybe, but I don't think so. What I can say in my own defense is that I felt that I had entered into another state of being, as Sheridan March might say. I had put aside enlightened self interest in favor of pure voyeurism, an affliction endemic to newspaper readers, television viewers, peeping Toms, secret agents, and, of course, writers. I was now just along for the ride to my own martyrdom and canonization, something like a suicide bomber blithely strolling along under a blinding sunlit sky to his appointment in Samara.

Our next stop was not Samara, however, but the very exclusive beauty salon of the fabled Veronica Banks who had been retained personally to attend to my cosmetic requirements. After the usual introductory formalities, Ms. Banks, a lanky, intimidating brunette dressed all in black leather looked me over and asked in her thick Scottish accent, "Who did your hair, sweetie? Lawn Doctor? Don't worry. We'll fix that. When you walk out of here you're going to be looking like Lockheed." She sat me down in one of the salon chairs and studied my face in the mirror. She frowned. "After we do your hair, we've got to do something with that skin."

I had no idea what she was talking about. I don't have acne or anything. Her assistant, the very gay Antonio, set to work right away clipping in an apparently random pattern that left me looking like he'd pulled my hair out in chunks. Then he tousled up what was left and had Veronica survey his handiwork. I looked as if I'd just crawled out of bed with a bad head which it turned out was exactly the look they were attempting to achieve.

"Okay, let's give that skin a little green tone and some bags under his eyes," she instructed her assistant. "You might want to try out some red blotches on his forehead." By the time Antonio finished, I looked like I'd been on a three day bender. Veronica wanted Barrington's opinion. "So what do you think?"

"Wonderful job," Barrington had to admit. "He looks just awful. I'll never understand why these young people want their idols to look like homeless, crack head bums, but I suppose that's their business."

"You really want me to walk around looking like this?" I asked incredulously. "I'll get arrested for vagrancy."

"That's the whole point," said Barrington and laughed. "No, you don't have to walk around looking like that unless you're performing. It's only stage make-up. The hair you'll just have to live with."

So they scraped all the glop off my face and combed my hair into a rude semblance of good grooming. Then it was time for lunch.

Barrington decided we should put in an appearance at La Chatte, a little bistro favored by well preserved older women and their gigolos. She explained this to me beforehand and told me our arrival together would set off waves of gossip and speculation about our relationship. "Keep them guessing," she said.

I didn't much appreciate being paraded around like an old lady's boy toy but I glumly went along with the program without a whimper. We were greeted at the door by the maitre d' Henri who welcomed Barrington effusively and gave me the old arched eyebrow and smirk routine. I thought this monkey suited fool was going to wink at me and give me the thumbs up but he led us to a table in the center of the room without making any further attempts to discomfit me. I sat down and looked around the place at all the other May – September couples, many of whom were staring at me with frank curiosity.

"Don't make eye contact with anyone but me," said Barrington quietly. "Do you like fish? The sole here is very good."

I went along with her recommendation and she ordered a bottle of Muscadet. After the waiter had poured the wine, she held up her glass in a toast. "To success," she said simply. "Nothing can go wrong now."

I hesitated before I spoke. "A young woman paid me a visit the other day."

"A lot of young women will be paying you visits if I'm not mistaken," she chuckled.

I stupidly plowed ahead. "Her name is Nuk Nuk Noing."

That stopped her dead in her tracks. She paused elaborately before she spoke. "I know Miss Noing. What did she want?"

Realizing I was already in too deep, I caught myself in time to clam up. "Nothing. Just a mild case of post-partum depression. She wanted to meet me." Why had I brought her up in the first place?

"I thought I'd made Miss Noing aware of the repercussions of violating her contract. I'll have to speak to her again."

"I don't think that's necessary," I hastily assured her.

"Maybe not," she agreed, much to my relief. "If she contacts you again don't have anything to do with her."

"No, of course not. I just wanted to let you know."

"If you're worried she might make trouble for you, don't."

"I'm not worried, I'm not worried. So when does my tour begin?" I quickly changed the subject.

"In two weeks. First you'll do Marymount and all the local colleges. Then it's on to the national bookstore tour. You should go to the gym and bulk up. You're going to need the stamina of a plow horse."

Going on tour was bad enough; "bulking up" was out of the question. "Yeah, I'll do that," I agreed affably.

"Listen, Martin, I know that Sparky's plans may sound a little bizarre, but he does know what he's doing and he does have your best interests in mind. You just have to think of yourself as a thing rather than a human being. You have to look at yourself dispassionately, like an object. That's the key to success."

I would have stolen her line if I were still writing the Buddha book. Now I was just agreeable. "I'll certainly try. I just have to focus on what sort of object I want to be."

"That's easy," she said. "If you had to be a vegetable, which one would you want to be?"

Vegetable? This "when did you stop beating your wife?" sort of question sorely vexed me. Any answer at all would make me look completely foolish. "Oh, I don't know. Can't I be an animal or mineral?"

She tittered. "You're so clever, Martin. I really can't see you as an eggplant. Don't you like vegetables?"

"Some of my best friends are vegetables," I said dryly.

She tittered again. "You have to write those lines down, Martin. They'll be very useful on the reading circuit."

And so we passed the next half hour agreeably enough, the sole was very good, and I left in completely delusional good cheer. As long as I was willing to be a thing, all responsibilities passed in to the hands of others and I had nothing to do but go along for the ride and enjoy the scenery as best I could. I was perfectly impregnable. When the curtain finally came down, it was the thing, not me, who would take the fall.

The good cheer wore off as soon as I got back on the train. In fact, I had a full-fledged panic attack as we pulled out of Penn Station. I was positive that the train was going to derail at any moment and I would be squashed like the bug I was. Terrorists were just about to bomb the railway tunnel under the East River and I would drown in a crush of sludge and PCBs and the only viable American export product, bullshit. Such were my fevered apprehensions as I contemplated me the thing on my grand tour of the boonies. Thrust into the limelight of a lynch mob waiting to happen. Made to perform like a trained bear for the yahoos. The utter shamelessness of it all! I did finally manage to calm myself by repeatedly chanting one of Sheridan March's many mantras: "Money isn't just anything; it's everything!", and I haven't had a strictly moral qualm since.

Mercifully, I drifted into a restless slumber for most of the trip out and just woke up in time to not miss my station. I immediately made a beeline to Cyrano's.

"We have a quorum!" Cyrano called out as I walked in the door. Pedro Barbez and Harry Poon were hunkered down at the bar trading off color banter. "Sit, young Martin," said Sandwort, "and tell us all about your expedition to the city."

"How did you know I went to the city?"

"The walls have ears," he chuckled confidentially. "I understand you are now embarked on the next phase of your ascent to the pantheon of celebrated scribes. A word of caution, though, Martin. Serious writers have nothing to say. The only thing that matters is how they don't say it."

"Hear, hear," said Barbez. "Buy the poor schnook a drink."

Poon was more charitable. "Don't listen to a word these two have to say. They are possessed by the twin demons of bitterness and envy."

"What's going on with the Sulema?" I asked.

"She is steaming across the sound in the company of a seagoing tug as we speak. She'll be back in a few days as good as new. Unless, of course, there is more foul play afoot and she is overrun by pirates on her wounded crossing."

"Yar, matey," Barbez growled. "There'll be no killing till I gives the ardors!"

"And what's this I hear," I persisted, "about you telling people that Redstone was responsible for the explosion?"

Poon was all innocence. "Now why would I say anything like that? Even if it were true?"

Cyrano cracked up. "You have no idea what slanders, calumny and outright nonsense Poon has been spouting the last day or two," he sputtered. "Redstone is a nobody compared to the other conspirators he's denounced. How about Pope Benedict the whatever number he is? How about Osama bin Laden? How about Elton John?"

"I'm telling you," Poon indignantly defended himself. "They're all in on it! What could be more obvious?"

Once again, Poon was making such a joke of any possible sabotage that I was now completely convinced that some person or persons unknown had indeed planted a bomb.

"If the Sulema's in Connecticut, where are you staying, Harry?" I asked.

"The Offenfussers kindly invited to me to spend a few days at the foundation. I believe they're calling me an artist in residence. For tax purposes of course."

"You're full of shit, Poon," said Barbez, echoing my own opinion. But then, Alicia can be a soft touch.

"Oh, ye of little faith," said Poon. "After the Sulema was raised from the muck, I cleaned out the previously submerged wine cellar and brought several cases of the very finest, mud caked vintages over to the foundation. My largess may have had something to do with my present temporary accommodations."

"Your largess?" said Cyrano. "What does Mr. Jifhraz think of your appropriating his wine?"

"After being buried in mud? He wouldn't touch the stuff and I'm not sure I would myself but Offenfusser seems to like the concept."

"And why not?" said Sandwort. "Ancient wine jugs recovered from Phoenician shipwrecks have turned out to be perfectly drinkable."

"If you're not too particular," Barbez concurred.

I finished my own drink and bade them all farewell. I was in a restless state of mind. I didn't want to be in company — that company anyway — and I didn't want to be alone either. Now that I had nothing to do or even worry about doing, I did not want to be confronted by my own bad self and so decided to take a run over to a touristy waterfront establishment on the other side of the bay that neither I nor anyone I knew ever frequented.

The Fat Tuna was only moderately crowded with happy hour revelers when I arrived and managed to find a seat at the bar where I ordered a draft beer. Around me, the men and women in their shorts and flip flops were living it up in what seemed to me was a rather forced conviviality. The men were talking too loud and the women were responding with tinny, annoying shrieks of laughter. I drank my beer and went back to the house.

CHAPTER THIRTEEN

The next morning I wakened from my fitful, vaguely night-marish slumber to the sound of the ringing telephone. It was Alicia.

"Martin, I heard you met with Bunny yesterday. You must come over for breakfast and tell me all about it. Oh! Wick just fell off the ladder. Got to run."

Well, that didn't leave me with much choice even though I would have begged off if I'd been able to say anything at all. By the time I dawdled over there, Offenfusser had apparently recovered from his mishap and looked no worse than usual for wear. He and Harry Poon were attempting to pull a kitschy cement statue of a satyr on a dolly across what was left of the lawn.

"Mark!" Offenfusser called out. "You're just in time. Come give us a hand."

Poon was in a sour mood. "I bring over cases of Chateau Lafitte and get press ganged into hard labor."

"You're perfectly free to leave any time you like," said Offenfusser. "The foundation requires a certain amount of teamwork from its resident guests."

"Fuck you, Wick."

"Now, that's the spirit. Take this rope, Mark, and pull for all you're worth."

I did as I was told and we managed with some effort to move the thing to the place that Offenfusser designated.

"There," he said cheerfully. "Reminds me of working mornings on the farm."

"The funny farm," Poon growled.

"Now, now, Harry. No good deed goes unpunished and you are about to be rewarded with the results of another one of Alicia's cooking experiments."

"Yes, I thought there was a light at the end of the tunnel," said Poon. "I think I'll crack another bottle."

We all went inside where Alicia was busy in the kitchen. "Damn," she sputtered as she added a failed crepe to a pile of other mistakes. "Oh, hello there, Martin."

"Good morning."

"Mark was kind enough to help us move the devil statue," said Offenfusser.

"It's a satyr, Fuzzwick," said Alicia as if she'd repeated it one too many times. "There's coffee outside."

We adjourned to the terrace where Poon uncorked a bottle of Amontillado sherry. "Normally, I wouldn't touch this kind of stuff but it's so damn expensive I can't even exercise decent restraint." He poured himself a little glass and held it up in the sunlight. "To Edgar Allen Poe, wherever you are," he said and gulped it down. "Phew."

Eventually, Alicia came out with a tray of rolled up crepes and set them down on the table. The seafood stuffing wasn't so bad but the crepes themselves might as well have been made out of rubber.

"So, Martin, you must tell us all about your book tour," she said as I tried to gnaw through one of her creations.

"There making me play the part of a complete lout," I said. "I'm supposed to be loaded all the time, get in fist fights, and romance dubious women."

"I'm sure that Pedro Barbez would be glad to give you a few pointers," said Poon. "He's done a lot of research on the subject."

"Now, wait a minute," said Offenfusser. "You mean you're supposed to put on some sort of act for the press?"

"Of course he is," said Alicia. "He can't just be his old boring self."

Some people might have taken umbrage at a remark like that but I wasn't so vain not to realize it was true. After all, I was already divorced from the commodity I was about to become.

"I don't think Mark is boring at all," Offenfusser defended me. "He just doesn't have anything to say. I wish there were more people like him. Take Harry here, always babbling some nonsense. He could take lessons from Mark."

Poon smirked and kept his mouth shut.

"Believe me, Martin," said Alicia, "Bunny knows what she's doing. Just do what she tells you."

"Well, actually I'm being handled by Junius Flatmeat now."

"Who?" said Poon. "Flatmeat? He sounds like a bologna sandwich."

"He looks like a bologna sandwich. He's Sparky Goldflugel's nephew. Barrington says he's got his finger on the pulse of America."

They all guffawed.

"I didn't realize America had a pulse," said Offenfusser. "I thought it was in a state of suspended animation."

"And what's this Junius Flatmeat going to do for you," Alicia wanted to know.

"He's going to shepherd me around from one scandalous incident to the next. He's already got a whole itinerary of my public misbehavior laid out. Shoot outs, brawls, nightclub ejections, drug overdoses, you name it."

"Sounds like you've got a busy schedule ahead," said Offenfusser. "Do you have life insurance?"

"I think it's all staged. I might need a stunt double."

"I'd volunteer myself," said Poon, "but I'm getting a little old and infirm for that kind of thing. Besides, I left my crash helmet and knee pads behind with my ex when she ejected me from the premises."

"Really?" said Alicia. "That's when you should have been wearing them."

"They certainly would have come in handy when she was throwing plates at me. So, Martin, you're just going to fake all this bad behavior?"

"I believe that's the program."

Poon shook his head. "Damn shame. I mean if you have to acquire the reputation of a fool, why not really be one?"

"You might give that some thought," Offenfusser agreed. "Have you considered a lobotomy?"

"Why don't you two shut up," said Alicia. "You're just envious of Martin's rising star."

"That's true," said Poon, "but who said we had to try and hide it?"

"I did," said Alicia. "Martin will find out all too soon that it's lonely at the top. He won't know who his friends are anymore."

"Well, you've always got a friend in me, Mark," said Offenfusser. "A sort of in-law anyway."

"I'm grateful for all your support," I said with mock humility. "Where would I be without my cousin Alicia?"

"Not sitting out here enjoying this view," Offenfusser chuckled. "That's for sure."

I left them all there around noon and headed back to the house where there was a note on my door. It was from Redstone. "Please call me. Urgent." I didn't like the sound of that at all and decided to ignore it. Not that it did me any good. He emerged from the bushes before I could even open the door.

"Hello, there, sport!" he called out as he hurried over. "I've got to talk to you."

"Okay, come in."

We went into the house and he started pacing around like a caged animal. "Have you seen that thing on the road?"

"You mean the shrine?"

"Whatever you want to call it. I can't have that thing there in front of my house."

This was getting amusing. "Well, what are you going to do about it?"

"I want you to do me a favor. I want you to call the township and complain. I mean, it's got to go."

"It is sort of vulgar, isn't it?" I had to agree as I bit my tongue to stop from laughing.

"You don't know the rumors that are going around. People are saying I ran over that guy myself. People are saying I blew up A.J.'s boat. I know it's that crazy old bat down the road."

"Come on, Dack, don't you think you're being a little paranoid?"

"Even paranoids have enemies, Martin. Just remember that."

"I'm sure they do but I'm also sure that even Mrs. Bradley doesn't approve of the shrine. If it bothers you so much, why don't you just remove it yourself. Bust it up with a sledge hammer or something."

Redstone looked at me askance. "Can't do it, sport. I don't want to get the ghost of that Mexican after me."

I naturally assumed he was joking and I chuckled.

"What's so funny?" he demanded sharply. "I'm not much on religion but I don't go around desecrating graves."

"It's not a grave," I pointed out. "There's nobody buried there."

"Look," he said impatiently. "The damn thing gives me the creeps and I want the township to do something about it. I'm not exactly on their honor roll lately so I thought a word from you might help."

I had never seen Redstone in this state before. He was serious-ly bent out of shape. And how had Harry Poon's boat sinking story gotten back to him?

"Okay, fine," I allowed him, "I'll do something. I'll make the call. Why don't you come in and I'll do it now."

"Very good of you, sport. Thanks."

So I got on the horn to the town hall where I found out that the township did plan to remove the shrine but right now they were only giving it a ticket in case the owner showed up to cart it away. Redstone did not like this news at all.

"How long is this going to take?" he fumed.

I tried to reassure him. "No more than a day or two, I'm sure. They did say they were going to remove it."

"Well, I guess that will have to do," he said. "What's going on with you, Martin?"

"Nothing much. Just boring book stuff. How about you? What's that you just said about bombing A.J.'s boat."

"You haven't heard?" he said disgustedly. "There's a rumor running around town that I blew up the Sulema."

"Really?" I guffawed. "Who concocted that?"

"No idea. The problem is it's true."

This was so absurd it didn't even pull me up short. "Well, it's ridiculous but it's pretty original," I chortled.

He looked at me askance. "Didn't you hear me? I blew up the Sulema."

"Right," I played him along. "Just jumped in the water in your frogman suit and did the dirty deed. Aren't you ashamed of yourself?"

"I didn't do it myself, you fool! I don't like the water! Those were people I hired."

I had never seen Redstone come this close to flat out comedy. I hadn't even thought he was capable of it. "Now, why would you do something like that, Dack?" I coaxed him along like a good straight man.

Redstone winced, then he smirked. "You know why, Martin? You really want to know why? Because I'm a true patriot, a real American who refuses to stand by and watch a lecherous Arab defile young American women! Not only does he degrade our women, he is

153

trying to undermine the huge amount of gasoline and other petroleum derived products that true Americans consume in vast quantities everyday by selling crude oil to the Chinese. What I did was just a warning, but A.J. must come to learn the error of his ways!"

I called out "Hallelujah!" and gave him a well deserved round of applause but he doggedly kept a straight face.

"Laugh all you want," he said tersely and looked at his watch. "I've got to go. Just remember what I've told you is strictly between you and me. Am I right on that?"

"Yes, of course," I said. "I would never betray your confidence. Well, almost never…"

"Ha, ha," he said and walked out the door.

I watched through the window as he marched off back through the bushes and wondered why the whole town was making such sport of the scuttling of the Sulema. Was it just, "Let's have some genial, jingoist fun at the towel head's expense," or was there more to the whole thing than met the untrained eye? I really didn't much care, but it was a good thing to speculate on if you wanted to kill time. At that moment, I did not want to kill time. I had an appointment in town with the local dentist to look at a tooth that bothered me occasionally. Before my recent good fortune, I could not have afforded such a luxury and I had wisely taken advantage of what might only be a fleeting opportunity to get my teeth attended to.

I drove into the village and parked in front of the mini-mall where the dentist's office was sandwiched between a bait and tackle shop and an Off Track Betting parlor. Without going into the details of the tedious and slightly painful procedure that ensued, let me just say I left minus my last wisdom tooth with a harangue about taking better care of my mouth ringing in my airs. Of course, I immediately headed for Cyrano's to recuperate.

"Welcome, young Martin," the good publican greeted me. "You look like someone punched you in the jaw. Have you recently engaged in fisticuffs? Never a wise recourse to settle a dispute."

"My only dispute was with my own tooth that has now been evicted from my mouth," I explained. "May I bother you for a martini."

"Your wish is my command. Never been to a dentist myself. We Brits don't do that sort of thing. You Americans believe that anyway and I don't like to interfere with peoples' stereotypes."

"Like anyone else, we do nurse our illusions," I agreed.

"Some more than others," said Cyrano. "All the great philosophers were just hypochondriacs who took too much interest in their imagined symptoms. There you go." He poured my drink into an iced glass and plopped in an olive. "I've got to do a few things in back," he said and tossed a newspaper down in front of me.

Here is what I read. A newly minted country and western singer who had recently won a television talent show had gone on tour to rub up against his "fan base" and been trapped in a coal mine in West Virginia when the shaft collapsed during a hard hat photo opportunity. He had been in contact with people on the surface via a special emergency telephone but things didn't sound good. The last words he had spoken were, "I can't breathe, I can't breathe!" and the authorities had been trying to make contact ever since to no avail. This article was placed right alongside another story about a politician who had been pulled over in his car for driving erratically and refused to take a breathalyzer test. It didn't say whether or not he could breathe.

These stories sent me musing about the tabloid universe into which I myself had recently, if minorly, been inducted. The fundamental disembodiment of printed narrative, the "imagined symptoms" that Cyrano had just mentioned were the true staples of our lives. Food, water, shelter, motor cars, drugs, and alcohol were, of course, all necessary, but illusions manufactured by others were our real bread. The media and religion vied with one another in a tense standoff over who would control mythology and, if the outcome was uncertain, media seemed to have the upper hand at the moment. "There is but one God" had crumbled before an onslaught of deities both large and small cranked out on a daily basis by television and the newspapers. The foolish and gullible now had the choice to identify with either saints or pop tarts and the latter were clearly winning out in the battle for the hearts and pea brains of the masses.

These grey thoughts were interrupted by the entrance of a disheveled, heavily perspiring Pedro Barbez into the bar. "Where's Cyrano?" he demanded. Before I could answer, he bellowed, "Sandwort!" and the good publican quickly appeared.

"Ah, Pedro," he said, "to what do we owe the pleasure of this not altogether unexpected visit?"

"Shut up and get me a drink," Barbez growled but no sooner had Cyrano started to pour than the crunch of gravel outside announced another arrival. Barbez hurried to the door, looked outside, then raced back through the bar and disappeared. The reason for his departure soon became apparent. A stolidly built policeman walked in and looked around.

"Good day, Sergeant McCorrigal," said Sandwort. "What can I do for you?"

"Hello, Cyrano. Have you seen Pedro Barbez around?"

"I see him all the time. As you know, he practically lives here."

"Well, if you see him today, tell him it was all a mistake and the charges have been dropped."

"I'll make sure and tell him," said Sandwort. "Is there anything else I can do for you?"

"Well, I am on duty. I'll just have a double shot of Jack with a draft beer back."

"Excellent choice. Mustn't overdo it."

Sergeant McCorrigal took a seat at the bar and delicately slugged down his whiskey.

"Whatever happened with that Arab's boat over in the harbor?" Sandwort asked casually.

"No idea. The word is he did it himself to collect the insurance."

"Insurance? Sounds like pin money for a fellow like that."

"You never know," said McCorrigal. "These Arabs are too tricky for their own good. He probably did it out of force of habit. Couldn't stop himself."

"Yes, I see what you mean," Cyrano cautiously agreed. "This compulsion to blow up boats, it's in the blood."

"Exactly. Well, thanks. Just tell Barbez that everything's okay. This time." He left without even offering to pay.

When he pulled out of the driveway, Pedro Barbez emerged from wherever he'd been hiding.

"As you must be aware, Pedro, we have just been entertaining Sergeant McCorrigal of the local constabulary," said Sandwort.

"What did he say?" said Barbez urgently.

Sandwort almost gasped at the possibilities presented by this question. "You didn't hear anything?"

156

"No, no, what did he say?"

"Well, you're in some big trouble, Pedro."

"I didn't do it! It's all lies!" Barbez protested.

"We know that, Pedro, but Sergeant McCorrigal has a different opinion."

"I'm being scapegoated! They won't get away with it, I tell you!"

"With all the great powers of the state arrayed against you, Barbez? With a hanging judge waiting for you down a long, twisting, Kafkaesque corridor... waiting to seal your doom?! How long did you think it would be until they finally nailed your ass to the wall?! How long did you think they would go on ignoring your heinous crimes?!"

From my own point of view, Sandwort's delivery was high Shakespearian comedy but Barbez didn't seem to get the joke.

"And now you, even you, turn on me!" he spat out.

"You have only to confess your sins," said Sandwort sententiously, "and God will forgive you."

"I'll show you, I'll show you all!" Barbez hissed, pirouetting from right to left as if he were surrounded by an enthusiastic lynch mob. With those parting words, he spun around and raced out the door.

"I guess I laid it on a little thick," Sandwort acknowledged, "but how could I resist?"

"It was an opportunity that doesn't come along every day," I had to agree.

"With Barbez, it comes around more often than you think. Another drink?"

How could I resist?

"You know, Martin, I always wanted to be an actor. I wanted to strut across the big stage in borrowed finery - a painted ape, if you will - and declaim all sorts of nonsense in my basso profundo. However, I soon discovered that everything the theatre world viewed as high art, I regarded as low comedy. Take Hamlet if you will. Here's this story about this paranoid schizophrenic who has hallucinations and kills his stepfather. Is he incarcerated and shipped off to the loony bin forthwith? Well, you know the rest so this is obviously burlesque. But all these yorps take this fruitcake seriously and my own interpretation is consigned to the rubbish heap of satire."

This line of simple, good-natured badinage had a disturbing affect on me. I was soon to become a "painted ape" myself.

Danica rolled in later that afternoon and immediately began addressing the nuts and bolts of my up and coming book tour. "You're definitely going to need some new clothes," was her definitive first comment on my haberdashery. Now, as any but the most naïve fool knows, when a woman decides to redecorate you she is actually exercising a proprietary claim. You don't have to even guess who's the property. This is always a dangerous moment in any budding romance because the lady is almost surely going to throw out all your most comfortable, favorite clothes in favor of a new look of her own devising. Danica had decided I should look more authoritative, more professorial. I explained to her that Junius Flatmeat and Sparky Goldflugel had decided I should look like a dissipated man about town. This rather confounded her remodeling plans and forced her to arrive at a compromise. My new look was to be rakish visiting lecturer. To this end, I would wear expensive designer suits with no tie, suede shoes, and a British accent. The latter was out of the question but I reluctantly acquiesced to the other two.

"Then it's settled. I'm taking you to the city tomorrow to go shopping for your grand tour. I don't know whether I 'm going to miss you or not," she pouted.

"Well, how can you miss me if I don't go away?"

"Stop making fun of me. I can just see you out there on the loose with a bunch of dummy brain college girls."

"I don't know how you can talk about the future mothers of America that way."

She cuffed me on the nose. "Just don't let me catch you with one of those little floozies."

"Oh, no, I'll be very discreet. And don't believe a thing you read in the papers."

CHAPTER FOURTEEN

The next day, I woke to the sweet sounds of birds chirping in the trees outside the window and the crash of something breaking in the other room.

"Dammit!" I heard Danica cursing.

"What's going on out there?" I called out.

"Nothing. I broke the mirror."

I got up and walked into the living room where Danica was sweeping up broken glass with a whisk broom. "What happened?"

"I don't know. I was cleaning up and it just fell off the wall."

I'm not superstitious and I gave this minor accident no more thought than it deserved, which was none. Shortly thereafter, however, we boarded the train for my shopping expedition and debarked sometime later at Penn Station where Danica thought our first stop should be Macy's due to its proximity. I must tell you I hate shopping and had to be practically dragged by the nose into the fabled emporium. As we passed from the street into this gaudy temple of earthly desires, I felt dizzy and broke into a cold sweat.

"Don't be such a baby," Danica scolded and frog-marched me to the escalator. We got off on the next landing and were immediately assaulted by a swarm of young sales girls and sissy boys trying to spray us with atomizer bottles. I was absolutely terrified but Danica brazened her way through the crowd warding off these scent purveyors by flicking her wrists as if she were whisking away flies. Once we had safely passed through this odoriferous gauntlet, I tried to get a grip on myself and at least assume the appearance of someone who wasn't about to run off howling down the endless, labyrinthine corridors of this infernal place.

"You feel better now?" Danica cooed. "Don't worry, we'll be out of here in no time. I've just got to get you a couple shirts."

And so she dragged me along to the shirt department where she picked up a stack of linen shirts that she thought suited me, made me pay for them, and mercifully let me off the hook by allowing me to leave that accursed place as fast as I could. I vowed then and there to go and sin no more if I never had to enter a department store again. I made this resolution clear to Danica in the taxi uptown.

"You are such a wuss, Martin. You'd think no one ever tried to spray you with cologne before."

"In case you haven't noticed, I don't use cologne and I don't want to go around town smelling like the flower show," I said testily.

"Don't worry. From now on it's one stop shopping."

Following Danica's instructions, our driver delivered us to a small shop on Madison Avenue called Fermi. We went into the store where an odd little man whose face looked like a particularly garish piece of waxed fruit minced up to Danica in a double breasted blazer that was stretched under his arms so tightly he looked as if he'd been shoehorned into it. "Darling, where have you been keeping yourself?" he gushed. Then he looked me over in a way that made me feel as if some horrible fluid was oozing out of his eyeballs and covering me with slime. "Oooh, no wonder you haven't been around." Now, I have nothing against raving queens, but this guy was a bit long in the tooth to be coming on like someone who'd even been fucked up the ass in the last fifteen years. He most certainly would have had to pay for it.

Danica bussed him on both cheeks. "Max, this is Martin."

"My pleasure, I'm sure," said Max batting his eyes.

"Martin needs a suit and some shoes."

"Well," said Max crisply, "let's just see if we can do something about that."

We did and I walked out with two linen jackets, some trousers and a pair of brown suede shoes. I should also mention these late additions to my wardrobe set me back slightly over fifteen hundred dollars.

"You've been such a good boy, I should take you to lunch," said Danica.

"Very kind of you to offer. Where would you like to go?"

We wound up downtown at one of those chic little, newly minted places on Clinton Street where the relatively inexpensive cuisine is barely passable and the girl watching is very good indeed.

"Now that wasn't so bad, was it?" she said to me as if she were soothing a small child.

"Would you please stop with the baby talk?" I muttered.

"Goo, goo, goo. I didn't realize what a toll a couple hours of shopping would take on you. Have a double whatever you want on me."

I did and it helped. I felt as if a huge sartorial burden had been lifted from my shoulders and I wouldn't have to buy any more clothes for at least another year. I was grateful. "Hey, D, thanks. You know I would have never done it myself."

"Done what?" she said suspiciously.

"You know. Go shopping."

"Oh, well, you would have picked all the wrong things anyway."

I guess that was her idea of saying, "You're welcome." I veered off in another direction that was bound to interest her. "Redstone was over yesterday complaining about that thing on the road."

"The shrine? What's he worried about? Vengeful spirits?"

This keen observation surprised me. "Strangely enough, that's exactly what he said. When I suggested he remove it himself, he said he didn't want to rile up the dead man's ghost."

"I had no idea he was so superstitious. Maybe you should take over a Ouija board next time you see him." She paused. "The reason he's upset is because he killed the guy."

"Yes, the story's all over town," I said sardonically. "Redstone the monster. Why is everyone so eager to blame him for everything?"

"Oh, you are one simple soul, Martin. I know you think I'm crazy but someday you'll realize the man is evil incarnate."

"Look," I said impatiently, "can we drop all this supernatural nonsense. The next thing you're going to tell me is he's got horns and a tail. As near as I can tell he's just an insecure lost soul with a talent for making money."

Danica shook her head and snorted. "He doesn't have to make money. He never did."

"You mean he's an heir?"

She hesitated before she spoke. "Not exactly. I don't want to talk about it."

"Of course."

"Well, you brought him up. Not me."

She had a point. It set me to thinking though. Why did people need scapegoats? In all of human history, in every culture and society, there has always been someone to be held liable, someone to be sacrificed on the altar of the gallows, the electric chair, or the concentration camp. Someone else, that is. Not too many volunteers for the assignment. Now, for some reason or other, Redstone was being set up as the offering to palliate the gods. His wealthy neighbors disliked him for more reasons than they would care to reveal. The others reviled him for his innocent vulgarity, but the snickering behind his back also masked a deep well of envy and resentment. Baby D had her own reasons which would in no way constrain her from cheering on a lynch mob. Was I really Redstone's only friend? I shuddered to think it might be so.

"How are the Offenfussers?" Danica asked casually.

"I don't know. They had me over for breakfast or brunch or whatever yesterday and I had to lap up Alicia's fine cuisine with a smile on my face."

"God, why does she even pretend she can cook? What else?"

"Fuzzwick fell off a ladder."

"He does that all the time," she pooh-poohed.

"Harry Poon's moved in until the boat is fixed."

"You're joking," she said. "Alicia's doing Harry?"

"I have no idea. Sort of getting a fast start on the whole extra-marital affair thing, isn't it?"

Danica held her hand up. "Alicia is a free spirit. She spits in the face of bourgeois modes of behavior," she said dramatically, then broke into laughter.

"Well, that's about all the news from the Offenfusser Foundation," I said modestly. "I hope I made it sound more interesting than it actually was."

"That's your job," she said seriously. "Who wants to read about things the way they actually are? So boring."

"I agree entirely. Life is so boring that it's better not to write about anything at all. Unless someone else does it for you, that is."

Danica caught my drift and joined in the fun. "Exactly. What if you'd actually written your book yourself? You probably couldn't stand to even look at it anymore. But now it comes to you fresh, untouched by your own hang-ups and baggage. What on earth could possibly be better?"

"Yes, I've often thought I'd like to be reborn as a college girl with the fervent ambition to inflict my piddly, yet deeply meaningful, thoughts and experiences on the maximum number of people possible."

"Well, now you have," she said. "Tell me what it's like to be standing in her shoes."

"Actually, it's the other way around. I couldn't fit in her shoes anyway."

On the train back out to the island, Danica fell asleep on my shoulder and had a disturbing dream. I know this because she made worried little whimpers that broke up the rhythm of her breathing. When she woke up and I asked her what she was dreaming, she couldn't remember. When we got back to the house, the sun was only beginning its slow descent over the bay and the water glittered with so many evanescent flashes it was almost painful to behold. But what was that off to the left? A flailing human body leaving a trail of smoke from its charred wings plummeted from high in the sky right into the middle of the bay with a splash. None of the boaters seemed to notice and went on about their business as if nothing had happened at all.

"How would you like to have several million dollars and live on your own tropical island with as many sexual partners as you could handle?" the television set blatted away at Danica who was curled up on the couch. "Well, now you can!"

"What are you watching?" I demanded.

"I don't know. TV."

"Then you won't mind if I change the channel."

"Go ahead."

I clicked the remote and there was the same cheeseball huckster in a gaudy Hawaiian shirt standing on a beach with waves crashing behind him. "You say you're not satisfied! You say you're not getting enough for the time you put in on your horrible, boring, degrading job! Well, I'm here to tell you – "

I changed the channel again. This time his face covered the entire screen. "You want out! You want to leave all the horror of your dreadful life behind and – "

I turned the damn thing off. "Want to listen to some music?"

"I want to take a nap," she mewed. "Aren't you tired?"

I haven't really described our lovemaking, have I? I mean, not in the clinical terms that people like to read these days. Well, maybe later. For now, all I'm going to say is we got up as the sun was going down.

Having nothing else to do, we decided to drive out to the point and watch the sunset from the outdoor deck of the Sea Trout, a touristy watering hole favored by the sport fishing set. The inside of the bar was decorated with lacquered sharks, sword fish, and other sea beasts not even indigenous to the local waters such as a marlin and a sail fish. The crowd was strictly hog power boat with a three story tall tuna tower and they were living it up after a hard day of battling the elements and bad fishing luck. The surrounding waters were so depleted that the catch had plunged to practically nothing in the last few years but these hearty fellows persisted in the hopeful belief that the fish would return and all things would be as they were before. They might as well have staged a prayer procession carrying a carved, wooden Santo on their shoulders as they do in Italy.

Danica and I took a table overlooking the water and ordered a bottle of champagne.

"Why do women know that they're going to bed with a man for the very last time but men never figure it out at all?" Danica wondered.

"I don't understand."

"Of course you don't understand. You're not a woman."

"Then why don't fill me in?" I teased her.

"You think you're being funny, don't you? What I mean is that women always know it's over but men think things can just go on and on."

"Are you trying to tell me something?"

She laughed. "Oh no, I haven't finished with you yet."

"I guess I should be relieved."

"You better be. I think we make a wonderful couple. In bed, that is."

"I've got no complaints. Except when we're out of bed, that is."

"You jerk," she laughed and cuffed me on the nose. "I should —

"

But something had caught my eye. "Isn't that Fuzzwick's boat out there?"

She looked in the direction I was pointing and saw the same thing I was seeing; a candy apple red speedboat weaving erratically across the water with a rooster tail spuming from its souped up engine. "With any luck, he'll kill himself," she sighed. "But then again, he's not the type. No matter what kind of foolishness he gets himself into, he always seems to walk away unscathed."

"To a charmed life," I said raising my glass in a toast.

She started to raise her own glass but stopped herself. "I'm not drinking to Wick."

"Who said I was talking about Fuzzwick? I was talking about us," I said gallantly.

"Oh, well, in that case," she simpered, "cheers."

I was certainly in lust with Baby D. I was beginning to wonder if I was in love with Danica. What was she up to anyway? That little business about women leaving for good – was that a warning? I didn't like the idea of her walking out on me but there wasn't much I could do about it but go along for the ride.

"It's so beautiful," she said, stirring me from my brief reverie and drawing my attention to the last stabbing rays of an orange sun framed in blue rapidly sinking into the ocean. Then a voice spoke out behind me.

"Mr. Seward, I hate to bother you two, but…"

I turned and there were Mrs. Bradley and Chappie Wilmerding.

"Would you very much mind if we joined you for a moment?"

I could not imagine what these two were doing there but then I couldn't imagine why I was there myself. "No, not at all," I said politely.

"Thank you," said Mrs. Bradley, taking a seat. "I believe you've met my brother Chappie."

Wilmerding nodded and said nothing.

"Chappie's been looking into your family, Mr. Seward, and I see that you're the right sort of people."

I had no idea what she was talking about. Had she discovered that my ancestors hailed from Chowderhead Bay?

Danica was delighted by this confirmation of my social status. "Martin comes from the very finest stock, I can assure you," she said lubriciously.

Mrs. Bradley gave her a "Who asked you?" kind of look and moved on. "As you well know, Mr. Seward, my differences with our neighbor Mr. Redstone are many and various. Now Chappie here tells me that Mr. Redstone is suspected of planting a bomb on that yacht that exploded."

"Well, I think that's just a — "

"I heard that myself," Danica eagerly horned in.

"Yes, well it seems to be rather common knowledge, doesn't it. That, of course, is a matter for the proper authorities. My concerns are with that excrescence on the road across from Mr. Redstone's place. I understand that you yourself called to request its removal, Mr. Seward."

"Yes, I did, Mrs. Bradley. If there's anything more I can do to — "

"There is indeed, Mr. Seward. You can cease and desist from lodging any more complaints until the matter is settled once and for all."

I have to say this request thoroughly confused me. "I don't understand. What matter are you talking about?"

"The matter of Mr. Redstone's imminent departure from the neighborhood. I would like him to leave voluntarily and I believe that declaring that little monstrosity a township monument will help things along."

"You think a shrine by the side of the road is going to make Redstone move out?"

"I said it may encourage him to do so since it also appears that he may have run down that poor man in the first place. A daily reminder of his crime might have a certain effect."

"I agree entirely," said Danica solemnly. "Rub it in."

Mrs. Barclay ignored her. "If Mr. Redstone refuses to see the light, my brother here is in a position to further illuminate the situation." She stood up. "So, that's settled. Nice to see you." She and Wilmerding walked back into the restaurant.

"What's settled?" I wanted to know.

"You are now an official defender of the shrine," said Danica. "I myself shall assume the role of the Virgin of Guadalupe."

"That's a stretch. I least she didn't want me to sign a petition. Why is everyone in town trying to ostracize Redstone? Just because he has big parties? He must pay a fortune in taxes."

"If I caught Mrs. Bradley's drift, he may soon be paying a lot more. Don't you see? Dack has offended these peoples' delicate sensibilities and, unless he builds a new gymnasium for the high school, they will find a way to push him out."

It was difficult to think of Redstone as a sort of scrappy underdog but these people were so intent on making him a pariah that my sense of fair play came to the fore. Of course, your sense of fair play only comes to the fore when you're ahead. "I don't care what you or anyone else thinks of Redstone," I said. "I'm not going to just be a bystander at the gallows. Leave the man alone, for chrissake."

"It doesn't matter what you say now," said Danica. "Dack's made his own bed and he's going to have to sleep in it. What do you care anyway? I think you have more important things to worry about than some zillionaire's standing in the community."

If I did, I wasn't thinking about any of them at the moment. My mind was blissfully free of care or foresight. "Would you like some more champagne?" I asked.

"You know I would," she answered with her most alluring smile. Then she was suddenly pensive. "What were they doing here in the first place?"

"How do I know? Maybe they're regulars. Do you think they're following me around?" I teased her.

"Well, they went to enough trouble to determine that you're the right sort of people. They've probably got your whole family tree."

Now that I thought about it, Mrs. Bradley's strange assertion which originally seemed no more than comical began to take on a more sinister aspect. Why were these people interested enough in me to do some sort of background check?

Danica noticed that I was perturbed. "Don't get paranoid. Not yet. Just wait until you're famous. Every sordid detail, every humiliating episode from your past, every rattling skeleton in the closet shall be paraded before the mob like a procession of freak show attractions!" she said melodramatically. "Your life will be an open book… even if you didn't write it."

"Thank you," I grumbled. "I feel better already."

"Poor Martin," she said. "You're just a cork floating on an oil slick."

"Would you cut it out?"

"I'm sorry, darling. It's just that you're so malleable, so easy to bend out of shape…"

"I think we've had this conversation before," I said sourly.

"I don't think it was actually a conversation," she corrected me.

"If I recall correctly, I was just lecturing you."

We both laughed and decided to order another bottle. By the time we tottered out of the Sea Trout, we were both pleasantly inebriated and decided to go rent a DVD in the village. This did not turn out to be a wise decision. I saw the flashing lights in the rear view mirror when we were about half way to town and pulled off to the side of the road. The police car behind me did likewise. The patrolman got out of his car and ambled up to my window fingering his revolver. It was Sergeant McCorrigal.

"What's the problem, officer?" I said nervously. I didn't know if I wanted him to remember me from Cyrano's or not recognize me at all. After all, I'd seen him drinking whiskey on duty.

"That's for you to know and me to find out," he said amiably. "Why don't you just step out of the car and show me your license."

I did as I was told and he examined my license closely. "I see this was issued in New York. You're a visitor I take it."

"Well, actually, I'm out for the summer. I'm staying at the Wilberforce house."

"Ah, the Wilberforce house. I know it well. Just had a fire over there, didn't they? I don't suppose you had anything to do with that."

"Uh, no, it was a propane tank explosion."

He gave me a hard stare. "We've had a few other explosions around here lately."

I had no idea how to respond to that and kept my mouth shut.

"So, Mr. Seward," he said reading my name off my license, "I see that you're drunk and you're driving a car. Isn't that right?"

"No!" I protested. "I mean I had a glass of wine..."

"I want you to do me a favor," he said. "I want you to close your eyes, put your arms out, and touch your right finger to your nose."

I did as he requested.

"Okay, now touch your left finger to your nose."

Again, I touched my nose.

"Okay, you can open your eyes. You're under arrest."

"Hey, wait a minute! I touched my nose."

"So you did, my friend. Only someone who's been drinking could do that, you know. Can't do it myself. Turn around."

He didn't wait for me to do it myself. He spun me around and slapped on a pair of handcuffs.

"Is this really necessary?" I complained.

"You never know. Sometimes it's the wimpy ones who give you the most trouble."

With that, he marched me back to his car and more or less pushed me into the back seat.

"Hey, wait a minute!" Danica called out.

"I'm sorry, young lady!" McCorrigal called back. "If you can't drive the thing yourself, you'll just have to get a cab!"

We soon arrived at the town hall jail where McCorrigal had an assistant photograph and fingerprint me, then threw me in a small cell.

"I'd try and sleep, if I were you," he said. "If you can't, you should spend the time contemplating the error of your ways. Look at it this way. You're lucky you weren't babbling on a cell phone when I pulled you over. Then we'd have to execute you." He laughed merrily and left me there to stew in my champagne infused juices.

I sat down on the hard bed and looked at the graffiti scrawled on the painted, cinder block walls. Among these many expressions of fear, defiance, resignation, and simple, misplaced exuberance was, "Stone walls do not a prison make! Nor iron bars a cage! But why, oh why, my lord, my God! Did the walls get painted beige?!" - Pedro Barbez. For some reason it comforted me to know that Barbez had preceded my stay in this place and I went to sleep rather easily.

The next morning, they cut me loose with a scheduled court appearance and I found Danica outside waiting to take me home.

"I feel like such a gun moll," she said. "You want to drive?"

CHAPTER FIFTEEN

A relatively uneventful two days later, I received a call from Junius Flatmeat. He was in a rather agitated frame of mind.

"Goddamit, Seward!" he howled. "You get busted for drunken driving and I have to read about it in the police blotter section of that podunk paper out there! Do you have any idea what that was worth until you went and blew it by keeping your mouth shut?!"

"Would you please calm down?" I admonished him.

"No! No, I will not calm down until you get your head screwed on straight! If you had tipped me off, I could have got you on Page Six before you were out of the drunk tank! Now it's just yesterday's news!"

"So what am I supposed to do? Apologize? I guess I could go out and do it again."

"That would be a good start. Just make sure you crash into a night club next time. Now listen, Marty, all kidding aside, you've got to understand my position. I'm your advance man! I can't be the last one to know what's going on with you! Besides, I'm supposed to be the one who sets these things up. That way I know about them before they even happen. So stop getting into trouble without me!"

"I promise you, Junius. I'll do my best."

"That's the ticket," he said enthusiastically. "See you in town next week."

If I hadn't been in such a good mood, I might have been annoyed by Junius' phone call, but that morning I'd received the first half of the Buddha book from – bless her heart – Nuk Nuk Noing. I gave it a quick scan, found it fundamentally inspirational and immediately forwarded it to the delighted Sheridan March.

"Well, I guess my little pep talk really got you going, Martin!" she brayed on the phone. "My assistant's out of town this week, but I'll have her read it first thing when she gets back. I suppose you want more money."

"Well, that's not really..."

"Don't argue with me. I know what makes you tick, Martin, and I know I'm going to have the rest of this book before September.

The check's in the mail."

This largesse on her part put me in a quandary. Should I give Nuk Nuk a bonus? I'd have to think about it. Danica had gone into the city for the day so I was left to my own devices. I didn't feel like visiting the happy threesome over at the Offenfussers, I certainly didn't feel like having anything to do with Redstone although he had left a couple of "urgent" messages, no doubt having to do with the shrine, and I didn't much feel like going over to Cyrano's but that's what I did anyway. When I got there, I found out my reputation as a newly minted bon vivant and menace on the roadway preceded me.

"You must be more careful, young Martin," Cyrano cautioned me. "The police out here are very arbitrary in their choice of prey. Have you had your day in court yet?"

"Next week," I said.

"Well, don't worry. All you have to do is pay a substantial fine and attend a class where they show you picture after picture of gory automobile accidents. I'm sure you'll enjoy it. I know I did."

"Thanks for cheering me up, Cyrano. Now about that beer..."

"Coming right up," he said cheerfully. "Now you must tell me about your overnight stay in the hoosegow. I've been there myself, of course, back when I was younger and fairly bursting with arrogance and stupidity. Did you know that Pedro Barbez has a poem on the wall of every cell in the place?"

"Yes, I had the opportunity to read one of them. It was a rhyming complaint about the color of the paint."

"Haven't seen that one myself," he said setting down an iced mug in front of me, "but then I haven't been there lately."

"Do I detect a note of opprobrium?" I mocked him.

"Do I disapprove of an occasional lapse into intemperance?" he answered my question with one of his own. "Of course not. Just don't get caught."

We both heard the rather odd sound that high heels make on gravel outside and Gloriana walked into the bar. "Hello there," she said brightly. "Sorry I haven't been around lately. Where is everybody? Where's the boat?"

"It's my understanding that the boat is across the sound being repaired," said Cyrano. "As for everybody, I have no idea."

"Harry's staying with the Offenfussers," I volunteered.

Cyrano made her a Campari and soda. "Harry's got a few theories about the explosion. He said you fled town as soon as you realized someone had planted a bomb on the boat."

Gloriana looked at him as if he'd gone out of his mind. "What are you talking about? The boiler blew up."

"Harry seems to be of another opinion."

"I was there, Cyrano. I know what happened. Harry's living in fantasy land."

Yet another wrinkle in the story of the Sulema, What did we have in the pot now? Harry Poon running around blaming Redstone and half the town believing him, Redstone with his tongue in cheek declaration that he had indeed bombed the boat, and now Gloriana throwing a wet blanket on all the gossipy intrigue. My interest in the whole affair was beginning to wane anyway. Not that I'd had much to begin with. It was just one of those situations in life that impose themselves on you without asking for permission. Let me add that Gloriana was looking very toothsome in a no frills kind of way and I offered to buy the next round.

"Well, it's about time, Martin," she said coquettishly. "I mean now that you're famous and all."

"My pleasure, but don't believe everything you hear."

"Or read," said Cyrano. "Martin recently had the great privilege of an overnight stay in the Stanford White designed lock-up in the village, but the local scandal sheet has blown it out of all proportion."

"What are you talking about?" asked puzzled Gloriana.

"Okay," said Cyrano, "you don't know, I don't know, Martin doesn't know, and let's keep it that way."

"Stop it. Please," Gloriana demanded.

"I was arrested for driving under the influence the other night," I explained.

"Under the influence of what?"

"The moon and stars overhead, the intoxicating fragrance of pine and fresh mown hay, the very tenderness of the night," Cyrano waxed poetic.

"All that," I agreed. "and a bit too much champagne."

Gloriana looked relieved. "Oh, well, that's no big deal."

"Not to you, perhaps," said Cyrano, "but the local constabulary took a dim view of Martin's disgraceful condition."

"My disgraceful condition?" I protested. "Due to your own generosity, that fat cop was probably drunker than I was."

"Now, now," Cyril soothed, "as my sainted mother used to say; if you don't have something nice to say about someone - " His mocking regurgitation of this old saw was interrupted by the arrival of none other than Sergeant McCorrigal himself.

"A hale and hearty welcome, Sergeant," said Cyrano.

"Can the bullshit, Sandwort," McCorrigal growled. "Just a double Jameson's with a pint back. I've got a meeting with the mayor in half an hour."

"Coming right up."

McCorrigal gave Gloriana and myself a red-eyed once-over from down the bar. His face screwed up in recognition and he punched his finger in the air. "Say, don't I know you from someplace?"

I didn't know what to say. "I don't - ."

"Not you," he cut me off. "Her."

"I don't believe I've had the pleasure," said Gloriana with admirable sang froid. And I do mean froid.

"There you go, Sergeant," said Cyrano, cutting McCorrigal off at the pass with his whiskey and beer. "Meeting with the mayor? Must be something important."

McCorrigal grimaced. "Are you kidding? That jerk-off has nothing else to do but - " He caught himself and smiled crookedly at Gloriana. "Excuse my French, miss."

She rewarded his gallantry with a why-don't you-drop-dead half smile.

McCorrigal leaned forward as if he was going to grab Cyrano by the collar and hissed confidentially, although Gloriana and I could clearly hear him, "It's that Richy Rich guy. They're trying to make things hot for him and they want me to do the dirty work."

Gloriana was suddenly all ears. "You mean Ahmed Jifhraz?"

McCorrigal looked down the bar as if he'd caught her with her ear to the door. "Just between you and me, baby - not him."

I was confused. Did he mean me? He cleared that up right away.

"It's that Redstone guy. I've got nothing against him. Every time he throws one of those parties of his he always slips me a nice, fat envelope. He's a right guy in my book, but these people got some kind of bug up their ass about him. Don't ask me why."

Gloriana turned to me. "You live right next door to him, don't you?"

Now, I must say that I think Gloriana is a very charming, sexually charged creature deserving of all the respect accorded Aphrodite in her occasional descents from Mount Olympus, but, at that moment, I felt like strangling her on the spot.

"Do I?" was the best I could lamely manage. "I don't really have anything to do with the neighbors."

"You know something?" said McCorrigal, "You look familiar." He contemplated me for a suspense filled few seconds. "I seen your picture in the newspaper somewhere."

"You must be mistaking me — "

"Enough already," he winked. "Relax. Out here you're just another nobody. Thanks, Sandwort," he tipped his hat and ambled out of the bar.

I couldn't believe that he didn't remember arresting me.

"I always feel safe and secure in the knowledge that keeping the local peace is in the able hands of Sergeant McCorrigal," said Cyrano.

That got the laugh it deserved.

"What a jerk," Gloriana scoffed.

"Well, I have to admit he doesn't have much of a way with the ladies," Cyrano allowed. "May I refresh your libations?"

He did and we whiled away another half hour or so until Gloriana twisted my arm into giving her a ride over to Offenfusser's. She didn't have to twist very hard.

"Drive carefully," Sandwort called out as we left. "Sergeant McCorrigal may be through with his meeting and once again be prowling the highways and byways for wrongdoers!"

Actually, since I was a little tipsy, I took Cyrano's advice to heart and drove like the proverbial little old lady from Pasadena.

"So, who's that girl you brought to the party?" Gloriana casually inquired as we leisurely made our way to the estate. "Why did she just get up and leave you there in Frog's Lip Harbor?" The inquiring female mind always wants to know. Everything.

"Just a friend," I sloughed her off. "She had an appointment."

She laughed. "That's not what I heard."

"Okay, what did you hear?"

"I heard she practically lives with you."

"Yeah, so what?"

She put her hand on my thigh. "You know something, Martin? You're really cute when you're uncomfortable. What over-bearing, all controlling woman could resist such a naïve guy?"

This observation made me really uncomfortable because it was more or less what Baby D had said herself. The best I could manage was a, "Heh, heh." We arrived at the Offenfusser's shortly thereafter and I was tempted to simply drop her off and leave but that really wouldn't have done, would it?

There was no one to be seen in front so we walked around to the terrace in back and found Harry Poon nursing a glass of wine and reading the newspaper. Gloriana gave him a big smooch on the forehead but he didn't look all that glad to see her.

"What brings you out?" he wondered. "You know A.J.'s in Dubai."

"Of course I do. I just came out to see Martin."

This teasing remark not only caught Poon completely off guard but rendered him momentarily speechless. I must say I got a kick out of his astonishment because his attitude towards me had always been accepting, perhaps grudgingly, but with something of the condescending to it. He did, however, recover very quickly.

"Well, Martin, this celebrity thing is working out pretty well for you," he leered. "You're going to be getting more ass than a bar stool."

I let that one slide right into the bay. "Where is everybody?"

"The newlyweds are off for a brief honeymoon on Bricktop Island today. Barring bad weather, they should be back this evening."

"How romantic," Gloriana crooned.

"It is, isn't it?" Poon agreed. "Now, what did you two have in mind?"

"I just came out to soak up a little sun," said Gloriana. "With Martin."

"Can we cut the bullshit?" Poon whined. "I'm invited to the Cotton Mather Yacht Club regatta. You want to go?"

"And watch a bunch of sailboats?" Gloriana said dismissively.

"No, no, we just go along for the ride. Horatio Pombo invited me to the party on his yacht. I'm sure you two would be more than

175

welcome."

Gloriana was impressed. "The Horatio Pombo?"

Even I recognized the name of the legendary, perpetually tan, seemingly ageless playboy.

"Yes," said Poon, "the old Hor himself."

Well, what else did I have to do? We all got into my car and drove over to the Mather Club at Quetip Point where the sleek, ultra light, racing boats were assembling for the start of the big race. Poon pointed out Pombo's boat, the Peeping Pequod, an enormous sloop moored at the end of the marina docks, and we were soon mixing with the revelers on deck. They were pretty much the exact same people you would find at a Redstone party but attired more nautically if you consider mixing a striped French sailor's blouse with high heels and a miniskirt nautical. The other resemblance to a Redstone party, as Gloriana soon found out, was that our gracious host Horatio Pombo had departed a week before to attend to pressing business in Los Angeles and would not attend. Her disappointment knew no bounds for about the twenty seconds it took her to find a drink and get into the swing of things. I myself was sorely tempted to walk right back down the gangplank and leave but I soon discovered that this was not an option. The huge sailing boat suddenly lurched out of its berth with a shudder and we were underway out into the open sea where the racing boats were still waiting for the signal to start. We weren't the only craft angling for ringside seats although the Peeping Pequod was certainly the grandest. The crew tacked back upwind and the hooting and hollering tipplers at the rail held on tight as the boat hiked from one side to the other. The breezy air was fresh and clear, the water was churning up a few white caps around that swarm of full white sails stretching toward the blue sky above, and all seemed right with the world. A cannon sounded from the shore and, to the cheers all those on the boats ringing the course, the trim ultra lights were off with their multi-colored spinnakers, many with corporate logos, billowing out before them. It was the sort of sight that only a travel magazine editor could truly appreciate, a confectionary image of the leisure class at play.

The Peeping Pequod sailed on roughly parallel to the buoys that had been set out to mark the parameters of the regatta and all aboard got an excellent view of the racing crews frantically trimming sails and trying to block their competitors' wind. Even the slightest advantage in a short race like this might make all the difference at the finish.

"Such a lovely day," sighed Gloriana to no one in particular as she sipped vodka and cranberry juice from a paper cup. "I just wish that every day…"

THUNK! The Peeping Pequod came to a sudden and violent stop that sent not a few of those on the rail hurtling overboard into the drink, Gloriana among them. The keel had apparently hit a drifting, uncharted sand bar. In all the panic and confusion, Harry still managed to find a life preserver, one of those old fashioned, round ones that are more decorative than functional, and toss it to her. She didn't even bother to retrieve it. She just swam back to the side of the boat where we could reach down and pull her up. Soaked and bedraggled but none the worse for wear, she rejoined the party as the rest of those who had also taken the plunge were fished back out of the bounding main by the crew. The grounding of the Peeping Pequod had, of course, been observed by all the craft in the immediate vicinity and all the visible witnesses were convulsed in gesticulating, howling laughter. I would have laughed myself but getting the sloop off the sand bar turned out to be somewhat more difficult and time consuming than many of the party-goers found convenient. However, we did all manage to drink up a storm and consume untold hot dogs and canapés before a tug brought around the point from the harbor nudged the sloop off this water hazard some two hours later when the race was long over.

Now, as you know, I would usually fill you in on all the amusing conversations I overheard on the Peeping Pequod while we waited to be rescued but, I swear, I can't remember a single one. I'm not saying there weren't any. On the other hand, I'm not saying there were. My mind had drifted much further out to sea than our actual position into the heaving surge of unknown waters where sailing right off the end of the world was a very real possibility. I had visions of sea monsters and mermaids and sirens on the shore but they were actually just the crowd on the boat going through their usual motions with the fading, sucking sound of a whirlpool in a toilet bowl. This was my world now; the great, abyssal trench where all the flotsam and jetsam too waterlogged to continue bobbing on the surface slowly descended into the unplumbed depths where the sun don't shine. White, ghostly creatures clustered around boiling volcanic fissures and waited to see what would float down next. And there I was, a feast for the pressure-proof worms of Atlantis, the only creatures with a rat's ass chance of surviving the impending terrestrial surface catastrophe and setting the whole dreary biological multiplication of finite, personal catastrophes in motion once again. Only the impact of the tug pushing the Peeping Pequod from its sandy perch into open water jolted me out of my morbid reverie.

While I'd been out in fantasy land, it seemed that Gloriana and Poon had managed to get invited to a house party by one of the people on board. Did I want to go? Not really, but I went along anyway. When the boat docked, we drove over to a small beach house on the point where there were a few other cars parked in the driveway.

"Whose place is this?" I asked.

"I don't know," said Gloriana. "Some woman Harry met on the boat."

Poon tried to stifle a laugh.

"What's so funny?" Gloriana demanded.

We soon found out. It seemed that Poon had promoted "Princess Gloriana of Andorra" to our credulous hostess, one Muriel Zink, who was positively entranced to be in the presence of royalty. She even curtseyed as she greeted us at the door. Gloriana was, of course, puzzled by this bizarre behavior. Poon soon cleared the situation up "Mrs. Zink…"

"That's miss, Harry, but just call me Muriel," she gawped with a ferocious shit-eating grin.

"Miss Zink," Poon continued, "Princess Gloriana and her foreign minister, Sewardo San Martin."

"I'm sooo honored," she gushed with such groveling ingratiation I thought for a brief second she was going to lie down on the floor and piss all over herself. She did, however, manage to remain upright.

Miss Zink was a curious specimen, a fiftyish live wire who'd had every possible cosmetic surgery performed on herself and come out looking like a horror movie, lady vampire. The only thing missing was the fangs.

"Please don't stand on ceremony," Poon helped her along. "Princess Gloriana prefers to mingle with the common folk without fanfare or special treatment."

"So very modern of you," Miss Zink simpered. "So democratic."

Gloriana, who hadn't quite decided to play along with this masquerade or not, was non-committal. "Yeah, right."

"Well, I'm glad you're all here. A very good friend of mine is trying to raise money for her favorite charity, 'Morons On Hormones.'" There was a dead air pause. "I'm just kidding," she giggled, "but it's something to do with retarded people and she's got a little film she wants to show."

Actually, it wasn't a film at all but a videotape on television. It's difficult to describe what we were then forced to watch. I'll try to be brief. A twenty-four year old Downs Syndrome individual with a rich mother and father is presented as a bearer of joy for behaving like a three year old. His fine qualities are legion but they pale in comparison to the virtues of the aforementioned parents which are countless. Eventually, the screen goes black and we are informed that little Johnny died a year and a half ago but his brief life must be an inspiration to all of us. Carefully woven into all this saccharine bullshit is that little Johnny was farmed out on a daily basis to a "program" where he did assembly line piecework for the princely sum of twelve cents a day (before taxes). A useful citizen, all and all.

Now I know that I may sound a bit cruel and the whole purpose of the party may have been to show this piece, but I found it extremely weird to mix cocktails with dead handicapped people. The other guests must have felt the same way because they immediately began whispering among themselves and consulting their watches. The rush to get out of there was hardly subtle and the Zink woman had to quickly intercept Gloriana before she made it to the door.

"Princess, I'm so glad you could come…"

"My great pleasure," Gloriana cut her off brusquely. "Now I'm off to a state reception for my subjects. Ta ta."

As soon as we'd made our escape, Gloriana cuffed Poon on the back of the head. "You are incorrigible, Harry."

"I could have been worse."

In the car, Harry told a story. "Did I ever tell you about the time I won a grant and one of the conditions of payment was that I make an appearance at some institution or cultural center and put on some sort of talk or slide show. Of course, I chose a nut house on 24th Street. On the appointed date, I went there with my projector and set up in the cafeteria. Then the keepers herded the sullen, drooling nuts into the room and made them sit down. I started my little introduction and the nuts immediately began pounding on the tables and booing. Then they started chanting, 'I killed JonBenet Ramsey! I killed JonBenet Ramsey!' They were really excited, I can tell you. To make matters worse, the keepers made so effort whatever to control them. In fact, they joined in the fun and cheered on their charges' riotous bad behavior. I was forced to retire from the field where one of the keepers took me aside and confided, 'I'm sorry, man, but this is one tough audience.'"

"You are such an idiot," Gloriana growled.

I dropped them both back at the Offenfusser's without going in and went back to the house where Redstone nailed me as soon as I drove up the driveway. He looked plenty upset, but also plenty relieved to see me.

"Martin, where have you been? I was just leaving a note on your door."

"Why? What's the problem?"

"Follow me. I'll show you," he said and marched me off back toward the road.

I reluctantly followed him to the site of the shrine which he pointed to dramatically and hissed, "Look!"

"Listen, Dack," I protested, "they said they were going to..."

"Look here," he insisted, jabbing his finger at something mounted next to the picture of the deceased. I looked more closely at the small photograph of Redstone with the word "Asesino" neatly printed across the bottom. "Do you believe that?" he demanded furiously. "What are these people trying to do to me?"

"Why don't you just remove it?" I suggested.

He visibly recoiled. "I'm not touching that thing."

I reached down and peeled the picture off the plaster, balled it up in my hand, and threw it in the woods. "There, that better?"

"You think I'm crazy, don't you?" he accused me. "I didn't put that picture there."

"Why don't you come down and have a drink," I offered.

On the way back to the house, he fumed and vented like an overheated frustration machine, mechanically repeating, "They can't do this to me. They don't know who they're dealing with. They can't do this to me, etc." I had never seen him in such a state and I could say

I was alarmed – but I wasn't. I wondered whether to tell him about the budding conspiracy to run him out of town, but that would have only made matters worse. He would have tried to recruit me as an ally and drag me further into his problems.

I poured us a couple glasses of white wine and we sat outside on the deck overlooking the bay. I sat, that is. Redstone paced back and forth in front of me, gesticulating wildly and denouncing his persecutors, real and imagined. Eventually, played out from his exertions, he plopped himself down on the chaise lounge and buried his face in his hands. "I'm sorry, sport, I must be boring you."

I suppose he thought I'd tell him that wasn't the case at all. Instead I opted for the truth. "Ah, actually you are."

He became petulant. "It's just that everyone takes advantage. It really is tough at the top."

If he thought he was boring me before... "Yes, it must be," I blandly agreed. I might as well have been yelling, "Speech! Speech!"

Redstone leaped up and jabbed his finger in the air. "So you do understand!" he marveled as if I'd just revealed that I'd taken Jesus Christ into my heart. "The American Dream is the glue that holds this country together, it's what makes us great!" he proclaimed exuberantly. Then, suddenly all was dark. "The problem is, once you've attained it, they turn on you. All the parasites, the back-biters, the fair weather friends! They do everything they can to turn your American Dream into the American Nightmare! They try to take everything you've so painstakingly built up and tear it down!"

"Uh, listen, Dack, I know you're upset but you've got to give it a rest."

"Easy for you to say," he muttered, then, after a long pause, "You're right. I shouldn't let these people get under my skin. So what's going on with your book?" This was his way of making amends since the sole conversational subject in which Redstone has any interest is himself and it must have been a strain to pretend a polite interest in me.

"Well, there's quite a bit going on actually," I said. "There's a lot of promotional things I've got to do, a series of book readings, the talk show circuit, newspaper interviews...," I droned on until his eyes glazed over and he looked at his watch.

"Got to go," he said abruptly. "Sorry for bothering you."

"No bother at all."

With that, to my great relief, he was gone. Was this sort of non-sense going to become a constant in my life? Were the riches Redstone had showered upon me for so little effort coming back to haunt me in continuous, nodding and smiling accommodation of his hopes and fears. I shuddered to think of it.

CHAPTER SIXTEEN

"You're late, Martin," said Barrington Stoat, squinting over the top of her reading glasses. Glowering Dimitri Bobokoff, sitting off to one side of the desk in his caftan, gave me a once over that made my skin crawl.

Actually, I was five minutes early but I wasn't about to make an issue of it. "Sorry," I said and took a seat across the desk from her.

"We're going to do a rehearsal in front of a focus group today and I asked Dimitri over to evaluate your performance. You've been a bad boy, Martin," she wagged her finger with a sly smile. "You should have called Junius as soon as you were arrested."

"Well," I said, "that was just a rehearsal too."

She laughed. Bobokoff had no idea what we were talking about. "What did I tell you, Dimitri? Martin's a natural."

"Nobody is a natural," he pompously objected. "Not without the proper expert guidance."

"Yes, yes, of course," Bunny agreed. "Just remember, Martin, you don't have to read from the book at all. Just charm them, make them want to take you home. In print, I mean. Now, shall we go?"

We didn't go far. There was a conference room right down the hall where Bunny had assembled a group of what looked like earnest college girls who were sitting around an enormous conference table sipping coffee and exchanging information about their no good boyfriends. There was one token guy wearing pimples and glasses.

"Ladies, gentlemen," Barrington called them to order as Bobokoff took a seat right next to mine at the head of the table. "This is Martin Seward, the author of *Babyland*."

Much to my surprise, they all applauded.

"Now, you've all read the book, so I'm sure you have some questions for Martin."

A half dozen of them raised their hands. Barrington pointed one of the young ladies out. "Go ahead. Don't be shy."

Bashfulness was not this particular young lady's problem. She batted her eyes at me like a streetwalker and thrust her ample bosom forward.

"Mr. Seward," she started and I held up my hand. Time to get into the swing of things.

"Please, just call me Martin," I insisted and lamely attempted a flirty grin.

The little hussy lowered her eyes and then looked back at me with lewd intent. "Martin," she said. "Were there any particular women you had in mind when you were writing? You've done such a wonderful job of getting inside your female characters. Their heads, I mean."

It was hard not to work a straight line like that, but I resisted temptation. After all, this wasn't a comedy club. "None of my characters are based on actual people," I replied suavely, "but you could say that some of them are composites of women I've known."

"And loved!" said Barrington enthusiastically. "Next question?" She picked out another of the girls waving their hands. This one looked bookish and was wearing cats-eye glasses.

"I couldn't help but notice the symbolic aspects of Lena's relationship with her banana tree. Don't you think that's laying it on a little thick?" she asked.

"Well, you know," I replied, "as the good Dr. Freud said, sometimes a banana is just a banana." I had no idea what I was talking about but I got a few laughs.

"Now, don't be naughty, Martin," Barrington coyly tut-tutted. "Haven't you noticed there are young ladies present?"

Her little joke got another laugh.

"I'll try to remember that," I played along. We were all having such a good time. I continued the best I could for the next half hour with my evasive banter and then it was over.

"I want to thank you all so much for sharing your opinions with Martin," said Barrington as she ushered them out the door. When they were gone, she turned to Bobokoff. "So what did you think, Dimitri?"

Bobokoff put his fingers together below his nose as if in prayer and frowned. "He made it look too easy. There was no gravitas. There were none of the qualities that turn mere celebrity into living legend. He sounded more like a big brother than a messianic man of vision."

I didn't know if I liked being talked about in the third person but at least he wasn't talking to me.

"Thank you very much for your words of wisdom, Dimitri," said Barrington dryly. "Your help has been worth every cent I've paid you."

Bobokoff didn't quite know how to take this opaque compliment. "Don't you want me to continue working with him?"

"I don't think that will be necessary. Now, if you'll excuse us, Martin and I have a few things to talk about."

Bobokoff was not happy about this abrupt turn of events but chose to make a gracious exit. "If you need me, Bunny, I'll be there."

"That's sweet of you, Dimitri," she cooed. "I'll call."

As soon as he had closed the door behind him, she turned to me. "Don't listen to Dimitri. I thought you were just wonderful," she exulted. "You had those girls - if you'll excuse the expression - creaming in their jeans." She drawled those last four words as if she were doing a Mae West impersonation.

I didn't know what to say. "Well, thank you."

"Now, as you know, you'll be giving your first reading at Marymount in a week. It's to one of those crash creative writing courses they have there during the summer so they may be a little older than this group today but I'm sure you can handle it. I knew I had a winner from the moment I saw you."

"Listen, Bunny, I still don't have a copy of the book."

"You don't? Well, let's fix that right now."

We went back to her office where she poked around for a copy and came up with nothing. "You know, Martin, I must have sent them all out to the reviewers. Don't worry, I'll have one messengered to you tomorrow."

I walked out of the building into a wall of muggy heat and for some reason decided to take a walk in the park. Out in the country I never walked anywhere but here in the park, squeezed by towers on all sides, I could walk for miles. I meandered along the east side past the zoo where seals were splashing around the pool in the courtyard and continued on my way to the boat pond where model yachting enthusiasts were spread out along the shore with their radio controls. I don't know why but this peaceful scene conjured up a vision of a hundred miniature Offenfussers zooming around in an aquatic demolition derby, smashing into each other with reckless abandon. I took a seat on a bench along the gravel path and pondered my bright, bleak prospects. I was tired of the whole thing already and it hadn't even begun. Soon I would be whirled into a fast paced world where everything would run completely counter to my constitutional laziness. I would be forced to keep a schedule and suffer many fools gladly. I would be ejected from my comfortable cocoon and emerge as "Martin Seward - Author!"

But, for the moment, I could just sit on that bench and watch the girls go by. Better not to have a care in the world briefly than never at all. I bought a beer from one of the illegal vendors who ply the park selling their wares from icy green garbage bags and refreshed myself. Then I saw something that very much took me aback. Was that Baby D on the other side of the pond walking hand in hand with some middle-aged sonuvabitch? I squinted through the hazy glare. It was indeed! She and her older escort – her uncle? her father? – were walking slowly through the throng milling around the small refreshment stand. He must have said something funny because she broke into laughter. Then she pushed herself up against him with her arms around his neck as he drew her to him in a lingering embrace. Uncle, father, my ass! She broke from his clutches after a few of the longest seconds I have ever experienced and sashayed off into the crowd with a little pivot and wave. He stood for a moment looking after her, then walked off in the opposite direction. I immediately got up and hurried around the pond after Danica but she was nowhere to be seen. I searched for her frantically the next few minutes but she had disappeared into the heat and bad air. I wondered if I'd seen her at all or if it just been a mirage generated by pond evaporation. On the other hand, what business was it of mine? The part of my brain generating that sort of clear-headed logic, however, was instantly overwhelmed by a burbling, boiling stew of crazed jealousy and anger. I was in the claws of a demon that shook me like a rag doll, then flung me down into the pits of Hell where I crawled around on my hands and knees wailing and howling like no other terrestrial creature until I collapsed into my own despair. I guess that sounds pretty melodramatic but that's the way I felt at the time. Sort of. Maybe it was the heat.

I walked out of the park to Fifth Avenue in an agitated funk and grabbed a cab downtown. I subsequently arrived in front of an abandoned movie theatre on the eastern outskirts of Chinatown, paid the driver and got out. Passersby might assume the building was derelict but that was not the case. I pushed the buzzer and the side door was soon opened by an overweight, middle-aged man with a full white beard wearing overalls, my friend and sometime mentor Purvis Ames.

"Well, well, what do we have here?" he said by way of greeting. "Come in. come in. Long time no see." He led me through the lobby into the dimly lit, cool precincts of the gutted theatre which now housed a giant model of New York City with all its bays, rivers and canals rendered in actual water. It was Purvis' job to tend to this peculiar municipal project where various hydraulic theories were occasionally tested and he lived on the premises, rarely venturing further afield than the bodega and the liquor store down the block. "Welcome to Water World," he said grandly. "Would you like a beer?" I would indeed and he fetched a couple of cans from an ice chest on the floor. "I've seen your picture in the newspaper lately. I didn't know you'd finished your book."

"Yeah, well…" I trailed off.

"So what brings you here?"

"I need a second opinion."

"Well, you certainly have come to the wrong place then. How can I make matters worse?"

So I told him the whole dreary story of *Babyland* and when I finished he cocked his head quizzically to one side like a dog and gathered his thoughts.

"I know it sounds insane," I blurted.

"Insane? I don't think so," he replied. "You can try greedy, vainglorious, and foolish on for size but not lunacy. In fact, you're right in synch with all the most cherished values of our society — untrammeled ambition, sales-manship, and the willingness to trade integrity for creature comforts."

"I didn't come here for a lecture," I snapped back. "I know damn well what I've got myself into."

Ames chuckled. "Well, I guess you do, don't you. I shouldn't worry. Trust yourself to your fate. After all, it is written." He chuckled again. "In your case, in more ways than one. You should be glad. You're no longer a writer chained to the printed page, forced into the drudgery of committing words to paper. You're now an actor, soon to be adulated by adoring strangers and recognized everywhere. Just think of those tens of thousands of people out there futilely clamoring to be packaged and sold. You're the lucky one, Martin."

He motioned for me to take a seat on a raised platform above the giant model and pushed a button on a panel. Immediately, underwater mechanisms went into action recreating the tidal flow of the harbor. Miniature waves even came crashing ashore in Coney Island. "I find watching water move around very soothing," he said. "Clears the mind."

I could only think of Danica at the boat pond which certainly hadn't cleared my mind.

"So you want an opinion, Martin? You want me to ratify the path you've already chosen or try to dissuade you from going further. I say go for it. It's all an illusion anyway. Just like this fantastic simulation of the power of the moon. Now let me show you something else, a simulation of a tsunami hitting New York."

"This isn't an earthquake zone."

"No it's not, but out there in the middle Atlantic is a cluster of islands called the Azores which are highly volcanic and could explode at any time. I'm sure you'd like to see the result." He pushed another button and the water in New York Harbor drained out to the point where all the shallows were exposed. Suddenly a wave a mere eight inches tall rushed across the ocean toward the Verrazano straits leaving the shoreline of Brooklyn and Queens completely inundated for miles inland. Taking on even more power as it was squeezed under the bridge it rose to a full foot, took out the Staten Island lowlands, and smashed into lower Manhattan leaving the tallest skyscrapers looking like islands in the sea. I must say I was quite impressed with this demonstration.

"All right!" I whooped. "Let it come down!"

"So you see," said amused Ames, "nothing is what it seems. Those waters, once placid and serene, can become a raging torrent in a matter of seconds and drown all our hopes and dreams in a maelstrom of chaos and death."

I must say I was immensely cheered by this demonstration of the violent forces of nature and, as the water receded from the model of Manhattan, I even asked Purvis to do it again.

He held up his hand. "One show at a time, Martin. Consider yourself lucky to have witnessed this cataclysm even once. You realize if the fury I just unleashed had really transpired, you and I would be ten feet underwater at this very moment."

"I don't give a fuck!" I said. "I am saved! I am washed in the blood of the lamb!"

"I think it's time for another beer," said Ames.

When I left some two hours later, it was with a sense of liberation, a new found freedom that put a spring in my step and a song in my heart. I jumped off the curb and kicked my heels together in the air right before I was flattened by a double-decker tourist bus. No, just kidding. I stole that story from another book that better goes unmentioned. However, I did feel that the burden of all my transgressions had been lifted from my shoulders and I could go forth to meet whatever fate awaited me with a newfound confidence and resolve. Now there was only Baby D to deal with.

In the train on the way back out to the island, several fantasy scenarios milled around in my head contending for a little attention. I could not say a thing and push her into a brazen lie which I could then pounce upon like a tiger. I could confront her directly and let the chips fall where they may. I could do nothing at all because she probably wouldn't even be there. And such was the case.

After a Happy Hour cocktail at Cyrano's, I returned to an empty house. There was, however, another note from Redstone tacked up on the door inviting me over "for a chat." What could this possibly mean? I decided to ignore it. But not for long. Within minutes he was rapping on my door demanding I come over to his place for dinner. He looked haggard and confused.

"I understand that you're busy with the book and all but I'd really appreciate it if you could just join me for an hour so I can explain my position."

I hadn't the slightest idea what he was talking about but I was just toasted enough to be cajoled into going over there, but not before we were interrupted by a messenger with a package from Nuk Nuk Noing. I ripped it open and there – bless Nuk Nuk's heart – was the rest of the Buddha book. "Let's go," I said cheerfully but just as we walked out the door Danica's car pulled into the driveway and stooped abruptly about twenty feet away from us. I thought she was going to back up and flee but she eventually took her foot off the brake and rolled to a stop in front of the house. She got out of the car and walked up to us with frigid aplomb.

"Danielle...," Redstone sputtered.

"He thinks that's my name," Danica explained to me.

"I have to talk with you, Danielle," he pleaded.

"No you don't," she said curtly and brushed us both aside as she disappeared into the house.

"Well, at least I finally got to see her," Redstone said disconsolately.

I was curious. "How do you know, er, Danielle?"

"Oh, I've known your cousin for..,"

"She's not my cousin, Dack. She's my girlfriend. Sort of."

This news brought Redstone up very short indeed. "I thought you were with that blond!" he fumed indignantly.

I ignored that remark. "Whatever made you think she's my cousin?"

"Well, her last name is Seward, isn't it?!"

This strange assertion was certainly new to me though I did not, in fact, know Danica's last name.

"Please ask her to come out and talk to me," he pressed.

"Right now? I don't think that's a good idea."

"Just do it, dammit!" he exploded. "You owe me. Martin!"

So that's what this was all about. Redstone hadn't paid me to write his report. He'd paid me to get at Danica. "I'll see what I can do," I said. I went inside where Danica was sitting on the couch listening to everything.

"Tell him to go away," she said. "I'm not going to talk to him."

I was sorely peeved about being forced into the role of go-between in this bizarre encounter. "Tell him yourself."

"I'm not going to speak to him. He can stand out there all night as far as I'm concerned."

And so it was left to me but Redstone was nowhere to be found by the time I poked my head out the door. He had already disappeared back into the trees.

"He's gone," I said.

"Good."

"I think it's time we had a little talk, Danielle."

She pursed her lips in annoyance and looked away from me.

I was not about to relent. "Is your last name really Seward?"

"Of course it's not," she said. "Make me a drink and I'll tell you everything."

Strangely, I wasn't sure I wanted to hear everything but there I was doing the insisting. I poured her a glass of white wine and sat back.

"My name is not Danielle Seward," she said. "That's just the name I made up when I was seeing Redstone."

"You were his girlfriend?"

She laughed. "Are you joking? No, I wasn't his girlfriend. Let's just say I provided him with certain services for a fee. Like you."

It all began to dawn on me. "What services?"

"I never fucked him, if that's what you mean. I met with him on a weekly basis to beat him up."

"You what?"

"Well, it's a job, isn't it?" she said defensively. "Dack likes to be punished for his numerous sins and I did not spare the rod." She chuckled, then became serious. "It all seemed rather harmless at the time but the more he confessed to me, the more uncomfortable I got. He told me he was a Martian placed on earth to study and imitate the mannerisms of human beings."

I had to laugh. "That actually seems to make sense."

"It's not a joke," she brought me up short. "I didn't believe he was a Martian but I did begin to think he was some sort of demon on a mission to appropriate innocent souls. Like yours."

I couldn't stop her now. "I'll let that slide," I said. "So what happened?"

"I got another job."

"That's it?"

"No, that's not it. He's obsessed with me. I had to change phone numbers to get rid of him. I ran into him two years ago and the first thing he does is get down on his knees and beg, 'Beat me, baby, beat me! I can't live without you!' It was so disgusting."

I couldn't help laughing.

"It's not funny!"

I wasn't so sure about that but then I have a pretty morbid sense of humor. "So what's that got to do with Redstone being a demon?"

"I suppose he's told you his boring football story, his boring army story, his boring Wall Street story, and all that stuff. It's all crap. It's all made up. As far as I know, he just appeared on the planet with a shitload of money and he's been pretending to be a human being ever since. He just can't get it right though. There's something off about his delivery. He tries to play the part that people expect of him but he's on the wrong channel. He's not even really a masochist. He just did it because that's what all the other big time financial guys do. Stay away from him, Martin. He's trouble with a capital T."

"Why did you choose Seward as a last name? What is your last name anyway?"

"I picked Seward out of the phone book. My last name is Lethe. I thought you knew that."

"I must have forgotten. Who was that guy you were kissing in the park this morning?"

That certainly caught her flatfooted. "Excuse me?"

"You know. The guy at the boat pond."

Baby D briefly pondered her options and decided to go into an attack mode. "Are you spying on me?" she demanded. "Nobody follows me around."

"I wouldn't dream of it. I just happened to be at the right place at the wrong time." The whole conversation was beginning to give me a headache.

"I should ask you for a search warrant, you naughty little snoop." Now she was mocking me.

"All right, all right, I know it's none of my business."

"Oh, baby, you don't want me to leave you with lingering doubts, do you?" she teased. "The man in question, who is old enough to be my father, has promised me a grant from the Humanitas Foundation to form my own dance company. His name is Marshall Stanley and I didn't have to fuck him or even beat him up for the money."

"I thought you were retired."

"No more dancing. I want to be a choreographer. I want to have my own company."

Did I believe her? Did I even care? My jilted suitor act certainly wasn't getting me anywhere. What more was there to say? We snuggled up on the couch with a bottle of wine and watched the news on TV. The world flickered by in short, pithy segments, just a bunch of temporary, unconnected moments that someone or something desperately tries to string together in something called memory. We dozed off in each others' arms.

CHAPTER SEVENTEEN

The first thing I did the next morning was call up Sheridan March and tell her that the Buddha book was finished. She was, of course, delighted.

"Martin, you are a gem! I'll send you the last check as soon as I read it. It's coming out in two weeks, you know."

I was puzzled by this news. "How can you have a publication date without a book?"

"You don't know about print on demand? Oh, I forgot. You're just a first time author." And she hung up.

This dismissive phone call was followed in short order by another more enthusiastic inquiry. "Martin, it's Alicia. You and Danica must come over for brunch. I want to celebrate her grant from the Humanitas Foundation."

"Well, she's still asleep…"

"Don't wake her up. Just come over around noon. Isn't it wonderful? I mean, everyone's doing so well."

"How did you know about the grant?"

"Oh, my spies are everywhere, Martin. You ought to know that by now."

I was sure that Danica would not be interested in the invitation but, when I broached the subject, she was only too eager to accept. "I know what Alicia's up to," she snorted. "She just wants to use me to get next to Marshall Stanley."

"Oh, I see, you just want to go over there and gloat."

"Something like that. I've never been averse to a little ass kissing as long as I'm on the receiving end."

And so, propelled by these bright sentiments, we drove over to the Offenfusser's at the appointed hour where Alicia was out of the gate like a race mare as soon as we pulled up the front of the foundation, bounding out the door to greet Danica as if it were a much postponed but eagerly anticipated reunion of two bosom friends.

"Congratulations!" she gushed as she embraced a considerably less enthusiastic Baby D. "Come in, come in, everybody's here."

And so they were. Offenfusser, Harry Poon and Gloriana welcomed us with a more modest demonstration of conviviality than Alicia but good feelings, acting as a thin veneer over greenish envy, still suffused the bright pastel tones of the gathering on the sunlit terrace.

"Well," said Offenfusser, "I hear you hit the jackpot. I've been trying to snag a Humanitas grant for years."

"Never applied for one myself," said Poon "I always preferred the rough and tumble of commerce to the snug cocoon of philanthropic largess."

"Can it, Harry," said Gloriana. "Congratulations, Danica."

"Thank you. It was really quite a pleasant surprise."

Alicia was having none of this. "Surprises in the art world are few and far between. Your exceptional good luck must prove the rule."

Danica paid no attention at all to this comment.

"The way I look at it, the whole grant system addresses the only real pressing problem of our age — the desperate, shriveling middle class," said Poon. "Save the bourgeoisie! I say."

"Harry, you've got to stop drinking those rum drinks in the morning," said Gloriana. "I'm going down the road for a paper. Anyone need anything?" Nobody did and she was off.

"So, Martin," Alicia picked up the ball, "I hear you're giving your first reading next week at Marymount."

"No finer institution for horny Catholic girls," said Poon.

"God, Harry, you're living in the Stone Age," said Alicia. "It's all Jews and Chinese now."

The wonderful thing about this crowd was it wasn't necessary to say anything yourself, even if they were ostensibly talking to you. I could bend my head to, "I know those Jewish chicks are horny, at least when they're in college, but how about the Chinese?" then swivel back to, "The Chinese? Why do you think there are so many of them," without ever commenting or responding to anything. Impatient Offenfusser, however, broke it up with, "I'm hungry. I mean, all our guests are here, even the uninvited ones," with a pointed glance over at Poon, "so let's chow down." The Sulema was still missing in action and Harry the Houseguest was apparently beginning to get on Offenfusser's nerves.

"Hey," said Poon, "let's wait for Gloriana."

"She's not even uninvited," said Offenfusser. "She just showed up."

"Wick," Alicia scolded him.

"Sorry, Harry," he apologized. "Just kidding."

"Well, it's going to take a little time anyway," said Alicia. "I'll get things started." She disappeared into the kitchen and Offenfusser poured everyone another drink from a pitcher on the table.

"Alicia has this habit of dragging me off to movies I don't understand," he said. "The other night we saw this Iranian movie at the Frog's Lip Playhouse. I tried to make some sense of it before I fell asleep but I failed."

"What was it about?" Danica helped him along.

"Iranians. Don't they call themselves Persians? What's A.J. anyway?"

"A.J. is a man of the world, Wick," said Poon. "He has more passports than you've had hot dinners."

"Well, anyway, it was about these strange people in this Godforsaken place where everything was just yellow dust. My allergies started acting up just looking at it. That's all I remember. You'll have to ask Alicia what it was all about. She'll sit through anything."

"Don't give me a straight line like that," said Poon.

In far less time than I thought it would take her to go to the corner store and back, Gloriana reappeared at that very moment and tossed the Times on the table. "Read that," she commanded. The headline read: "Middle Eastern Financier Arrested in Vatican City."

Poon grabbed the paper and quickly scanned the first few paragraphs. "Oh shit," he moaned, "oh, shit."

"Don't just sit there whining," Danica scolded. "Read it out loud."

Dispirited Poon did as he was told. "Billionaire investor Ahmed Jifhraz was arrested by the Pope's Swiss Guards at the request of the F.B.I. which is seeking his extradition on charges of human trafficking, money laundering, bank fraud, and drug smuggling. He is expected to be flown to the United States within a week. Mr. Jifhraz, a Maronite Christian, was apparently seeking sanctuary in St. Peter's but Vatican authorities refused his request and had him detained. An American co-conspirator, under sealed indictment in New York, is being sought by Federal agents."

If not exactly dumbstruck, the party was not immediately

forthcoming with a response.

"What's going on out here?" Alicia wondered as she emerged from the house with a tray of napkins and silverware. "A silent prayer meeting?"

Offenfusser was first off the mark. "It seems Harry's benefactor, A.J., has been arrested."

Alicia set down the tray and wagged her finger. "He shouldn't drink and drive."

"I think it's a bit more serious than that."

Danica looked out across the bay and murmured. "I'll bet you anything I know who that co-conspirator is." And, as it turned out, she was right, though the suspect didn't have to suffer the indignity of being hauled off in handcuffs because they don't handcuff dead people.

When Danica and I returned to the house, police cars with flashing lights were lined up and down the street. Strangely, I knew exactly what was happening though I didn't know anything at all. Redstone was sprawled in front of the shrine in his Sulka robe with a bullet through his neck. Dried up blood that had originally run in a torrent now looked like a small, rusty lava field. It was the first time I'd ever seen a convincingly happy expression on his face. A bower of brightly colored plastic flowers placed in memory to the deceased busboy framed his head and the cameras were flashing. I turned away and there were Danica and Mrs. Bradley standing together a distance behind me looking on with the sort of curious detachment reserved for an extraordinary plant. Mrs. Bradley did not tarry but faded back into the small crowd of gawkers who had gathered to watch the ambulance attendants and the police go about their business. I joined Baby D.

"Well?" I said.

"There's nothing to say."

"Aren't you curious about who did it?"

"Who cares? The possibilities are endless. You don't think I had something to do with it, do you?" she said with a dismissive arch of her brow.

We watched as Redstone was tagged, bagged and slid into the ambulance on a gurney.

"Excuse me." I turned and it was Sergeant McCorrigal. "Aren't you the young fellow staying down the road at the Wilberforce place?"

I had to admit I was.

"Strange," he mused with insinuating false bonhomie as if he were playing the part of a clever detective on a lame television show. "You and the late Mr. Redstone being neighbors and all, I mean. You ever see anything funny going on around here?"

"Funny? What do you mean?" I said cautiously.

"You know, like strange people running around in the bushes. Arabs, Mexicans, that sort of people."

"No, not that I've noticed." I thought it best not to mention Redstone's own penchant for running around in the bushes.

"You wouldn't be holding back on me now, would you, young man?" he asked with a fixed, hard stare.

"Why would I do that?"

"People have their reasons. Believe me, people have their reasons." With that, he turned abruptly and walked away.

People do have their reasons, whatever they are. The press certainly had their reasons splattering Redstone's mysterious demise all over the place. Neither Reynolds nor Guillermo was anywhere to be found which, of course, fueled an explosion of speculation ranging from the sinister workings of Opus Dei to a vendetta by the Aztec Brotherhood. Junius Flattmeat called and insisted that I confess to the crime. "I'll make you a bigger lead story than... than..." he sputtered as I firmly refused. "Why are you letting that bitch steal the spotlight?" he moaned. The bitch in question was, of course, Megan Fillywell who, dressed all in mourning black, now graced the morning talk shows tearfully confessing to her longtime affair with Redstone. The locals were only slightly less florid in their prognostications.

"The man died for all our sins!" bellowed Pedro Barbez at Cyrano's.

"Not yours, "Cyrano rejoined. "The whole town would have to drop dead to make a dent in your numerous peccadilloes."

Barbez didn't even hear him. "I raise my glass in a toast ... to the Great Redstone!" And that's what poor Dacron has been called ever since.

I myself had other things on my mind. Barrington Stoat hadn't managed to get me a copy of my book and there was only a week to go until the first reading.

"God, Martin," she admonished me, "the things you worry about. We've got to think about your hair, your latest romantic interest, real stuff." I suppose she had a point. "Sparky and Junius are all over me to build up this Redstone thing," she added. "You've got to help us out."

To the relief of Offenfusser, Harry Poon and Gloriana had been obliged to flee back to the city since their boat was never coming in. I think Alicia missed them though.

"It's just so boring around here without Harry. Wick says he likes it that way. He doesn't know I'm thinking of divorcing him. By the way, how's Danica?"

If Redstone even had a funeral I had no idea when or where it was. He was forgotten so quickly even I could barely remember him. But I do remember him now. I remember him quite well. Perhaps it has something to do with his meteoric plunge from a grand somethingness to nothing but a charred cinder on the vast landscape of folly. A month after his death I could certainly relate to that.

Didn't someone once say: "First the gods raise to great heights those they would destroy?" Or something like that. Since I suffer from acrophobia and was only raised to very moderate heights, my destruction was hardly a blip on the radar screen.

The seeds were planted at my Marymount reading which actually went very well except that I was absolutely appalled by the drivel I'd written. I had no idea Nuk Nuk Noing was that bad. Anyway, the crowd of middle-aged women seemed to like it and expectantly lined up for me to sign their copies. Some of them were positively flirty, which made Barrington Stoat, Sparky Goldflugel, and Junius Flattmeat very happy indeed.

In the limousine on the way to the party that Sparky had arranged in his Park Avenue apartment, Junius enthused, "You were great, man! You really got those old koozies going."

"For God's sake," Goldflugel berated him.

"Sorry, Bunny," Junius apologized.

She didn't even bother to acknowledge him.

The party was a strained affair with many strangers from the literary world briefly congratulating me and then moving on in search of bigger prey than a mere author. Danica, whom I had invited, did not show up, perhaps instinctively sensing the swirling storm sweeping in from just over the horizon.

Goldflugel's apartment was decorated in I-can-get-it-for-you-wholesale Byzantine, all gold mirrors and flocked wall paper. His guests were assembled in the spacious living room where I first met my publisher, Raj Kapoor of Hotgroove Press, the house of the moment, who had made a fortune cranking out books for the "sixteen to twenty-eight year old female demographic" as he called it. Junius ushered me around into a number of awkward and embarrassing situations largely due to his own extravagant charm.

"Berenice, this is Martin Seward and, believe me, he's a real terror. Don't be surprised if he shoots up some smack and pukes all over the rug!" he introduced me to an ancient crone who it turned out was Goldflugel's mother.

"Oh my," she gasped in a thick Lawn Guyland accent, batting enormous false lashes over her rheumy eyes, "it must be wonderful to suffer so for your art." There really is no coquette like an old coquette.

Junius pulled me away and we were off to meet a huddle in one corner of the room where a small group of junior agents were kibitzing. "You guys all know Martin, don't you?" he said. "He's going to be the biggest thing since prepackaged, sliced baloney!" Well, it least he was being accurate for a change. The agents weren't much interested since I wasn't making any of them any money.

When I finally escaped from this trying event, I caught the train and headed home in the fading twilight. The lights flickering on from the houses and other buildings along the rail bed seemed to dance around me like fireflies as the sun settled in the west behind the clattering train and, just for a moment, I felt that all was right with the world. Talk about delusional.

The next day I was wakened from my solitary bed (Danica was nowhere to be found) by a frantic call from Sheridan March who had just discovered that *Buddha; The First Entrepreneur* had been lifted more or less verbatim from another inspirational author's work, *Games Spirits Play*. The other author was not pleased with this appropriation and had filed a complaint in a court of law. "How could you do this to me!" she shrieked in my ear.

How to respond? I was worse than a plagiarist. I was a plagiarist's agent. I couldn't possibly tell her that I had nothing to do with it because, of course, I had everything to do with it. Nuk Nuk Noing had really fucked me over.

"I'm sure this is all a misunderstanding," I smoothly reassured her. "I've never even heard of *Games Spirits Play*." At least that was the truth.

"You're lying. Martin, "and you're going to pay for it!" she screeched and slammed down the phone. Of course, there wasn't much she could do without admitting that she didn't write her own books. That was not, however, much solace to me. At the very least, I would have to return my fee.

I immediately tried to call Nuk Nuk but all I got was a computer voice on an answering machine. "Miss Noing is too busy to answer. Please leave a message and she will get back to you when she has the time."

There was nothing to do but make myself a stiff drink, slug it down, and then make myself another. Fortunately, Sheridan March's book had not yet been distributed to the bookstores so a disastrous scandal could still be averted. There was a light tapping on the door and I opened up for Danica who looked me over with curious appraisal.

"You're in a lot of trouble, Martin," she said flatly.

I was taken aback. How could she know about the Buddha book fiasco? She handed me the Flash. "Author Accused of Stealing Book" read a small headline on the second page. "Martin Seward, whose new book, *Babyland*, was just released this week has been accused by Columbia creative writing student Virginia Chesterman of publishing her book under his name."

"That's not the name of the girl who wrote my book," I absurdly protested.

"Maybe not but she's the one taking you and your publisher to court."

Right at that moment I had an epiphany, a glimmer of understanding what it's like to be a coal miner when the roof in the shaft behind you caves in, leaving you trapped in the dark with nothing to do but wait for the air to run out. As I found out later, Nuk Nuk Noing had simply Xeroxed *Babyland* from one of her classmate's manuscripts.

"What are you going to do?" Danica pressed me.

"Find a hole and hide." Which is what I did. I knew that the press was already tracking me down and I would soon be faced with a carnival of smirking scorn and humiliation. I had to get out of the house and take refuge at the Offenfusser's until I could make my escape. "Are you coming?" I asked Danica.

"I have to go into the city and meet Marshall Stanley," she said. "I'll see you at Alicia's when I get back."

She never showed up and I did not see her again. Ever.

Without going into all the sordid details of my public disgrace and personal ruination, let me say that, after getting dragged out to the woodshed and whupped good, I have recovered my ironic detachment, as Alicia would call it, and I can look back on the whole trying episode with a sense of relief. Getting derailed on the express track to fame and fortune may, in fact, have been the best thing that ever happened to me.

After a short, furtive stay at the foundation, with the press sniffing around like a pack of baying hounds, I managed to elude my various pursuers and fly off to Mexico where I holed up in a beachfront casita a little south of Tulum. I might tell you that I spent my time there mulling over my mistakes, taking stock of my life, and resolving to press on in the face of adversity, but that would not be true. Actually, I became a bit more of a wastrel than I already was and whiled away several months on the beach and in the local drinking establishments, chasing and often bedding the young, adventurous tourists who passed through until I abruptly came to the sobering realization I needed to get out of there and make some money. I determined to follow in the footsteps of one of the brightest lights in the American literary firmament and become a paid escort for wealthy older women in Palm Beach, Florida. To this end, I flew back to Miami, signed up with an agency, rented a small apartment in West Palm, and set to work. All I needed was a tuxedo, gracious manners, and my natural wit and charm. I must say, I was the quintessential walker. But that is a whole different story which I may write about someday Suffice to say, my Florida sojourn afforded me enough leisure time to sit down and crank out a book. I published under a pseudonym, of course, and what you have just finished reading is the fruit of my labors. May the Great Redstone rest in peace.

※

THE GREAT REDSTONE